FREEDOM

BLACKSTONE
BOOK 3

J.L. DRAKE

CAST OF CHARACTERS

CAST OF CHARACTERS

Mike: Agent at Dusk but originally from Shadows. Scary-looking teddy bear, covered head to toe in tattoos.

Catalina: …you're just going to have to read to find out.

Charlotte: Mike's little sister and Catalina's best friend.

Keith: Member of Blackstone. Secretive. Savannah's 'big brother.' Husband to Lexi and father to Brandon, Jr.

Lexi: Keith's wife and Brandon, Jr.'s mother.

Cole: Owner of the safe house in Montana called Shadows. Fell in love with a picture of a victim.

Found, saved, and married Savannah. Leader of the Blackstone special ops team.

Savannah: Held for ransom in Tijuana, Mexico for seven months. Saved by Blackstone, married Cole Logan, has a daughter named Olivia, lives at Shadows.

Mark: Best friend to Cole Logan, Blackstone member. Uses humor to escape the pain from his past. Married to Mia, has twin boys.

Frank: Blackstone contact for the Army, lives in Washington, DC, Mia's father.

Mia: Mark's wife, nurse, Frank's daughter, mother of twin boys (second round of kids to enter the Blackstone team).

John: Blackstone member, twin sister almost died.

Abigail: Mark's adopted mother, Cole's childhood nanny, and now house aide. Dating Dr. Roberts.

Dr. Roberts: House doctor, kind soul, snappy dresser, dating Abigail.

Davie: Member of Blackstone, specializing in diving. Lives at Shadows.

Denton Barlow: The American from *Broken* who was obsessed with Savannah, wore gold- tipped cobra boots.

KIDS IN THE ORDER THEY ARRIVED

Olivia: Savannah and Cole's daughter.

Lopez Twins: Names will be revealed in this book.
Brandon, Jr.: Keith and Lexi's son.

DEVIL'S REACH MC

Trigger: Scary as hell, president of the Devil's Reach Motorcycle Club in Santa Monica.
Tess: Trigger's old lady.
Brick: Trigger's VP of the Devil's Reach, Tess's best friend.
Rail: Member of Devil's Reach, a tad *metrosexual.*
Morgan: Member of Devil's Reach, Sergeant at Arms, bartender.
Gus: Trigger's uncle.
Zay: Trigger's half-brother he never knew he had.
Crawford: New Dusk member.

TEAM NORTH ROCK

Steve
BT
Greg
Danny
Beast
Mike
Ryan

BLACKSTONE CODE NAMES

Cole: Raven One
Mark: Raven Two
Keith: Beta Seven
John: Fox Two
Mike: Delta Six
Crawford: Hawk

SOUNDTRACK

It's Tricky—Run-DMC

The Weight—The Band

Chicken Fried—The Zac Brown Band

Save A Horse, Ride A Cowboy—Big & Rich

Los Tiempos Van Cambiando—Franky Perez and Los Guardianes Del Bosque

In Hell I'll Be In Good Company—The Dead South

Assassin—Muse

Same Blood—Aleo Blacc

DEDICATION

To North Little Rock Police Department Swat Team, for all the fun and laughter you brought to my readers and me, as you blended fiction with reality.

Thank you for protecting the line of good and evil.

PROLOGUE

Location: Tijuana, Mexico
Coordinates: Classified

MIKE

"**M**ark!" I screamed through the roar of the storm. "Move to your three o'clock!"

He dipped down and rolled into the gully, while I slammed a bullet into the neck of the sniper perched in a nearby treetop. I snatched his ammo bag from where it landed at the base of the tree and raced to catch up as we headed for the next checkpoint.

"Delta Six," Cole's voice broke through my ear, "ETA?"

"Five…" I heard a snap from behind me and twisted to scan my surroundings. Rain poured off my helmet in a sheet, so I tilted it to break the curtain.

"Delta Six, repeat," Cole ordered.

I knew I wasn't alone, so I clicked my radio two times slow, then three fast to alert them that I couldn't respond.

Mark suddenly showed himself. As soon as his eyes met mine, he knew something was up. He moved to my side and lifted his gun.

"Anyone?" he whispered.

"I'm thinking four." Every sense in my body was on high alert. Rain pelted our battered bodies and smeared our war paint into different patterns across our skin. No matter how bad the elements were, I trusted my gut to guide me and alert me of any danger.

Mark's shoulder tensed when something caught our attention. "Seven o'clock."

"You feel it?"

"Yeah." He nodded. "We need cover."

We were sitting ducks against this cliff. The only cover we had was the rain coming down like a waterfall around us.

This isn't good.

"Cover me," I grunted to Mark, and he gave me a quick nod. "Raven One," I called to Cole.

"What's going on?" I heard him huff like he was on the run.

"We have company."

I caught a flash of red and lifted my weapon again. "I see you."

"I see three." Mark chewed on his gum. "I want to spray."

I waited until I locked in my targets before I agreed with the only option we had left.

"One." I took a breath and thought out my path. "Two." I blinked to free my eyes of water. "Three!"

Bullets sprayed across the forest. The sound broke through the thunder, and the flash of gunfire joined in with the lightning. We were storm, nature, and man working as one to take out the scum who dared walk this Earth. This was vengeance; this was freedom. I could feel the adrenaline flowing through me, and it felt right.

Two thick ropes dropped behind us, and we wrapped our wrists around them and waited for the signal to start climbing.

"Delta Six and Raven Two, go!" Keith yelled over the radio. We didn't miss a beat as we turned, flipped our guns onto our backs, and started to climb up the slick rock wall.

A year ago, Cole had us training up on the peak at Shadows. We had to climb a sixty-foot rock wall with a fire hose blasting in our faces. It was grueling, but it prepared us for moments like this. Our muscles screamed and our lungs fought for air, but we made it to the top and raced to catch up with the others.

"We have twenty minutes left before our window closes," Cole informed me. We had lost an extra thirty because we got separated at the lake's edge.

We fell into formation and headed back to the boat. I noticed one of the hostages had lost a shoe and was struggling to keep up.

Not having a moment left to spare, I scooped the woman and slung her onto my back. She wrapped her arms around my neck and buried her head into my shoulder. With my size and strength, I knew she wouldn't slow me down.

Keith had the younger woman by the arm. Her face was white with fear, and she shook from head to toe.

Pop!

Pop!

Pop!

The sound of gunfire quickly grew closer, and we knew someone had tipped off our location.

Shit!

"Start the motor!" Cole screamed into his radio just as we hit the sand. We jumped into the boat, and John revved the engine.

We flung ourselves flat in the hull as their bullets flew, and we could hear them striking the boat as we sped clear.

We slowly sat back and took a moment to breathe once we knew we were far enough away.

The extraction, although well planned, went south fast when we were only able to secure the mother and one daughter, Luna. Elena, the second daughter, had been moved unexpectedly, and we couldn't locate her. We had to go before we were exposed and lost them all.

Salvador and his men hit us as we headed back for the boat.

"No! *Mija!*" Martina had her daughter's head on her lap.

"Oh, shit." I ripped open my pack then did the same to Luna's dress. I started to pack the cork-sized hole that gushed blood.

"Please!" She covered my bloody hands and made me look up at her. "Please save her!"

"I'm going to try," I reassured her, but I could tell by the color of her daughter's skin she wouldn't make it long.

We had made a deal with Martina that we would get her and her two daughters out, in exchange for information on Salvador's operation. Martina had been deep inside Salvador's life for eight years, but once her daughters started to get old enough, she knew something needed to change. She took a huge chance when she made contact with our brother unit, North Rock, to ask for help. As I watched Luna and thought of Elena, I knew it was not good. Not only had we failed them, but the information we so desperately needed on the cartel would have to wait.

Luna didn't make it back to Dusk.

ONE

MIKE

The music was loud, and the place was packed. It definitely wasn't my comfort zone, but the guys wanted to blow off some steam after the last trip. So here I was, towering over most everyone, in a dance bar. I stood in the corner and watched people's faces for any sign of aggression or for any sudden movement that could possibly mean a fight would follow. I had an urge to manhandle someone, and that wasn't good. Maybe I'd just been spending too much time with Trigger. In his world, the law was just a word and not something to follow.

Oh, that reminds me.

"Cole." I signaled for him to follow me. I led him outside to the poorly lit patio where a bouncer checked kids' IDs.

"What's up?" He downed a bottle of water and tossed it into a can.

"I just spent some time with Trigger." I saw and understood Cole's discomfort with the topic. He knew Trigger and I had a past, and he made the effort to respect that. It was important for me to keep my friendship with him. Cole knew Trigger and I were a lot more alike than most realized.

"How's he doing?"

"Good. I know he carries his uncle's death on his shoulders, but he'll bounce back."

"Mm," Cole grunted. None of us were shy on the topic of death.

"He gave me this." I handed him the scrap of paper. "It's the location of Salvador's summer house." Cole smiled wryly at my description. The *summer house* was where Salvador kept his drugs and where his crew cut and bagged it for distribution.

"How legit is this?" He pulled out his phone.

"If Trigger gave it to me, it's legit."

Cole nodded his agreement and held his phone to his ear. "Tell him thanks." He hit my arm and headed down the road for some privacy. "Frank, I've got something for you."

I sagged against the cool bricks and closed my eyes, needing a moment to shake off Luna's death. Now the hunt for her sister was that much larger. Poor Martina was a mess when we'd left her at the safe house.

Fuck the cartel!

My phone vibrated in my pocket, and I thought about ignoring it. It wasn't until the fourth buzz that I gave in.

"Hello."

"Hi, Banner." My mother greeted me with my childhood nickname. "Are you still coming by tomorrow? You never answered my text."

Damn! I rubbed my head and tried to slip back into *this* life. It was hard to go from scaling cliffs and scoping out a kill to doing laundry and attending your sister's birthday party.

"Sorry, Mom." I turned my back to the bar door. I had completely forgotten about my sister's birthday. "Yeah, I'll be there. Four, right?"

"Okay, good." She paused. "What's wrong?"

"Just a hard week."

"Well, you come by and let your mama take care of you."

I grinned like a child. No matter how old I got, she still loved to care for me.

"Are the rest of the boys coming?"

"Mark mentioned about leaving a day early, but I think he just wants to find an excuse to get out of his son's friend's birthday party."

"Well, you tell Marky he's more than welcome. We always have extra food."

"I will." I chuckled. I knew all I had to do was

mention a barbecue and Mark would be game. "Love you."

"Love you more, Banner. Night."

I slipped my phone back in my pocket and began to head inside when I heard someone softly curse behind me. I turned slowly to find a girl on her phone. The lighting was poor where she was standing, so I couldn't get a good look at her face, but her long, lean legs under her black skin-tight dress did catch my attention. Her sexy curves had me moving closer.

"You need to call me back, Javier." Her Hispanic accent was there, but you could tell she had spent a lot of time learning English. "And I want the camera back that you *stole*!" She brushed at her hair like she was upset. "You just...I need to know where you are." She dropped her arm and swung around but jumped as she saw me.

"Sorry." I raised my hands to show I wasn't a threat. I'd learned through time that even when I was trying to be kind, people saw me as scary. "Didn't mean to eavesdrop."

Her shoulders sagged as she sighed. "It's fine," she said, trying to be nice. "Just a shitty night."

"I hear ya on that one."

Her gaze shot up to mine, and I saw the fire that smoldered behind her hazel eyes. She squinted and seemed to really look at me for the first time. For whatever reason, she reined herself back, and the embers faded from those eyes. I found myself wanting to fan the flames so I could see it again, but I left the thought alone.

"Rough night with your mom?" She snickered.

I couldn't help but laugh at that. She must have spotted me when she left the bar.

"You always listen to other people's phone calls?"

"I could say the same about you," she shot back. "You were in my spot."

"Spot?" I stepped a little closer, feeling like it was all right to do so, before I leaned my weight into the pole and hunkered down.

She tucked her phone into her tiny purse and folded her arms like she was chilly. "Yes. It's one of the only well-lit spots around this dive of a bar. The place creeps me out."

I nodded. She was right. The place did cast a lot of shadows.

"So, imagine my surprise when I go to step outside and see you," she dragged her finger in the air, gesturing up the length of me, "in my spot chatting away to your mother." She couldn't help but smirk again.

The look on her face told me she was intrigued by me, and I kind of enjoyed that.

"Well, you're in the one percent that didn't turn away screaming."

"You exaggerate, but why would I scream?" She seemed genuinely curious.

I held out my arms so she could get a good look. "What do you see when you look at me?"

She paused as she took me in. "I don't know you."

"I know, but first impressions matter, so tell me what you see."

"Okay." She stepped a little closer, which drew her into the light. My stomach twisted when I took in her slim body, long dark-brown hair that curled to the bottom of her back, slender legs, and a face that made my world tilt for just a moment.

"Stand," she commanded like she took it seriously. There was about a foot of space between us when I pushed away from the pole and slowly pulled myself up to full height. She kept her eyes locked on mine as I towered over her and let her take in my mountain-of-a-man appearance. To my surprise, she didn't react. She only twisted her mouth like she was thinking.

"So?"

"What is it that you do?"

"Army," was all I offered.

"I see. So, a protector?"

I liked that answer.

"I wasn't aware you could have tattoos, scruffy hair, and a five o'clock shadow," she touched her chin, "when you're in the Army."

I smirked. "It's allowed in my division."

She raised a sexy eyebrow as though impressed with what she saw.

"So, I don't scare you?" This was new to me.

Her face fell slightly but she caught it. "Why would you scare me?"

I stood six foot six, two hundred and sixty pounds of solid muscle and tattooed from head to toe—although not my face, per my mother's request. I gently reached out and took her hand in mine, so we were palm to palm, and I denied the fact that something charged through me. My hand was nearly twice her size.

"Because I'm big."

She left her hand against mine and studied my tats. "You're colorful too."

"I am."

"Those are impressive." She pointed to the ink on my arms.

"Thanks." I held them out and admired my beloved artwork that had been added to over the years. My right shoulder had an eagle clenching a ripped American flag as it was in mid-flight. The fringes of the flag waved in the wind, but if you looked closer, you would see the details traveling up the loose threads were actually names of our fellow brothers we'd lost. I brushed my thumb over Paul's name and felt that jolt of pain that came when I thought of him. We all knew our job was risky, but you were never ready to lose a brother.

My right arm looked like a bionic piece of machinery, with steel plates and bolts holding it together at the joints. It ran right down to my fingers where red and black lines weaved around like wires. To anyone, it was an intense piece of metalwork, but what they didn't know was the wires were drawn a certain way, so if my eyes couldn't see the bomb I was trying to defuse, I could use the path on my fingers to guide me. It was a tool, and one I used often. On the inside of my left arm, nuzzled into the steel, was a tribute to a fight I had many years ago. Deep in the belly of Iraq, my team fought off a wall of enemies while I worked to defuse a bomb that was set to kill us all. I could still remember I had one eye on the bomb and one on their leader, who stood across the cannon and watched the entire show play out. That was the day I knew I was born for this.

"Catalina?" a guy called out from the parking lot. "Come on back inside."

She waited a beat before she dropped her hand and gave the guy a wave.

"I guess I should get back." She turned to leave, but I stopped her in one stride.

"Catalina?" I tested out her name. "Stay out of the shadows."

She walked backward with a sly grin. "Stay out of my spot, then."

Once she turned back around, Mark popped in out of nowhere with a shit-eating grin, "Gotcha self a little Latina flare, there, do ya?"

"Shut it." I tried to hide my smile.

"Hey, man, I get it." He bumped my arm. "We are a rare breed."

"Says the man who was born and raised in Montana?"

"Yes, but Latino blood runs thick in these veins."

"Mmm." I rubbed my mouth as we walked toward the bar.

Once back inside, I spotted Keith with some drunk chick wrapped around him. He peeled her off and joined me.

"I hate drunk chicks," he muttered. "You good?" I nodded and scanned the crowd. I spotted Catalina with some friends on the dance floor. I wasn't one to dance in public, but I had been known to bust a move at a wedding or two. I believed there was a video that circulated after Cole tied the knot, and Run-DMC *It's Tricky* had made an appearance.

Catalina was tall. My guess would be five-seven, but her heels made her six feet. I loved a woman in stilettos; they were such a turn-on. Her sexy curves had my gaze rolling over her lines as she moved about.

I headed for Cole, who sat at the table on his phone. When I joined him, he leaned over. "Location checks out. Frank is looking into it, but it looks like we could be scoping the house sometime next week."

"Elena?" I mentioned the missing sister.

"Very good chance he's holding her there."

I leaned back and was relieved Trigger's tip had led to something valuable for us.

"You guys ready?" John slumped into the seat next to us like he had a few too many.

"Doesn't matter to me." I spoke without thinking, and he and Cole turned to me in confusion.

"What's going on?" John looked over my head then

turned to scan the crowd. It was hard to miss Catalina. "Oh, you see something you like?"

I reached back and cracked Mark in the thigh, and he yelped in pain and tried to breathe through the charley horse while Cole chuckled in amusement.

"Son of a nut hair, that hurt!" Mark continued to bitch.

"I've always wanted to know what your type would be." John checked out Catalina again. "Damn, she's fine. She has spicy written all over her."

Truthfully, I had no idea what my type was. I dated randomly, but no one really caught my interest but Lizzy, and that was only one-sided for too long.

"You get her number?" He pushed on.

I shook my head.

"Why?"

"Didn't have the chance."

"Was that before or after you told her to stay out of the dark?" Mark jumped out of the way when I took a second swing.

"Go ask her," Cole suggested. I was surprised. He normally would let us guys ride each other and sit back and be entertained. He rarely commented.

Somehow, I found myself on my feet, moving through the crowd. I glanced around the room, but she was gone.

Shit.

I looked back at the guys, and Cole shrugged then motioned it was time to go.

Maybe it wasn't meant to be. With one more glance around the room, I joined the guys in the SUV and headed home.

———

My pillow never felt so good.

Traffic was light, and we made good time. I was pleased to see there was still parking left in the driveway.

"See, smart pants." Mark pulled at the waistband of his pants to show how they expanded. "Now I can eat all I want and not feel tight."

I shook my head as I locked my truck, and he followed, still in conversation, all the way up to the bright red door.

Before I could turn the handle, my sister swung open the door and leapt into my arms.

"You came!" Charlotte laughed like she was a kid again. My baby sister was my world, and I was shamelessly wrapped around her little finger. I wasn't sure if it was because I was six years older or what, but we'd always been that way.

"Like I'd miss your twenty-fifth. You're almost thirty!" I set her on her feet and kissed her hair.

"Where's Keith?" she joked when Mark went in for a hug.

"He's coming. He had to run an errand for Frank." Mark snickered before he followed me into the kitchen.

None of the guys' families knew the truth about

what we did. All they knew was we were in the military. They also knew that, due to security reasons, we weren't able to talk about our missions. The only one who knew the whole truth was my pops. He and I were as close as any father and son could be, so when I joined Blackstone, it didn't take him long to figure out the type of work I did. We just didn't talk about it much. My family didn't pry, and I didn't talk about work. It was an understanding. It was nice to have one confidant I felt safe talking to now and then, and Pops was always there for me.

"Banner." My mother flew from the living room into my arms for a hug. "I'm glad you were able to make it."

"You act like I'm never here." I swiped a piece of apple from my aunt, who was making a pie. She blew me an air kiss and went back to her work.

"I just wish you were here more."

I rolled my eyes at my father as he caught wind of the conversation.

"Shall I move in…" Someone pinched my ass. "Hey!"

"You flaunt it, I taunt it." Keith's dirty little Nan grabbed the sides of my face and planted a kiss directly on my lips.

*And there it is…*Nan at her finest.

"Where's my Brandon?" She looked around like he would emerge out of thin air.

"He's coming." Mark wrapped his arms around her from behind. "We just knew you wanted us to yourself first."

"Oh, you and your lashes." She batted his arm, and he blinked like a chick.

Christ, I wished Cole was here.

Mike: ETA?

Keith: Let me guess…my Nan and Mark are at it?

Mike: ETA?

Keith: Ha! Almost there.

Mike: Drive faster.

"Come on." Charlotte pulled my arm to follow her out back. "I want you to say hi to everyone."

I loved our back yard. It was a huge piece of property that was nestled in the woods outside Asheville, North Carolina. It was only twenty minutes from Dusk, which made things a lot easier when I wanted to visit.

My parents had strung lights throughout the trees to give it a whimsical feel. They ran right down to the edge of the lake. There was a pond full of koi fish and a large gazebo on the other side, which was great for their parties. For as long as I could remember, my parents loved koi. It was the reason I had one tattooed on my head; I wanted to carry them with me everywhere.

Both my parents were musical and loved to rock out to good music with friends. I loved bringing Mark along. He had told me the story of his family, and it had always bothered me. The guys all knew our families were part of who we were, and Mark had found himself with a big family like no other.

My dad handed me a beer as I walked out and tossed me the cap. I slipped it into my pocket and went to join my sister. As I stepped out, I came to a dead stop.

TWO

Char insisted I join her family and friends for her birthday. I wasn't good at the whole big family thing, but for her, I would give it a try. Her determination to befriend me, in spite of the fact that I made an effort to keep everyone at arm's length, made it impossible not to like her. I was born and raised in Mexico, and we were known for our big, loving families, but sadly, that wasn't the case with mine. Not at all.

It took me three hours to decide on a dress, but I settled on a short tropical floral sundress that crisscrossed in the back, exposing most of it. My tattoo showed, which worried me a bit, but I was willing to take the risk. The dress was so pretty and hugged me in the right places. I had twisted my hair into a thick, messy mermaid braid, and a small gold necklace adorned my neck.

Charlotte and I worked at Brew while we paid off our school debt. We were fortunate enough to have landed a job straight out of college, but the money wasn't great. We needed to work our way up, so the brewery helped the bills, and it was a great place to make quick cash. Drunk guys tipped well.

I fiddled with the gold bracelet that hung from my wrist while people arrived. I felt a little out of place since everyone seemed to know one another well.

"Here," Lizzy handed me a glass of white wine, "you look like you could use this."

"Thanks." I raised the glass to take a sip when I heard her giggle as though something had caught her attention. When I turned around, I almost lost my balance.

"That," Lizzy whispered, "is Mike. Char's yummy older brother."

Lock your knees, lock your knees.

Mike's gaze met mine from under his ripped ball hat, and his lips parted in a smile. Holy shit, his size was almost breathtaking. I found myself unsure what to do, so I shamelessly stared. Charlotte looked between us, her face curious to know what our connection was.

"Ah, Catalina, this is my brother Mike. Mike," she pointed at me, "Catalina. She works at the Brew and the ad agency with me. Mike is an intelligence sergeant with the Army."

His huge, colorful arm came out for a shake, and when I slipped my hand in his, he gave me a wink.

"Nice to meet you, Catalina."

"You too, Mike." I fought a grin when he didn't let go right away.

"And this is Chris and Kyle. They work at the Brew too, and of course, Lizzy."

Mike's eyes moved over to Lizzy's, and something strange passed over his face. I dropped my hand from his, and his gaze immediately fell to his empty hand.

"There's my Brandon!" The old lady, who made Betty White look like Mother Teresa, rolled her wheelchair over to another big dude.

"That's Keith." Charlotte filled me in once Mike stepped back. "He's another Army guy, and that's his Nan. She's a riot, sheer entertainment. Mark," she pointed to a cute guy filling a plate for three as he shoved a bun in his mouth to free up a hand, "is part of their group too."

"They're all in the same unit?" I tried to follow.

"I think, but they call them teams." She shrugged like it didn't bother her. "Whatever it is, they don't talk about it much."

Huh.

After we had eaten and had the cake, I found myself wandering to the shady parts of the property. The humidity was high in summer, and I needed a break from the sun. I was wishing I had worn a hat.

My heels clicked on the wooden planks that led down to the water, and my fingers skimmed along the tops of the long grass as I walked. I breathed in the cool summer breeze as I stopped at the side of the dock. I hung my arms over the edge and closed my eyes, taking a moment to turn my head off.

I tuned in to the sounds of the water lapping the shore, the birds playing in the air, and someone talking. I looked around and saw Mike and Mark talking down by the sand. I could tell by the way their arms were crossed it was a serious conversation and something private.

Oops.

As I turned to move away, Mike's head shot up to me, and one hell of a sexy smile raced across his lips. My shy smile reflected back before I turned on my heel and headed back up through the grass.

I didn't want him to think I was eavesdropping.

Chris and Kyle were in the gazebo with Charlotte's parents, who had started to play the guitar and keyboard. To my surprise, they started to play *The Weight* by The Band. His father took the lead on the vocals while he strummed on the guitar. For some reason, I expected a Jimmy Buffett song, or a Neil Dimond.

"Damn," Chris laughed, "I wasn't expecting that."

"Me either."

Lizzy rushed over to Charlotte and squeezed in between her and her aunt. I felt a little ping of discomfort when she appeared. Lizzy and I were friends, but it was only because of Charlotte. She always made sure I knew I was second to Charlotte, which I found a little strange. I could have accepted that type of schoolyard behavior if we were kids, but we were grown adults, and it was tiresome. I wasn't looking for anything from anyone. I just wanted to keep my head down and grow my career.

Speaking of keeping my head down…I pulled my phone free and checked for any missed calls, texts, perhaps an email—or, shit, even a PM—from WhatsApp. Of course, there was nothing.

Where are you, Javier?

"Mikey, come over here!" Lizzy squealed from where she sat. Her voice had risen about ten octaves, and I noticed Char cringed.

Mike had come up from the lake and now lazily leaned against a pillar. His long, lean legs were crossed at the ankles, and his thumbs hung loosely from his pockets. He totally ignored Lizzy. One thing I noticed about him was he was completely comfortable in his own skin, and I found that to be very sexy. I moved a little closer to get a better view.

I allowed my eyes to wander over his massive muscles. On his left arm was a titanium shield like you'd see on a battlefield. The detail was incredible, right down to the hinges holding the steel plates in place. His right was more colorful with a bald eagle on the side of his shoulder with its feathers spread open, and tiny lines created its texture. A ripped American flag hung in the claws of the eagle and wildly wrapped around the rest of his arm. They were impressive tats, although when he moved, I noticed a little troll laced in between the fringes of the fabric.

It was spectacular.

Once my gaze shamelessly climbed his body, I met his

eyes that were locked on mine. One side of his mouth curved, then he tilted his head toward the lake in a gesture for me to join him.

I waited for him to leave before I followed him down to the dock. With a quick glance over my shoulder, I made sure Lizzy hadn't spotted me.

"Hi." He stepped into view at the edge of the dock.

"Hey." I fought the urge to grin like a child. Mike made me giddy for some reason. "So, it seems we both know your sister."

"What a great surprise," he retorted with a laugh. "To think when I went back into the bar to give you my number and you weren't there, it *wouldn't* be the last time I saw you."

"You came looking for me?" I rubbed my hand down my arm, feeling the temperature change now that the sun was going down.

"I did."

"Well, I'll have to give you mine before I leave."

"How about now?" He pulled out his phone and handed it to me. "Just in case."

"Are you leaving?" I blurted, realizing I didn't want him to go.

"We're on call all the time. I could be leaving in five minutes or next week."

I nodded and plugged my information into his phone then handed it back to him.

"Catalina Mendez," he repeated like he was memorizing it.

"Mike?" I waited for his last name even though I knew what it was.

"Mike Irons."

"Well, Mike Irons, your parents have a lovely home. This must have been pretty great. Growing up here, I mean."

"It was." He looked around with a happy smile like he really agreed with me. "What about you?"

A heavy weight pushed down on my shoulders, so I smiled and kept it light. "Let's start with you for right now."

He pushed off the railing and stepped closer to me. He reached for my hand and entwined our fingers. Mike was forward with me, but in a respectful way. I wanted more of it.

"For now. I see I'm not the only one with ink." He brushed his fingers down my back, and a small shiver followed their path.

"She's my guardian angel," I confessed.

"She looks a little dark and sad to be a guardian angel."

"Well, perhaps I'm hers," I whispered, and his eyes grew somber.

"May I?" I nodded and gathered my hair as he turned me around to study it better in the orange light of the evening sky. Again, his fingers swept across my skin and traced her battered wings. She was curled into a ball. Her wings were clipped and tucked in, and her head was turned to the side, looking down, so it was just her brittle profile. She was almost the length of my entire back with no color, just a black outline of a fallen angel.

"Beautiful." He matched my tone, although I thought he was calling me beautiful, not her.

"Thank you."

He eased my hair out of my hold and slowly ran his fingers through it as I turned to face him. It was an intensely intimate moment that caught me completely off guard. How could someone so big be so tender?

My sightline was at his chest level, and I wanted to reach up and feel how solid his body really was. He was a chiseled masterpiece.

"Are you dating anyone?" he asked quietly.

"No."

"Good."

I smirked. "If I was?"

"Then I'd have to find a way to get your attention away from him or her."

"Him. You definitely have it."

"And you have mine."

The wind suddenly picked up, and goosebumps broke out across my skin, but it wasn't from the cool air. I'd dated before, but no one had ever piqued my interest like Mike. He was kind and respectful but with *mucho* alpha.

"So, what now?" I playfully challenged him.

His mouth rose but immediately fell the moment *her* voice broke through our moment.

"Mikey?" Lizzy called, and we both dropped our hands. "Char was looking for you."

"Okay." He looked back at me and smiled. "I'll catch up with you in a bit." He began walking up toward the house.

Lizzy gave me a strange look. "I'm going to offer you a little advice, Catalina." She folded her arms. All signs of sweetness evaporated, and I could see she wanted me to really hear her. "You're new to the Irons world. We all have our place and know where we stand. It's best for you to learn what you can touch and what you can't."

"Meaning?"

"Meaning Mike is off-limits."

Okay…

"Are you two dating?"

"He's been in love with me for years. That's a lot of history to sniff around in." She held my gaze a little longer before she turned on her heel and raced to catch up with Mike.

She didn't answer my question.

Once again, the feeling that I didn't belong swept over me, so I hung back and waited until they disappeared from sight.

Something must have happened, because Mike didn't reappear for the rest of the night, and I left disappointed. What made it worse was he never texted or called either. Maybe I was crazy, but he had seemed interested. Or was he a player? I pushed that thought away. That wasn't fair. I might not know him, but I sure had never gotten that vibe from him.

The Brew was busy, and we didn't stop once, but at least the tips were piling in.

"Catalina." Char pulled me from my thoughts and eyed the beer I had overfilled. "I need two Blackbirds and a Stella."

Sometimes we'd pick up extra shifts to help out Andy, the manager, when someone called in sick. Tonight was one of those nights, and frankly, I was more than happy about it because I really needed the money, and Andy needed me to train the newest member of the Brew Crew.

"Got it." I shook my hands dry and pulled the beers before I entered the order into the system.

"Hey." She came behind the counter and stood next to me. "You okay?"

"Yeah," I sighed inwardly, "I just have some stuff on my mind."

"Well," she handed me the cash for the drinks, "come by on Friday. We're having a barbecue and a bonfire down on the beach." When I didn't bite, she wrapped her arm around me. "Come on, Cat, you've been stuck in a funk for a month now. Why won't you share what's going on?"

I wanted to cry. My life was so different from hers. What I wouldn't do for some warm family moments of my own. A dark shiver went down my spine, and I scolded myself for thinking of *them*. I looked normal on the outside, but inside there was a constant war happening, one that chipped away at my strength.

Tears threatened to surface, and I felt my walls start to shift.

"Cat?" She studied my face. "Oh, honey, I'm sorry. I didn't mean to pry."

"It's okay." I sniffed and swallowed down my sadness. "I'd love to come. What time?"

"Yay!" She faked her excitement. I could tell she was worried about me. "Let's say five?"

"I'll be there." As she went to leave, I hooked her arm and hugged her. "Thanks."

"Of course." Her arms tightened.

My shift was long, but I managed to get through it with very little interaction with Lizzy, though I caught her staring at me a few times.

Was she seriously still stuck on last week's topic? No worry, he hasn't called.

My walk home was nice, but damn, it was hot. I stopped in at the corner store and bought a three-color popsicle for fun and some relief. The ice felt wonderful inside but melted fast under the morning heat.

"Are you trying to get my attention?" Jeff, the jerk who owned the basement I rented, locked the door to the top floor where he lived. He was as sleazy as they came. I'd caught him in my place before, claiming he was checking a pipe, but later I found my underwear drawer had been tossed around.

"If you get bored with that treat, I have a different one for you." He thrust his hips in my direction.

Yuck.

I pushed by him to get to the stairs that led to my door.

"Hey," he grabbed my arm, "it's rude to ignore me. You know I could jack your rent up at any point," he snarled.

I ripped my arm away and fiddled with the key until it finally opened. I quickly secured all three locks and sagged against the cool brick wall. Why was I always surrounded by dicks? What was it about me that attracted them?

He had no idea what I was capable of, but I would never stoop that low. I would not give in. I was different.

I dropped my bag on the chair and headed for the shower.

"Dammit!" There wasn't any hot water. Jeff often turned it off whenever we fought, or when he wanted me to come up and ask for it to be turned back on. He loved me at his mercy. I couldn't wait to move, but right now it was all I could afford. Jeff was attractive and knew it. He was forceful and often tried to manhandle me, and *not* in a good way. I knew my time at this apartment was going to have to end, and soon.

The icy water woke me back up after my shift at the Brew. My bed looked inviting, but I had no time to waste. I quickly did my make-up, got dressed in a paisley sundress with a wraparound neckline, pulled on heels, and finger-combed my hair. It would have to dry on the way to job number two. I grabbed my keys and rushed out the door.

Charlotte was already at Duncan and Wayde Advertising when I arrived, on time by the skin of my teeth. Normally, I was an early bird, but today I was running behind, as Andy had begged me to teach the new guy how to do inventory at the Brew, and I couldn't say no. He was, after all, the one who employed me when no one else would. I owed him a lot.

"Good morning, sunshine." She handed me a cup of coffee as I hung my bag up and shook my mouse to wake up the computer.

"Thanks." I sipped the delicious coffee and sank into the seat. I felt the lack of sleep tug at my chest.

"How was work?"

"Good. Just got off an hour ago."

"Damn, girl." She made a sad face. "Look, Duncan is here and looking for the mark-up on the gel line for Opal."

I opened the bottom drawer and pulled the file free. "Here."

"Is it finished?" She skimmed the pages. "When did you have a chance to finish it?"

"Remember when I disappeared last shift and missed lunch?"

"Yeah."

I gave her a shrug. "I wouldn't have had time to have finish, otherwise."

She leaned her bottom on my desk and shook her head. "You're a pretty impressive person, you know that, Cat?"

I squeezed her arm as a thank you.

My phone rang, and I snatched it to see an unknown number.

"Hello?"

Oh, please be him!

Silence.

"If it's you, hit a key. You don't have to say anything. Just tell me if you're okay."

Charlotte gave me a concerned look but kept her head down while I pleaded with whoever it was to give some indication it was Javier.

The line went dead, and so did my hope.

It wasn't until the end of the day that Charlotte stopped by my desk again with her bag.

"Look," she pulled her keys from her purse, "I know you like your privacy, but something is clearly going on, so I will only say this once. If you need anything or just someone to talk to, you know you can call me, right?"

I knew, and I wanted to so badly, but I wouldn't burden anyone else with my problems.

"Thanks, Charlotte." I gathered my things. I desperately needed some sleep.

"Can I drive you home?"

"Sure." I smiled my thanks at her.

I didn't remember crawling into bed or when I hit the pillow. I just let sleep carry me away.

THREE

Keith laid the laminated map on the conference room table then took a red Sharpie and started to outline our next trip, another attempt to locate Elena. Her mother was still mourning the death of her youngest daughter, and we promised her she could stay at our North Rock safe house until we were able to extract Elena. We would hit Salvador's summer house, but not yet. Trigger informed me last night that they had changed their security. We would have to get our guy over in TJ to watch over the next few days until we knew their new schedule.

"There's no reason to think Martina is playing us." I turned to Keith as he answered Crawford's question. Ben Crawford came in last year and had proven to be a great asset to the house.

"All I'm saying is most people would have gotten the hell out of Mexico, given how much trouble they were in, especially if Salvador finds out she was on his computer…"

"When you have a child, you'll understand. I wouldn't have left either." Keith glanced outside to where Lexi and his son played on the swing set. Little Brandon was a great kid and had really tamed Lexi's *fight or flight* behavior. Under her hard shell, she was really a sweet girl. She had just been through a lot of shit. Plus, Savi was good at getting through to the nitty-gritty of people's problems. She was still in constant touch with Lexi on FaceTime calls.

"Mike, do you have what you need?"

"I do," I nodded at Keith, "and I'm ready to go at oh-four-hundred."

"Great. Get some sleep and see what we can find out tomorrow."

Just as I arrived at my room, Mark called, "Hey, man." He held up his radio. "Where are you keeping the extra batteries?"

"Crawford just ordered a new shipment. He's charging them now."

"Thanks."

"Mia giving you shit for being gone so long?"

He laughed and pulled out his ringing phone and held it up. "Mainly because the boys are being little dicks again."

"Well, they are part of you."

"Touché." He laughed and held the phone to his ear. "Wait, Mike!"

"Yeah?"

"Catalina…" His eyebrows pinched together while he thought. "Should I get Cole to vet her?"

I shrugged, knowing it was protocol, but I didn't think we needed to go there yet. "Let me get back to you on that."

He nodded before he pointed at his phone as Mia answered. "Hey, baby." He cringed as the yelling from his boys rang out. "How are ya?"

I chuckled and headed inside my room. Once I was packed and had my things by the door, I opened my closet and peeled back the wooden panel. I wanted to add the newest addition to my collection. My mother, who still insisted on buying me trolls, had gotten me the Bravery edition. Careful not to knock over the rest, I set him on the shelf next to his new friends. I smiled at how funny it would be if anyone ever found out my secret. Sixty-five trolls stood in their places waiting for me to return. That was the point; they would always be there for me. My mind slipped back to how my childhood was anything but free.

"Hey, Lurch!" A neighborhood boy and his stupid friends chucked a soda can at my back. "What's it like being a giant? Can the giant even run, or does your head get stuck in the clouds and you lose your way?"

*I rolled my eyes and ate my lunch alone, like always.
I was in fourth grade and was almost five-one. My
father was six-three, and my mother was six feet, so
I was bound to be one tall human. I was the butt of
a lot of kids' mean tricks and comments over the
years.*

*I didn't have many friends, and the ones I did have,
I didn't trust to have my back.*

*"Andre the Giant is coming!" one of the little brats
called as I jumped off the step from the school bus.
"Quick, he's going to eat us!" The kids scattered and
screamed, and once again I walked home alone.*

*I never had to say anything when I got home; my
mom just knew.*

*"Mike, look at what I found today." She turned a
box around and showed me the Bruce Banner
edition of the troll dolls. "You know who that is,
right?"*

*"The Hulk." I held it in between my hands and
studied the little monster.*

*"Why don't you go introduce him to his new friends?"
I dropped my book bag and grabbed the snack she
had made me and headed to my room.*

*I sat on the floor and inhaled my cookies while I
ripped open the box. "Guys, meet Bruce Banner. He
will be head of security while I'm at school. No one
messes with him."*

*"Do they like Banner?" my mother asked from the
hallway. I grinned at her.*

"Of course. They don't have a choice. He'd crush them all."

"Right, but he only hurts the ones who hurt him. He was misunderstood because of his size, but he has a huge heart. Just like you." She took a seat on the floor and started to play with me. "I guess we should call you Banner."

I shrugged, but a smile crept over my lips. The name stuck.

———

My boots sank into the thick mud as we raced along the back of the property. Normally, we'd attack at night with the darkness on our side, but our sources confirmed that between thirteen-hundred hours and thirteen-thirty-five, they left to do a check-in, and we'd be clear to enter the house. We weren't ready to storm Salvador's summer house yet; we wanted to clear the others first. Elena could be anywhere, so we'd start small, then work our way to the big house later. Besides, Cole mentioned possibly going in undercover to see what we could find out if Elena still came up MIA.

Keith signaled for me to enter through the back of the house. I kicked in the door and used my laser to sweep the place and check for any cartel.

"Laundry room clear," I whispered into my radio. I moved around to a small room and checked the closet. "Room in back clear."

"Living room and family room clear," Mark checked in.

"Barn clear." Keith followed suit. "Hawk, check in."

Crawford was quiet. Where the hell was he? He was new but understood the rules, and we didn't have time to waste.

Without moving, I glanced at my watch. 13:14.

"Bedroom's clear." I moved about but stopped when a dusting of stucco landed on my shoulder from where Mark was above me on the second floor. Water damage, most likely from a pipe.

"Raven Two, the floor is weak where you are."

"Ten-four, Delta Six, floor is weak," Mark repeated. "This house is in bad shape."

A cold rush swept down my back under my gear, almost like an invisible warning something was wrong.

"Beta Seven and Raven Two, do you feel that?"

"Delta Six, share." Mark caught my tone.

"Something feels off," I whispered. "Hawk, click your radio."

A single click cracked over the radio, and along with it, the realization that my gut was once again correct.

I moved to the bottom of the stairs and nodded at Mark. He joined my six, and we slowly moved around the corner and caught sight of Keith about to join us from outdoors.

"Hawk, stay put. We're making our way to you." My heart thumped in my throat. I wasn't scared. I was just hyperaware of my sixth sense and what it was telling me.

I blinked to better my vision and carefully opened the door the rest of the way.

"Hawk," I whispered to his back, "I'm coming up on your left." I raised my fist to tell Mark to wait. "I'm at your eight." I reassured him he wasn't alone. "Moving to your nine." I was good at walking people through my process. It was something Cole prided me on, and he often used me in situations with children.

As soon as I was at Crawford's side, I scanned his rigid body.

"Okay," I kept my tone light, "tell me what's going on."

"I heard a click," he whispered. "Not a click from stepping on the floorboards, a heavier click."

"'Kay." I glanced around the room, moving only my eyes in case I triggered another device.

"I kept waiting for a boom, but it never came. We learned about landmines in training, and that even the slightest movement could set it off."

"Yeah." I listened, but my mind was elsewhere. Mark checked his radio, and I knew the clock was ticking. If we were found, the hunt for Elena could be deadly. Sooner or later, Salvador would make her pay her family's debt for leaving. That was what they did. If someone left a debt, it had to be paid, no matter what cost. Needless to say, we were running out of time.

I quickly disconnected his radio so he wouldn't be distracted and stayed focused on me. The way the wooden board he stood on was disconnected from the rest confirmed my fear.

"I see it," I whispered. "Don't move."

"I can do that." His hands shook at his sides, and sweat dripped off his sideburns.

"Raven Two, I have a situation here."

"Oh, shit." Mark stood guard at the doorway. "What do you need, Mike?"

"I'm not sure." I bent at the knees and laid my body flat on the ground. I studied the short floorboard and how much of Crawford's shoe was actually on the trigger. "Mark, something heavy."

"Ten-four." He disappeared from my vision, and I removed the switchblade from my pocket.

"What do you see?" Crawford's leg shook.

"Your sister home from Italy yet?" I needed him to stay cool. I hadn't been in enough situations with Crawford yet to know his level of calm.

"Next week." He swallowed hard.

I shifted and rolled to my side, and with the tip of my knife, I lifted the board next to his and clicked on my flashlight to see multiple wires sticking out.

Dammit! It was a homemade landmine like ones they often used to blow up our tanks.

There was enough shit in there to flatten the entire house.

"This is what you're known for, right?" Crawford started to tap his fingers on his leg, "You're the bomb guy."

"I am." I studied how the wires were connected. One, two, three, four, and five, but the fifth and third were wrapped around each other. It was a goddamn freak show of a bomb.

"So, have you seen anything like this?"

"I have."

"And?"

"Different units of the cartel have a signature way they make their bombs." I used my knife to pull a wire free. *One down, four to go.* "They like the attention and, since bombs create different patterns once they go off, there's no mistake who made it. Yup, they are fuckin' attention seekers."

My wrist slipped, and I almost pulled the two entwined wires out at once. I blinked and studied my hand again, using my tattoos to line up my eye, and popped one free and left the other. Most people thought my tattoos were my personal stories, and most were, but they also were my guides for when I was working.

"What's the pattern look like for this one?"

"This is most likely a signal, a bomb they leave in an unused room to alert them that someone was in the house when they were gone." I moved to my knees and glanced around the room as Mark arrived with a handful of bricks.

"That explains why there isn't any furniture."

I held my tongue not to remind him of his training and how that was a dead giveaway not to enter a room.

"Will these bricks work?" Mark huffed.

"Let me see." He handed me the stack of six bricks on top of each other, and I felt their weight. Not heavy enough. *Think, think…*I clicked my radio. "Beta Seven, are you inside the house?"

"Delta Six, I am. I see we have possible company in roughly fifteen minutes."

I glanced at Mark, and he raced out of the room and returned with a large clay pot.

"Between the weight of the pot and the bricks, I think we're at seventy pounds. Will it work?"

"It will have to." I stood and carefully moved in front of Crawford, who was now covered in sweat. "You want to live to tell your sister this story?"

"Yes, sir."

"Good. Do exactly what I say and ignore your own head."

"Yes, sir."

"Mark." I pointed to the clay pot, and he dragged it over. "Gently, now." We ever so carefully inched it on the small piece of wood, and when it was next to Crawford's shoe, we started to fill it with the bricks, one on top of the other, making sure they lay perfectly so the weight was even.

"Okay, Crawford." I held his shoulders. "Look at me." He did. "We're in this together. You blow, I blow, so either way, I will see you on the other side."

"Okay," he whispered, "I'm ready."

"Mark," I held Crawford's gaze as I spoke, "leave."

"Fat chance, brother."

I cleared my head and took a deep breath. "On three, you will step off, turn, and run down the stairs to Keith, where you will follow his orders. You will turn your radio back on once you're safe. Understand?"

"Copy that, sir."

Mark's hand landed on my shoulder, so we were all connected. It was something Blackstone had done since I joined.

Live as one, die as one.

"One, two," I gripped his jacket in my hands and mirrored his step as I said, "three."

Silence.

Mark grabbed my head and kissed my cheek. "That's my brother!"

Shit.

Crawford let out a strange sound as he realized he was alive. He took one look at me, and he stepped back into line and raced downstairs.

I dropped to my knees and went to work.

"T-minus five minutes," Keith ordered.

"Copy that." Mark went for the door, but when I didn't follow, he yelled, "What are you doing?"

"Karma." I pulled a push charge from my pocket and stuck it in where wire number two once was. I set my watch for sixty seconds.

"Now what?" Mark asked as I stood.

"Now we fucking run."

We raced down the hall, down the stairs, through the kitchen, and out the back door just as our company arrived. For one so big, I could outrun most. Speed was something I worked on often so it wouldn't be a weakness.

As we hit the tree line, I heard Keith on the radio.

"Location?"

"I see your back," I yelled as I glanced at my watch and hauled Mark to the ground.

Boom!

The blast was so big we could feel the shockwaves from where we were. Hot wind tore over our exposed skin as the oxygen was pulled from our lungs. It was over in a matter of seconds.

"Whoa!" Mark rolled onto his back and laughed hysterically. I joined in and met his fist for a bump. "Damn, you are one badass dude."

"Thanks for staying." I smiled up at the sky and watched the forest dust swirl in the air. I loved the brotherhood of the Army, of Blackstone, of my family. I wished they were around when I was younger, but as Cole explained, our past shaped us, molded us into who we were. If we didn't have the bumps, scrapes, and scars, we might not have each other today.

"Nobody is walking out of the house, boys," Keith cheered through the radio. "No sign of our vic, so get your ass to the chopper. I want to get home."

"Copy that." I coughed as I pulled myself to my feet. "Let's go home."

"Shoulder." Mark pointed before he checked himself out. I glanced over and saw my shoulder was torn open and bleeding badly. It could wait. I wanted to get across the border before more company arrived.

FOUR

I changed into my yellow bikini and jean shorts and shrugged on a loose tank top. I put three necklaces over my head, and I slipped on some thin matching gold bangles. I then packed warmer clothes for when the sun went down. Gathering my hair into a high ponytail, I raced to the fridge. I was starving. Of course, it was empty. I hated to go to the store because I couldn't carry much home.

I decided on an apple and downed a bottle of water to fill the hunger void.

Kyle honked his horn twice to let me know he was here. Just as I locked up, I heard Jeff snicker about my outfit. He hopped off the step and blocked my path.

"Where are you going?"

I rolled my eyes and sighed heavily. "Move, Jeff."

"Just answer my question, and I will." His gaze dropped to my chest.

"Beach." I held up my hands as he moved to touch me and stepped around him.

"Mmm, tan lines," he cooed after me, and I wanted to throat punch him.

"Hurry up, *chica*!" Kyle yelled from the driver's seat, more to get Jeff to go away. Kyle and I were close, mainly because neither of us allowed ourselves to live in the past. We lived in the here and now. I knew he had his demons to deal with, and I had mine. That was the funny thing about hurting. You could spot it in others, and there was an unspoken understanding to leave it alone.

"What did the Slytherin want?" He pulled into the street.

"Just giving me his daily dose of creep."

"You really need to move."

"Tell me about it." I angled the air vents to face me and basked in the cool air until we arrived at Char's parents' house.

"Hi, Mrs. Irons," I greeted Charlotte's mother as we entered the kitchen. "How are you doing?"

"Hi, Catalina." She wrapped her warm arms around me and pulled me in for a hug. "My goodness, you smell yummy."

I laughed and showed her my coconut beach spray.

"Would it be too much trouble to ask you for some help?"

"Not at all." I waved off Kyle, and he held up my bag

to indicate he'd take it down to the beach and left to say hello to the rest of gang.

"Can you peel the apples and cube the avocados?"

"Sure." I was more than happy to help her out. She was feeding all of us, and it was the least I could do.

"So," she joined me at the island, "tell me a little about yourself."

I flinched but continued to peel.

"Um, I was born and raised in Mexico. I moved here when I was seventeen and haven't been back since."

"What about your parents?" She glanced at me, genuinely curious. I swallowed past the lump in my throat.

"They didn't come. They're still in Mexico."

"Oh." She paused. "I'm sure that's very hard on all of you."

"It is," I answered honestly. "Lonely too." That last part slipped out.

"I bet. Do you have any family here?"

"My aunt, but she's not really around anymore." It didn't take long for my aunt to meet someone and kick us out so she could start a new life. Thank God we were resourceful.

"Catalina, where did you stay when you came here?" Her tone was concerned. "Did your aunt take care of you?"

Ha! Not even close.

I shrugged as I remembered that day. "A lot of promises were made, and a lot of them were broken. But I was here, and I managed to get myself a place, a job, and enrolled in school."

All by myself, with no help from them.

Mrs. Irons dropped the butter into the dish and turned to face me. "So, you're here without anyone?"

Kind of.

"No, I had my brother, Javier, but he had different plans for when we arrived. It wasn't so bad." I tried to reassure her while I flat-out lied to that sweet woman. Those times were horrible. Dark corners and alleyways were my home for a short time, but I was resourceful and was book smart, so it didn't take long. But she didn't need to carry that burden, so I chose to move on. "It could be worse, right?"

Her red eyes told me I wasn't convincing anyone.

"I want you to know you're always welcome, no matter if Char is here or not."

That was such a kind thing to offer, not that I would ever.

"Thank you, that's very nice of you." I went back to peeling.

"Do you get to talk to your parents very often?"

Not unless I have to.

"It's been some time," I whispered.

"That's pretty heartbreaking to hear. I'm sure they miss you."

I changed the topic while we finished up, and I helped her carry out the food to the barbecue. Mike's father was knee-deep in steaks but flashed me an Irons-huge smile when I handed him a beer.

"Thanks, hon. How was work?"

I loved their use of terms of endearment for me. "It was good. Busy, which is always nice."

"Good. Happy to hear it."

I didn't leave right away. I liked standing near him while he cooked, and I enjoyed his company. He was easy and had such a positive outlook on life.

"How is the sunscreen campaign going?"

"Good. We're just starting it this week, so not too much has happened."

"Well, it sounds like it's off to a good start." He closed the hood on the grill.

"She's being modest," Char chimed in behind me. "Dad, she pulled straight As in school. Cat won lead on the sunscreen project."

He held up his large hand for me to high-five him. I did and felt a hint of pride kick in.

"It was unexpected."

"Why?" Char shrugged. "You're super smart and beautiful. You're the entire package."

I appreciated her compliment, but I wanted to talk about something else now.

"No one fear, the men are here!" Mark boomed from behind us. I welcomed the interruption as a trickle of excitement bubbled up from somewhere dormant. "For you." He handed Mr. Irons a strange-looking wine. "A treat for some of my favorite people."

"Oh, would you look at that, dear." He held it up for his wife to see.

"How lovely." She beamed. "That was thoughtful, Mark."

"You feed me, so we're even." He laughed and winked at me. "How are you, Catalina?"

"Fine, thanks. And you?"

"Happy not to be sitting in mud." He jammed a handful of Charlotte's chips into his mouth. I wanted to ask where he'd been, but I noticed no one else asked, so I let it be.

"Catalina, swim with me?" Kyle waved me over to the dock.

"Yes!" I loved the water.

I dropped my shorts and ditched my top by the boat and rushed to join him. He pointed to Chris and wiggled his eyebrows. I knew what he was going to do.

Kyle full-out football tackled Chris, who was fully dressed, into the air, and they both hit the water with a huge splash. I covered my mouth to control my laughter. Chris was going to kick his ass once back onshore.

I started to pull my hair free from my ponytail, only to feel a vibration behind me. I didn't get a chance to think before Mike grabbed me around the waist from behind and lifted me up over his shoulder like I weighed nothing.

"Oh, my God!" I shrieked as I clung to him. "Where did you come from?"

"Can you swim?"

"No!" I lied.

"She's lying!" Chris spat out. "She's a fish."

"Screw you, Chris!" I laughed.

"I guess I'll have to come in after you." I felt Mike's muscles contract as he lifted me straight up and tossed me into the lake.

Once I was submerged, I stayed under and swam a little way out. When I heard him hit the water, I waited and squinted through the air bubbles. Where did he go?

I came up for air and looked around.

"Your six!" Mark shouted, but I didn't know what he meant until I felt him grab my sides and twist me around.

"Oh!" I yelped. My hands flew reflexively to his shoulders. His muscles were like bricks. How was that even possible? "Damn, you can swim fast." I yanked my hand back when I noticed his gash. "Jesus, are you okay?"

"Just a scratch." He brushed me off.

"No, it's not," I elaborated, and he let me, totally ignoring what I was saying.

"Banner," his mother scolded playfully, "are you being nice?"

"No." He grinned.

"Banner?" I questioned, and he moved his attention back on me. "What's that stand for?"

"Go on a date with me, and I'll tell you."

I stroked backward a few feet, but he didn't like that, so he closed the gap and treaded water, making the current hard for me to handle.

"I'm busy."

"You're busy on a date and time I haven't put forward yet?"

"Yup."

"Nah," he shook his head, "I call your bluff."

I started to swim back to shore, but he blocked my path.

"What's up?"

"You didn't call or text, so I'm dating someone else now." I tried to hide the excitement that he just asked me out. I swam away from him, but he hooked an arm around my waist to stop me.

"Trust me?" he asked, but before I could answer, he dipped us both under the water and up and inside the walls of the dock.

"Wow." I thought it would be gross or creepy, but it was well maintained underneath.

"You think I blew you off?"

I dipped underwater and popped up to pull my hair out of my face.

He held on to the wooden plank to stabilize himself, and I was suddenly aware we were in our own private area where no one could see us.

"There are a few things you should know about me, Catalina." His gaze fell to my lips as I licked the lake from them. "One, there will be things I can't share with you. Like how I was out of the country since I saw you last. I'm not always allowed to take my personal cell with me for safety reasons. Two," he inched closer while the water lapped around us, "I like you, and I don't normally like many people. And three," he came so close I felt the pressure of the undertow created by his legs, "I don't give up very easily. Don't mistake my silence for me not wanting to speak with you. Understand?"

"Yes." I matched his hold on the wood.

"Good." His muscles flexed under his drawings, making them come to life momentarily. The eagle caught my attention, and without thinking, I reached out and ran my fingers along the feathers. When you focused on their detail, you could see names etched into the lines.

"Who are they?" My fingers kept moving about.

"People I don't want to forget." His tone wavered slightly.

"Family members?"

"Yes, but not in the way you think." His hand stopped mine and brought it to his chest. He seemed to enjoy my touch.

"This place is cool," I muttered to fill the silence.

"It got you alone with me, so I like it." He flashed me a charming smile.

"Why do you want to be alone with me?" I felt my stomach clench as someone jumped in the water and the wave tossed me into him. His strong arms wrapped around me, and suddenly he was standing. *He can touch?*

"So I can look at you and know that no one else is," he whispered. I fell into his trance as he shifted me against the side rails. "So I can do this." His finger ran from the top of my bikini strap, wrapped around my neck, and made a trail down to the top of my breast. I sucked in deeply, which lifted my chest, and his expression grew hungry. I could burst just from his touch alone.

"How is someone so smart and beautiful still single?" He let his hand trail around to the other breast while I held on to his shoulders and treaded water the best I could.

"I could ask you the same thing," I huffed, completely lost in his warmth.

His eyebrows pinched, and he gave me a lopsided grin. "You think I'm beautiful?" I nodded, and he thought for a moment. "No one has ever called me that."

"That's a shame." I tipped my chin, wanting his lips on mine. I was so wound up I could scream.

The water splashed as his body pressed into mine, and I couldn't miss his huge erection. *Holy…!*

"You cold?" He ran a hand over my goosebumps while I shook my head. He urged my legs to wrap around his waist, and now we were face to face. The water lapped between us, and he pressed his chest to mine. "What do you want right now, Catalina?" The way he said my name made my legs flinch, and he cleared his throat. It had been a while since I'd been with a man, and holy shit, I missed it.

"Anyone see Mike?" A shadow passed over his face, and Lizzy's voice cut through my lust.

His mouth moved to my ear before he grunted, "Tell me."

"Kiss me," I responded from somewhere far away.

His lips started at my earlobe and traveled south. Each

peck came with a swirl of the tongue and a low moan like he was trying hard to control himself. I wished he'd let loose so I could.

Curling his finger around the bow at my neck, he tugged, and my top let go, offering my bare breasts to him.

"Jesus," he murmured as he palmed one gently and then went back to kissing my neck. The water was my friend and helped keep my breasts nice and high as they bobbed between us. He bent and licked my nipple then drew it into his mouth slowly before he gave it a deliciously hard tug. My hands moved to his head to encourage him to keep going. I wanted him to taste every part of my body, to devour me completely. I could feel the buildup within, and I knew I might be about to experience a world-class orgasm.

"Mike," I panted in his ear. "Mike, I…" I squeezed my legs, needing more. Pushing past his arms, I reached down and wrapped my fingers around his erection and fisted him tightly.

He growled and sucked harder. I didn't care that Lizzy was above us somewhere or that anyone could swim by. I really needed this right now.

I pumped harder, and he moved up my breast and started to suck on the side of it. We were lost in our foreplay, teasing the hell out of one another. I felt the heat of my arousal pool in my suit in spite of the water, and I secretly begged for him to do something about it.

"Mark," Mike's mother called, "could you please let the others know dinner is ready?"

"Sure thing," Mark replied.

Mike pulled away and closed his eyes like he was trying to calm himself. I, on the other hand, wanted to cry at the loss of contact.

I pumped him one last time, and his eyes opened, flashing a need that I mirrored.

"I could have you right here under a dock." He chuckled. "That's one for the books."

I glanced down at my breasts and saw the hickeys starting to form. I'd never had one before, but they were proof Mike Irons was there. Oddly enough, it was sexy as hell.

His fingers brushed over the markings. "I wish I could say I'm sorry, but I think there was a part of me that wanted to stamp you as taken."

"Taken?" I raised an eyebrow. "Says the man who hasn't kissed me on the lips yet."

He stepped closer to me and pressed my breasts into his massive chest. "Says the man you have your body wrapped around." He leaned down and hovered over my lips but paused. "I think I'll savor this moment a little longer." He kissed my neck, pulled back with a wink and a grin, then dipped under the water and swam back to shore.

Damn that smile.

My stomach flipped into a tight knot of excitement. Mark stood at the end of the dock with his phone to his ear. I squinted through the slits of the dock to see him better.

"Oh, Christ, Savi, Mike just Code Forty-Fived Catalina." His laugh boomed across the water. "I really wish you and Mia could have been here to witness it."

Code Forty-Five?

After dinner, I tugged on my oversized pink sweater that always fell off one shoulder and ran my fingers through my wavy hair so it wouldn't dry too crazy. Charlotte handed me a rather large glass of wine and stood to block my path.

"Do you like my brother?" I laughed a little then took a long sip to buy myself some time. "Okay," she smirked when she got her answer, "look, he's fantastic, quite possibly one of the best guys out there, but there's a lot of unknowns that you might not like if you start to date."

"Like?" I was curious as to whether she was going to mention his work.

"Mike works for the Army."

"Okay?" I shrugged. "That's not a big deal."

"No, like, special forces Army. As in, he disappears for days on end, and sometimes he returns fine, and other times he returns, well, with a lot of baggage. Sometimes he could have cuts and scrapes, broken bones, even. We don't ask, because we never get an answer. And…"

"Honestly, Charlotte," I held up a hand, "I have a lot I don't talk about too. I get that."

She started to say more, but we could both see Lizzy heading toward us. We stopped talking.

"What are you two talking about?"

"Work," Charlotte said, and I appreciated the lie.

"Oh." She rolled her eyes. She hated that we worked together. "I'm going to the fire pit."

We followed her down the path to the sand where everyone sat around in folding chairs.

"Here, Catalina." Mike stood and offered me his chair. I began to protest, but he turned and snatched another from a pile near the bushes. I noticed a neat little shed nestled into the scrubby trees just above the waterline. They must have stored all their beach stuff there. Nice.

"Thanks." I watched as Mark handed him a beer and Mike tucked the cap into his pocket.

I tuned in to the conversations around me and tried to picture what it would have been like to grow up in America with money. How normal it might have felt to have properties that went for miles, where you could walk at all hours of the night and not feel the fear that at any moment you could be shot or raped.

I quickly pushed the thoughts out of my head and focused on the right now. That was all I could control.

"Do it, Cat." Kyle pulled me out of my fire trance. "Please talk dirty to me, baby."

I chuckled. Kyle loved when I spoke Spanish. I normally just recited parts from my favorite books, but instead, I went with whatever came out.

"*La manera en que me miras hace que las mariposas de adentro aletear a la superficie y pelear para ser liberadas.*"

The way you look at me makes butterflies inside flutter to the surface and fight to be released.

I noticed Mark glanced at Mike, who was watching me intently.

"Go on," Kyle encouraged me dramatically like he was trapped in my love spell.

"*Tu no conoces el miedo hasta que se palmeado a través de tu vida controlando tu próximo aliento.*" You don't know fear until it's webbed through your life controlling your next breath.

I paused to see Mike lean his arms on his thighs as if to get closer to me.

"*Pero luego estás tú, tú entraste en mi vida y me hiciste sentir segura.*" But then there's you, you walked into my life and made me feel safe.

Everyone was silent, and I took a deep breath and shook my head.

"*Yo te protegere,*" Mike whispered, and I froze.

I'll protect you.

FIVE

MIKE

"What did you say?" Lizzy moved her seat to be next to me.

"It's just a line from a song." Catalina brushed her question off and gave me a quick glance before she moved her attention to my sister.

Kyle held his chest like her Spanish made him happy. "Oh, I love when you roll your Rs."

"Seems your girl may have some secrets too." Mark bumped my arm with his.

"Hey." Lizzy slipped her hand into mine. I was so used to her touching me, I didn't even think about it anymore. "Can I steal for you for a moment?" She nodded for us to move away from the group.

"What's up?" I broke her hold and tucked my hands in my pockets.

"Well, I was wondering if you're busy. I need a date."

"Not unless something with work comes up. Why?" There was still a part of me that fell into old habits with Lizzy. It was comfortable.

"I need a date, and I thought maybe you'd like to take me." She flipped her blonde hair off her shoulder and gave me the same eyes she did when she really needed me. I had been in love with her since we were kids, so I found myself agreeing without a thought.

"Sure. Text me the details."

"Yay! Thank you!" She leaned up and kissed my cheek.

Mark gave me a funny look when I pulled out my phone to add the date to my calendar.

"What was that about?" He looked worried.

"Lizzy needs my help."

"Of course, she does." He snickered into his beer.

I ignored him when something flashed up on my phone screen.

CRAWFORD: SEE ATTACHMENT

I opened the link and was taken to YouTube, and the title came up as *US Army Black Ops*. The video started with someone watching us on our mission when we ran across the beach with Martina and Luna.

My stomach sank, and I felt sweat break out across my

skin. It was unbelievably imperative that we remained faceless with the cartel for everyone's safety, not to mention that video proved we did indeed have Elena's family.

"Shit!" I cursed without thinking. Mark was by my side in a flash and snatched the phone from my hand, and we both walked away from the group.

"Call it in." He handed me his phone as he kept watch and I dialed.

"Logan," Cole answered.

"Cole, did you see the video?"

"No."

"Mark." I nodded, and he waved back. "The link just went through."

"Did my night just go to shit?"

"Shit doesn't describe what you're about to see."

There was a long span of silence before he spoke again. All I could hear was the sound of our boots as we raced by the hidden dick with the camera. "I need to call Frank. Everyone is to hold tight until you hear from me."

The line went dead.

"So?" Mark took his phone back.

"We sit tight."

"Oh, shit," he huffed, "Mia is going to kick my ass."

"No way!" Charlotte yelled, and we looked back at the group. Everyone was laughing. "Okay, okay." She waved her arms around. "Lizzy, go!"

Mark slapped my shoulder. "Well, at least we're here and not sitting in a mud pit. Let's have some fun."

"Umm," Lizzy closed her eyes, thinking, "never have I ever gone commando to a work party." She slowly raised her drink, and so did Catalina.

"Your turn, Cat!" Charlotte directed.

"Never have I ever shot a gun." She raised a sexy eyebrow at me as she took a sip of her drink.

Interesting…

"What kind?" I smirked.

"Kimber semi-auto."

"That's a serious gun."

"It is." She leaned forward, and one of her arms tucked under her chin and the other motioned for me to come closer, so I mimicked her movement. "So, then, the question is who's a better shot."

"Ha!" Mark hit my shoulder, clearly entertained, not that it took much.

My curled lips broke through my poker face, with no help from Mark, and I squinted at her through the flames.

"We need to hit a shooting range."

"I mean," she leaned back and crossed her legs, "if you want to be humiliated in front of everyone, so be it."

"Nah," I shook my head when everyone cheered, "you and me."

And just like that, I got my date.

"Mike." Lizzy tugged on my arm, but I wouldn't break my hold on Catalina's gaze until she did.

"That's it," Mark pulled out his phone, "Mia and Savannah need to hear about this."

The rest of the night went by in a blur. Every so often,

Catalina would sneak a glance in my direction, and I would be ready with a smile, which made her smile back. *Every time.*

"So," Catalina came up behind me as I finished up a call with Keith, "can I ask you something?"

"Maybe." I leaned against the table and enjoyed how the light from the torches made her honey skin glow. I so wanted to lean into her and kiss that radiance.

"What's with the bottle caps?"

"Huh?"

She stepped forward and tapped my pocket. "Something tells me it's not the best place to keep them."

"Why?"

"Three times, you slipped your hand inside your pocket before you took a beer from Mark."

I removed her bag off her shoulder and set it next to me. I didn't like the idea of her leaving. "So, you were watching me." I sounded a little cocky, but I wasn't trying to be.

"Maybe." She wiggled her nose when I called her out. It was rather cute. "So?"

"I like control." I laughed more to myself than to her. The Blackstone team all had the same issue. We needed control in any way we could get it, since most things in our lives were out of our control. "We all do. The caps keep me in check. I know my limit and don't like to cross it."

"I like that." She moved to sit on the table next to me and looked up at the clear summer sky. "You speak Spanish?"

"I do."

"Wish I knew that," she muttered with a chuckle.

"I meant what I said."

"Mike," she dropped her head, "you don't know me, and it seems to me that you do enough protecting."

I moved to stand in front of her, and my arms landed on the table by her legs, trapping her in. "You're right, I don't know you, but I want to."

She studied me for a moment, and I took the time to drink in her heavenly scent of coconuts and lake water. Images of my mouth on her skin and her hands wrapped around me sent a surge through my veins.

"We come from very different worlds, Mike," she whispered sadly. "Worlds that I don't know can coexist."

"Then let's create our own and see what happens," I challenged, not giving her an out.

"Mike."

"Catalina." I leaned down and gently kissed her cheek, and to my surprise, she turned to me, so I let my lips linger as I spoke. "I'm not asking you to marry me." I nudged her ear with my nose. "I'm just asking you to give me a try."

She turned into the crook of my neck, and a soft huff of air brushed my skin. "I'll try."

I wasn't sure what it was about Catalina that drew me to her, but I was determined to figure it out.

"Kiss me," she whispered, and I chuckled, as it was the only ammo I had against her.

"Go on date with me."

A sexy smile tugged at her lips, and her eyes glowed with interest. "I'm off this Tuesday."

I brushed the pad of my thumb over her bottom lip with a happy sigh. "I'll pick you up at five."

"You play dirty." She chuckled.

"You have no idea."

She leaned in and pulled on my shirt to draw me down. "Game on, Mr. Irons."

With that, she hopped off the table, snagged her bag, and gave me a wink as she walked away.

Damn.

———

I barely slept that night. Dusk was abnormally loud as the word quickly spread that we were not on call tonight, so the new recruits partied. I didn't blame them. It wasn't often we were allowed to blow off steam without some kind of order.

I had one of the biggest rooms in the house. Keith said it was one of the perks of being number two, but frankly, I thought it was because I was so big, they figured my room should be too. I didn't care. It was a place for me to keep my stuff and a quiet place to think. The cathedral ceilings had steel plates that lined the edges, and the rustic lamps that stuck out from the walls gave it a castle feel, and in my head, it seemed to belong to Thor. I kind of liked that. A seventy-inch TV hung over a stone fireplace directly in front of my bed. That was nice but not something I'd use much. It was a great room, but it still didn't feel like it was mine.

The guys of Blackstone were finding love, some new, and some old flames were rekindled. Then there were John and me, the last two bachelors of Blackstone.

I had been in love for years, and the wear of Lizzy's constant rejection had taken its toll on me. I had been convinced she'd really see me one of these days, but now…my mind went to Catalina. Now things were different. Someone new had stepped into the light and lit something dormant inside me. Whether it would develop into something, I didn't know, but I sure wanted to give it a try.

With my arm tucked under my head, I stared up at the ceiling fan and let my mind wander to Catalina's angel tattoo. Something about it tugged at a memory. I swore I had seen it before.

My legs became restless when the memory of her skin under my tongue surfaced. It had taken everything inside me not to rip her suit off and plunge inside, but I wanted to savor the moment with her. Catalina was like a smooth whiskey that you swirled around and sipped, appreciating the taste as it absorbed into your senses.

My phone buzzed, and I pulled it off the charger.

Keith: Can't sleep, kicked the guys
inside, having a drink on the deck.
Join me?

Mike: Yeah.

It bothered me that Keith wasn't always a part of Blackstone since Frank had him working on the admin side of Dusk. We knew it was only temporary, so when we had the opportunity to hang out, we took it. I was pleased to hear he would be joining us for our next mission. It wasn't the same vibe when he wasn't there.

I slipped into some shorts, skipped the shirt, and joined him outside. Dusk reminded me a lot of Shadows in that it looked out over a lake and was nestled deep in the woods. Though we weren't surrounded by the Montana mountains, it still resembled home. The house was just as big, if not a little larger, and had an indoor pool and a giant gym. The only difference was it didn't have the same family feel. Time would develop that, but Keith and I often found ourselves reminiscing about home.

Once I hit the main floor, my bladder screamed at me. I rushed to the restroom, dropped my zipper, and moaned at how good it felt to...

"Fuck!" I jumped and shot piss straight up the wall.

"I like to watch," the little stuffed Furby monster chirped at me as its eyes moved up my front.

"Lopez!" I boomed, and a roar of laughter spread throughout the house.

"I swear to God." I closed my eyes and tried to calm my nerves. If only Olivia knew what her toy was being used for.

I smiled as my dicky side took over. I grabbed the fucking creature and hurried up to his room, held down the button and recorded, "What's another set?" I stuck a sewing needle in its hand and sat it in his drawer next to his condoms. I spread a few of them around its lap and feet.

I hurried down the steps and spotted Crawford still laughing. "There's a mess in the bathroom."

His face dropped, and he groaned as he went to grab the mop. It was a dick thing to do to make him clean it, but he was on bitch duty this week since he'd ignored a rule and gotten our team into trouble.

With a deep breath, I pushed back the urge to smoke Mark in the head, but I knew that would only give him the satisfaction that he'd gotten me, so instead, I would play it cool.

"Hey." Mark waved at me and went back to his phone call with Mia. I knew she'd been missing him, and the twins were quite a handful.

"Lexi left for Shadows tonight." Keith handed me a drink. "She and B will stay there for a week."

"Should be fun." I took a seat and propped my feet up on the unlit fire pit.

"I pity Olivia." He laughed, but I knew he hated it when they left. Little Brandon barely left his father's side, and Keith loved it.

"She's a Logan. She'll have them in line soon enough," I said and laughed.

Mark ended his call, and we all sat in silence mulling over the fact that we were a YouTube sensation tonight. There were already 1.2 million views, and every hour it grew. Thankfully, the rain marred our war paint, so our faces were a blur. I was concerned that one of my tattoos was visible when I carried Martina on my back. No one said it, but we knew it would make me more of a target the next time I stepped over the border.

Mark plucked his drink from the table and started to mouth the straw. I glanced at him and shook my head, but he went on like a dummy trying to move the plastic into his mouth.

No man should use a straw while drinking an alcoholic beverage. Ever.

"You should have seen him with the Chapstick the other night at the bar." Keith slapped Mark's shoulder. "He fisted the length of it and proceeded to rub it in a circular motion over and over."

"What?" He grinned, happy he got a rise out of Keith. "I like to moisturize."

"I can't with you." I held up a hand and closed my eyes for a moment to keep my laughter in. If you gave Mark an inch, he'd run a mile and then some.

Keith's phone lit up, and we all stared at it, our stomachs tightened in case Cole told us to gear up and leave. Though we were clear to stay home, things could change at any time. Elena could surface, and minutes could make the difference between life and death.

I set my untouched drink down and stood while Keith read whatever it was.

"What the hell?" He tossed his phone on the table and covered his eyes like something just stung him. "I'm going to be sick!"

Mark snatched the phone, and to my surprise, he broke out laughing. Not just a little laugh but a full-out hoot which brought on tears.

"What?" I looked at both men, completely lost. Mark tossed me the phone. It took me roughly a full minute of staring at it to realize what I had read.

A dirty text from Nan.

> Ruth: Wear the tight white slacks I got you for Christmas. They always make me feel moist. Hot damn! The outline of those is something to be desired.

Suddenly, Keith ripped back his phone and called her. He pointed to Mark, who was about to open his mouth.

"I will straight-up nut punch you, Lopez, if you make one comment. It's bad enough I have to address this behavior."

Mark pressed his lips together and eyed me like it took every ounce of his willpower not to go there.

Oh, this was awesome.

"Seriously, Nan!" Keith shouted while Mark and I crumpled over with laughter. "Don't yell at me. You were the one—" He paused and went red in the face. "No, you need to check who you send that stuff to, and who was it that you were—" Again, he was cut off, which only made the situation that much better. There was nothing like seeing a grown-ass man get manhandled by a seventy-some-year-old grandma with a set of brass balls.

"She used the word 'moist.'" Mark laughed through a hiccup. "Oh, shit, Savannah is gonna love this one!"

Thankfully, that made our night turn around, and we laughed into the wee hours of the morning, drunk on the word *moist*. Laughter really was the key to our survival.

I pulled into the parking lot, took my normal spot, and eased out with my bag in hand. The bell on the door rang, and Tom granted me a nod.

"Morning, Irons."

"Morning, Tom." I set three ammo boxes on the counter. "How are you today?"

"Thoroughly entertained, actually."

"Oh, yeah? How so?"

"Blue Water just dropped off a team of seven soldiers, and, well, they got a treat." He pointed out the window where I spied Catalina in the center of the group.

I wanted to be a fly on the wall out there, as I was sure she was giving them all shit on their form.

"You know her?"

"I do."

"She's a trip. Definitely a nice change from the normal riffraff that walk in here." He laughed, pointing his comment at me.

"Agreed." I chuckled.

It was true. This was mostly a military range, and not many locals came around. Mountain Ridge Shooting Range was where most of us went to shoot. Tom had these jet engines and water machines that he turned on so we could practice working in the different elements. You could never be too prepared.

I signed the bill and waved him off, and the warmth of the sun hit my face as I stepped out onto the gravel and made my way around the corner.

Jesus.

Catalina stood by the bench in army boots and black jean shorts with a camo tank. Her hair swirled around in the breeze. It was like a soldier's wet dream. Two men were trying to get her attention, and she was giving them shit right back. She really fit in well with men. She could hold her own for being such a tiny little thing.

When she spotted me, she pulled her aviators forward and raked her gorgeous eyes down my front before she turned her smile into a sexy grin. I had the opposite on, black t-shirt and camo pants, my normal getup when I went shooting.

With my bag flipped over my shoulder, I headed in her direction and dropped it heavily at her feet.

"Morning, solider." She beamed up at me while the men moved closer. "Ready to get your ass kicked?"

I couldn't help but drop my gaze down to her breasts, and I saw my mark. I was pleased she hadn't tried to cover it with make-up.

I wanted the vultures to know she was with me, but I reined in my alpha tendencies for the moment.

"Hey," she flicked her head, "eyes up here, Irons."

I licked my lips and tried to behave, but my head and my erection had very different ideas.

"My apologies, Mendez. I see you made some friends."

"I did." She shrugged. "Taught them a few things too."

"That she has." One of them laughed and elbowed his buddy.

"Like how Smith, here," she pointed to the guy, "flinches every time he shoots, so he pulls to the left."

"Ohhh." The other guys hit his shoulder playfully.

"Got a bad hand," he said, trying to make an excuse.

"Well, let's see what you got." I ignored them and pulled my gun free and started to load its clip.

She waited for me to get into position and lined up on the bench when I did.

"Ready?" I asked once as I adjusted to the wind speed.

"Yes."

Pop! Pop!

I hit the center, and so did she, to my utter shock.

"Again." I nodded as I lined up my eye.

Pop! Pop!

Again, we both hit the bullseye.

Damn, that's sexy!

I glanced over my shoulder and eyed the men who were watching us, and they all separated and went back to their drill.

"Pull the rifle into your shoulder with your forward hand." She tried to do it but struggled. "Here." I stood and went to show her, and I caught sight of part of her ass hanging out of her shorts.

She's killing me.

She looked over her shoulder to see where I went. "Problem?"

I huffed out a breath and shook my head. I was stronger than that. I could do this.

Using my hands to draw her backward into me, I tapped her legs to spread a little farther. "Hold the gun like this. I wrapped my body around hers and tried to touch as much of her as possible. She wiggled when I set my hand low on her stomach. "Hold your core tight."

"Okay," she nearly moaned, and it hit right in the heart of my erection.

"Breathe in." I waited for her to do so. "Exhale, start to take up the slack in the trigger." I paused then started to count. "One, two, three."

Pop! Pop!

She nailed the bullseye.

"Perfect."

"You doubted me, Irons?" She laughed, and I pulled the gun out of her hand and removed the clip. "What are you doing?"

"I want to take you to my spot."

I grabbed my bag and took her hand so we could get away from the gawking men. Down a hill and through the shrubs, I showed her the hidden hut that was used for long distance shooting. I pulled back the little door and waved her to go ahead. Once inside the tiny shack, there was enough space for two people to either stand or lie down and shoot.

"Welcome to my thinking place." I set my bag down and watched her squint at the target that was three hundred and sixty yards away.

"You can hit that?" She bent over to finger the mat we used to lie on.

"I can."

She studied me. "That's pretty impressive."

"So are you." I folded my arms so I wouldn't reach out and touch her.

"My father taught me how to shoot when I was younger. He said it's better to know how than not to."

"He had a point."

"Mmm," she agreed while in thought.

"Have you had to point a gun at anyone before?" I felt like there was a lot more to her story then she was sharing.

"I have."

"Did you pull the trigger?"

"I did." She rubbed her arm. "It was the first and last time I ever missed."

"What happened next?"

She shot me a quick glance before she flipped her hair back out of her face with a sigh. "Have you ever missed?"

"No."

"Never once?" She stepped a little closer, and I dropped my arms.

"No."

"You never get distracted and miss your target?" She slid her arms up my chest and over my shoulders while I closed my eyes with a gasp. "Your mind never slips back to a dirty thought or feeling?"

"Not when I have a gun in my hand."

Her head tilted flirtatiously. "Are you thinking a dirty thought now?"

I nodded, and she smirked before she leaned in and hovered over my lips.

"Show me."

I slipped my hands around her waist and down to the bottom of her ass that peeked out of her shorts. I gave it a good squeeze before I lifted her up into the air and placed her on the table.

Hooking her shirt, I pulled it down and popped out her breast. I played with her nipple and watched as her face pinkened. She had the plumpest pair that begged to be fondled. I did the same to her other breast so both nipples were puckered and alert. I licked the hard nubs and gave them a little suck. Her hands were on my back, dragging her nails across my skin.

I kissed her neck and whispered, "You're a goddamn tease with those shorts." I kissed up to her jaw. "I wanted to throat punch those guys out there for looking at you."

"You're pretty protective."

I leaned back and studied her eyes before I cupped her face and leaned in. "You…" I paused. "You make me protective. Something about you stirs up every single alpha gene in me, and it comes out all at once when you're near."

"Why is that?" She moved her hands over my chest, needing to touch me as much as I did her.

"I don't know." I squinted and tried to find the answer in her chocolate eyes. "I'm still trying to figure that out."

"Well," her hand fell forward out of my grasp, "I like it."

Something inside me shifted, like I had the green light to be me.

"Catalina," I lifted her chin, "I really like you, so know that about me, okay?"

"I like you too, Mike," her hands stroked down my arms and back up again, "even if we shouldn't."

When I started to ask her what she meant, she lifted her head.

"You know, you promised me something when we were under the dock."

"I did?" I tried to think back, but all I could remember was how good she felt in my arms.

"Banner?" She grinned.

Right.

"I was a big, scary kid, and no one would play with me. My mother called me Banner, like Bruce Banner the Hulk, to show me that my size could be used for good. That I wasn't scary, my size was a gift, and if I worked hard enough, I could be a superhero too."

"Oh." Her tone held no pity but sounded more amazed that a parent could be so kind.

"She would buy me these ugly troll dolls, and we'd play with them together."

"Troll dolls?" She grinned. "Is that why you have this?" She held up my arm and ran a finger over the troll tattoo.

"Yeah. She told me that no matter how crappy my day was, my friends would always be here." I let a smile escape from the memory. "She promised me that someday I would find my people. Joining the Army was the best thing I ever did."

"You were lucky to have a mother like that." I couldn't help but feel a sense of sadness with her statement, but she quickly shook it off. "Do you still have the trolls?"

"Maybe."

She moved in for a kiss. "Would you ever show me sometime?"

"Maybe."

"I would like to see them."

I eyed her more for show and pressed my lips together like I was thinking, when really, I just liked to watch her squirm. "It's a secret you'll have to take to the grave."

She laughed lightly. "I can safely say I can keep a secret." She brushed her fingers through my hair. "How can you have hair like this, a scruffy beard, and a body full of tattoos when you're in the Army? I thought that was a huge no-no."

She had asked this before, but I knew she was looking for a better answer.

"I only had a few when I joined, and now I'm not on active duty. I'm in a special forces division and sometimes go undercover, so I have to look different." She nodded like she was satisfied with that answer. Her hands continued to roam. "Do you not like it?

"I do. I am *not* trying to be nosy. I'm just curious about you." She sighed happily, and I loved how at ease she made me. I didn't have to try like I did with Lizzy. Catalina saw me for who I was, and that was good enough. It was beyond refreshing. "So," she leaned back to look me in the eyes, "you brought me to your thinking spot?"

"Sometimes I need to clear my head, and this is where I do it."

"Ever had a girl in here?"

"Nope."

"So, this is a first for you."

"It is."

She grinned like she liked that answer too, then pushed past me to sit where I lay to shoot. "You lay right here?" I nodded. "Like this?" She wiggled onto the mat and sprawled out with her arms above her head. I nodded again and dug my heels into the floor to stop my impulse to jump her. "Will you promise me something?" Her breasts, which were now tucked back into place, nearly spilled out of her shirt. "The next time you're here, all alone and ready to shoot, think of me like this, under you." She grinned devilishly.

I bent down and grasped her bent knees and hauled her to me. I hovered over her, careful not to crush her with my weight, and stroked her hair back off her face. Her legs hiked up and crisscrossed around my waist.

"That, I can promise."

We spent the next hour shooting. I loved that we had that in common and that we both liked silence to think.

A few times, she flipped her hair out of her way, and I had to hold my breath because her perfume drove me wild. It didn't help that her outfit left nothing to the imagination.

We were both hungry, so we left the range, and I helped her into my truck. We were ravenous by the time we spotted the taco truck. She had told me she'd never eaten here before, so we had to stop.

"Try this." I held up a taco so she could take a bite.

"Oh, my God, this is so good." She licked her lips, and I shook off the effect she had on me. I never thought I would get over Lizzy as easily as I had, and it was friggin' nice.

I pulled my phone out to see a text message from Mark.

> Mark: North Rock is moving into position.

"Who's that?" she asked around her straw. She must have caught my sudden change of mood.

"Mark."

"Everything okay?" I knew she was just asking, but it did slap a dose of reality down on me that I was flirting with a line that could never be crossed. Maybe she should be vetted. I chased that thought away, hating the idea, but it lingered in the background like an annoying tick.

"Yeah," I looked away, "work stuff."

"Are you leaving anytime soon?" Her tone softened.

"I could leave in five minutes." I shrugged.

"Mark, Keith, and Cole all have someone, right?" I nodded and tossed my wrapper in the trash. "How did that happen? I mean, if we can't know all the details, how do they make it work? Where do they live?"

I swallowed hard and tried to say the right thing to end the conversation.

"Luck," I lied. I felt bad saying that about Savannah, but I needed to shut down the conversation.

"Luck, huh?" She finished off her last taco. "Well, damn, we're screwed, then."

I knew she was joking, but it still bothered me. I waited for her to finish before I walked her back to my truck.

"Mike?" she whispered from the passenger seat. It was dark, so I couldn't read her body language. "Can I ask you something at the risk of upsetting you?"

Sweat broke out along the back of my neck. Here it was, the dreaded conversation that always hovered on the sideline of my life. I slid my hands over the steering wheel and took a deep breath, waiting for it. "Okay."

"Maybe we shouldn't be doing this." She turned in her seat to see me better. "I'm not trying to be dramatic, here. I'm trying to be realistic. There are things that could get in the way. Are you really ready to dive into a relationship, knowing we have things we can't talk about?"

I reached for her hand and kissed her fingers and placed her hand on my leg. Words weren't coming to my head. Why couldn't I be that guy who knew what to say? I just couldn't find any words that I knew wouldn't mess things up. I could tell my silence made her uneasy, but she didn't say anything else as we drove. We arrived at her place while I still wrestled with what to say. I got out and opened her door for her.

"Thank you for the fun today. It was the best date yet." She squeezed my arm as she started to walk away, but I grabbed her hand and pulled her backward, and in one swift motion I took her by the hips and sat her on the hood of my truck.

"I need this." Both hands moved into her hair, and I held her still while I dove down and caught her lips. Her arms wrapped around my neck, and her tongue danced with mine. As I expected, she tasted amazing, and her lips were soft as silk. Her spine softened and formed into my body, sending a flicker of excitement to my chest while heat licked everywhere else. A tiny huff of pleasure brushed through her lips when my fingers crept up her thigh and pulled her tighter around me.

I hoped we weren't giving any neighbors a good show because I wasn't about to disconnect from this moment. Her legs flexed, and the heel of her boot drove into my hip. It was obvious she wasn't worried about our public display of affection, and I loved that it didn't bother her right now either.

Although we should go inside.

She started to massage the base of my neck and kissed deeper, destroying any rational thoughts that tried to surface.

Between her taste and her perfume, all sense left my head. I wanted to bottle and indulge in it whenever I pleased. I was a junkie addicted to the right kind of drug, still dangerous but worth the heartache.

I forced myself to pull myself together. It took every ounce effort I had, and I pulled away. I rested my forehead against hers, giving myself a second for my brain to kick in, but all that came out was the bare truth.

"It's hard to be a gentleman around you, Cat."

"If that's how a gentleman kisses, I've been dating the wrong kind of men." She smirked playfully. "Okay." Her hands landed on my chest and gently pushed me backward so she could hop down. I took her arm to make sure she didn't hurt herself. "I wouldn't want to be a bad influence on all that hard work Mrs. Irons has done."

She leaned up and gave me a long, gentle kiss on the lips. "Thank you, Mike, for today. It was really fun and much needed."

"Happy to hear it. So, we're okay, then?"

She licked her lips then pressed them into a hard line like she was thinking. "Just…" She paused and bit down on the side of her lip. "Just think about what I said, and I will too. We both have parts of our lives that could be upsetting to the other."

She alluded to a lot but always stopped herself like she was trying to share but couldn't or wouldn't. I saw the red flag but ignored it because I wanted—no, needed this. I had this amazing woman in front of me, and I wanted it all.

I crossed my arms and asked her anyway. "Like?"

"What did Mark's text say?"

I made an annoyed face. I couldn't be honest with her.

"Exactly." She leaned up and kissed my cheek and rested her hand on my arm for a second. "Goodnight, Mike."

"Goodnight, Catalina."

My truck roared to life, and I pulled out onto the quiet street, not ready to be alone yet. My head spun at the red light. I hated that we both had secrets, but I was shocked at the depth of my feelings for her. This wasn't what I'd felt for Lizzy, not even close. I realized this might be the real thing. Catalina might actually be the one. *Shit.* I couldn't mess this up.

I needed some sleep.

————

I woke to my phone ringing beside my head. I immediately glanced at it and didn't answer. When it stopped and started to ring again, I knew she wouldn't give up.

"Morning." I coughed to clear my throat.

"Morning would imply it's early. It's one in the afternoon, and you're late for our lunch date."

I rubbed my eyes and tried to recall last night's events, and she wasn't in them. We both knew I had an epic memory, but classic Charlotte liked to trip me up.

"Bullshit."

"Meh, get out of bed and meet me. I want to talk to you about Cat."

I sat up and tossed the blankets aside.

"Ha," she chuckled smugly. "That got your attention, didn't it?"

"Where and when?"

"Brew, twenty minutes."

"I'll be there in thirty."

"And that's why I said twenty." She laughed harder before she ended the call.

I tossed my phone on the bed and hurried to the shower. It wasn't long before I was out the door.

My grin made her roll her eyes when I arrived at the Brew in under twenty. I hated to be late and took pride that I often wasn't. The Brew was busy with its lunch rush, and I glanced around to see if Catalina was working.

"She's out back changing." Charlotte pushed out a seat with her foot, and I sat. "The soda gun decided to spring a leak and drenched the girl. I didn't know curse words could sound so good in Spanish." She grinned, amused, at the breakroom door. "She pulls out her Latina edge when she gets pissed off. No wonder she does so well here. Takes zero shit from anyone."

"Okay." I plucked the menu from her and started to decide what I wanted. "Why am I here?"

"We've always been extremely open with one another, right?"

"Um-hm. Do I want a burger or a chicken sandwich? I'm hungry but not starving. We have…"

"I think I'm in love with John."

My head shot up, and my face twisted into a scowl.

"Pardon?"

"Have you decided what you want?" She folded her arms. "You ignore me when food is involved. Christ, you're just like Mark!"

"First, don't swear. Second, John is too old for you, and third, yes, we've been open, so spit out what you need to say so we can order."

She rolled her eyes. She hated that I could do two things at once but let it go. "Fine, whatever." She sipped her Sprite slowly before she went on. "How much do you like Cat?"

"On a scale of one to ten?" I raised an eyebrow skeptically.

"Look, Mike, I've known her for eight months, and I've spent a good deal of time with her outside of work. Kyle would most likely know her better because…"

"Stay on topic, Char." I yawned. I loved my sister to no end, but her storytelling left something to be desired.

"Blah!" She swung her arms in the air, frustrated with me and herself. "I'm just saying every time I ask about her personal life or ask anything about her past, she shuts down."

"So, she has a shitty past. Look at Mark." Mark had been welcomed into our family like a second son, next to Keith. Since he met Mia, he'd been pretty vocal about his past and how he was trying to overcome it.

"No." She slammed her hand down on mine. "Mark has PTSD from child abuse caused by his now dead, thank God, mother. Catalina has something that is affecting her right now. I have a bad feeling, Mike. She has some real hell going on."

I leaned back while a waitress I didn't recognize set a water in front of me. I smiled my thanks at her.

"Thanks, Judy. This is my brother, Mike. Judy is new."

She looked mildly terrified and nearly dropped the cutlery she carried.

I smiled to show her I wouldn't eat her, in spite of my size, and ordered before she scurried off. I was used to that.

I turned back into my sister. "And how do you know this if she doesn't open up to you?"

"Because I watch and listen and maybe even snoop a little."

"Char!" I pretended to be mad, but she held up her hand.

"It's not as bad as it seems, big brother." She lowered her voice. "I heard her on the phone speaking to someone. She spoke half English and half Spanish, something about some guy named Javier and how much she despises her father."

"Hi!" Catalina eyed both of us before she tucked a loose piece of hair behind her ear. I was sure she could feel the mood in the room. "Sorry for interrupting, but I'm finally dry and de-stickied," she laughed as she looked at me, "and I wanted Char to know I finished the mark-ups for the first meeting on Friday." She turned to Charlotte. "I was wondering if I could use your eyes to see if everything looks right."

"Cat," Charlotte laughed lightly, "you were given the assignment notes yesterday. When did you possibly have time to finish that?"

"My guess," Kyle slipped into the chair next to my sister, "she didn't go home last night."

"Kyle." Cat shook her head. I could tell it wasn't anything that involved our date last night.

"Cat," Charlotte reached out for her hand, "you can't let him scare you into not going home. You know I've overhead enough to—"

"Who?" I interrupted. I wanted to know who would scare someone as sweet as Catalina.

"No one." She tried to shut us all up with a glare.

"Just have Mike walk you home one night, and all your problems will be solved." Kyle shrugged. "I apparently do nothing."

"Maybe that's because she knows you attract men rather than repel them." Charlotte bumped his shoulder.

"It's my shirt, isn't it?" he joked. "Or is it my long lashes that makes them insecure?"

"Bit from column A and a bit from column B." Charlotte wrapped her arm around his shoulders in an attempt to soothe him before she looked over at Catalina. "Of course, I'll look it over, but you know the meeting isn't until August first, right? That's three weeks away."

"I know, but I have a lot of work to prep for first." She touched Char's shoulder warmly. "Thanks." She jumped when her phone went off in her back pocket. She turned and answered quickly. "Hello? Javier?" Charlotte shot me look as if to make her point just as the food arrived.

She switched to Spanish, and I tried to listen over the

noise in the place but couldn't catch that much, only, "Please say something if that's you. Just anything to show you're okay."

Her hand flew to her forehead before she lowered the phone and straightened her shoulders.

"Everything okay, Cat?" Charlotte dove into her burger, but I knew it was to look nonchalant.

"Yeah," she shook her head as if to clear it, "just waiting on a call."

"A guy?" She wiggled her eyebrows. Catalina's gaze shot to me, and I saw concern race across her face. She seemed as if she was stuck.

"Kind of. My brother, he's been missing for a while."

Char glanced over at me, and a piece of burger fell from her mouth.

"You should have told me," I blurted, completely forgetting our company.

"It's not a big deal. I'm just worried, that's all." She forced another smile. "It's happened before. I'm sure he'll call."

"If you need any help, I can make a few calls," I reassured her.

"No," she cut me off quickly, "I wouldn't want to bother you with it."

"Catalina?" a customer called and pointed at his empty beer glass. "May I have another?"

"Sure." She rushed over to help, with Kyle right behind her asking about a beer.

"Wow." Char chased down her burger with a swig of

water, and her greasy fingers shone in the light. "She has never opened up like that before."

> Mark: Come back. Cole needs us.

> Mike: On the way.

"Sorry, Char, I have to go." I stood and tossed a couple of twenties on the table as I grinned down at my baby sister. "Seriously?" I pointed at the food droppings around her. "And you wonder why you're single."

"Who said I'm single?" She winked, and I remembered and wanted to kill someone.

"I'm callin' Mom." I pointed a finger at her. I leaned in and kissed her head, the one place that was food-free. Just before I turned to leave, I swung around and said, "He's too old, but I love you, girl."

"How could you not?" Charlotte called after me. "Thanks for the burger."

I waved over my shoulder and caught Catalina's eye. She stood over by the bar. She gave me a little wave, and I shot her one of my charming smiles. It was all I could offer at the moment, but by the way her chest lifted a little, I knew it worked. Mom always said I oozed charm, but I'd never used it purposefully, until now. I held up my phone then lifted a shoulder toward my ear as I looked at her with a little grimace. She nodded and gave me a weak smile.

With that, I left.

I pulled up to the house, and I could feel the vibe was off. Crawford met me at the door and gave me that same look he did every time Cole called us in this way.

"What's up?"

"You've been called out."

SIX

CATALINA

My fingers skimmed the table as I bent and eyed up the wine glasses to make sure they were sitting perfectly in place. The company only had one spot open in advertising for women's fashions and make-up. That was it. So, it came down to Brent, Tina, and me, and this pitch meant everything. Linda would take the lead, and I would assist her, but this entire pitch was my creation.

"Ready?" Linda shut the door behind her and smiled at my white pinstriped dress with its matte black belt. "This," she pointed, "is gorgeous."

"Thanks." I popped the cork on a bottle of wine.

"Should I ask?" She gestured to the line of wine bottles.

"You could," I leaned my head to the side to see past her, "but we have company."

Linda cooed as Nicole Miller fell into step with her company's head of marketing.

"She's something else, isn't she?" She said it quietly, hardly moving her lips.

"Sure is," I breathed, and I too fell into the love spell that was Nicole Miller.

"Okay," she smiled at me, "here we go."

The Miller team of eleven came in and actually gushed over the display I had created. It had taken me all morning and was based on what I had gleaned were Mrs. Miller's personal likes.

"Ms. Mendez, could you hold on a moment?" The head of marketing caught my attention. It was right after I had pitched my idea for their new commercial and billboard ads. Everyone in the room went quiet, and I placed my papers down and gave her a friendly smile. "You certainly did your research on Nicole." She waved a graceful hand toward her boss. "I welcome you to share with us what you discovered."

I paused to gather my thoughts, and I felt all eyes on me. "I would be happy to."

I moved closer and took a seat at the head of the table. It was a bold and daring move, but my purpose was to show I was comfortable in this world.

"Mrs. Miller," I addressed her politely, "*Time Magazine* quoted last year that you wanted to move away from the mainstream to more street chic. That you wanted things much edgier and forward." Nicole Miller smiled at me and nodded for me to continue. "I also learned that your favorite chocolate comes from a small shop in New York City." I gently opened the box to show her the little drops of heaven. Her eyes lit up as she reached for one and popped it in her mouth. "And," I reached forward and turned the label around so she could read it, "your favorite wine is a 2011 St. Michelle Merlot, your favorite because it was the bottle you had when your husband proposed."

Her eyes sparkled as I carefully tipped the bottle and poured a small amount into the glass. Linda gave me a nod and a grin to show she was impressed.

Her marketing director began to speak, but Nicole held up a hand to stop her.

"Ms. Mendez, I'm very impressed. Not many would have taken the time to do such research. I will be in touch with my decision. But for now," she took the bottle from my hand and filled another glass and handed it to me, "we celebrate a wine that is laced with wonderful memories." Her glass tapped mine before we both took a sip.

My hands were frozen by the time the presentation was over. Char was in the back with Kyle for moral support.

"Holy hell, Cat, that was amazing! Who knew you knew so much about Nicole Miller! We held our breath there a couple of times when the marketing director asked questions. Thankfully, we know how seriously you take your work, but you must have done a boatload of research."

I beamed and allowed a little of my own pride to sink in. I did kick ass today. It also helped that I took the owner of the downtown boutique out to lunch to get the real skinny on Mrs. Miller. It turned out they were good friends. There was nothing like getting to know someone through the eyes of a friend. I learned Nicole loved wine. Sometimes a little dash of something personal went a long way.

"Come on, our weekend awaits!" Charlotte pulled me from the conference room.

"Wait, Catalina." Linda stopped us at my desk. "That was impressive." She looked over her shoulder at Brent and Tina, who were trying to act like they weren't listening. "What was even more impressive was that you won over Nicole." Her brows pinched together. "How did you know about the wine?"

A smile broke free. "Her college roommate's best friend owns a shop downtown, and it turns out after a little Moscato, she had some stories to tell."

Linda's eyebrow perked up. "I think I need to keep my eye on you. Well done." She turned and walked away but stopped at the others. "The bar just rose."

Charlotte's eyes nearly bulged out of her head as she gave a silent scream of excitement. I grabbed her arm and my bag, and we rushed outside.

We linked arms and chatted the entire way back to my place. I was on a serious high. Sadly, we came to a standstill when Jeff stepped off the stoop and blocked our path to my door.

"I can keep that smile on your face permanently if you'd just come inside."

I rolled my eyes, but he stepped closer. "Jeff, stop."

"Come on, baby girl." His hand brushed down my shoulder, and I wanted to shiver.

"She's not interested." Charlotte batted his hand away. "Never has been and never will be. She has a boyfriend, you creep."

"Tame your dog," Jeff said and snickered at me.

"What did you say?" Charlotte went to get in his face, but I pulled her away, and we went inside. Jeff was an asshole, but he was also my landlord, and I didn't need my stuff out on the front step when we get back from our weekend.

"You need to do something about him, Cat. He's really creepy." She sat on my bed and kicked her feet up. "Peek through a hole, stand behind a curtain kinda creepy."

"I'm agreeing with you, Charlotte, but what can I do?" I tossed her a water before I started to pack my bag.

"My brother needs to set him straight."

"Your brother would actually need to be around for that to happen."

Her face twisted like she was concerned. "Are you finding his coming and going too much?"

"The last time I saw Mike was with you at lunch three weeks ago."

"If he hasn't texted you, it's because he can't. I hope you know that." I loved that she defended him.

In fairness, Mike did say he couldn't text or call sometimes, but three weeks was a very long time, especially when we'd only had one real date. "I know, and honestly, it's okay."

She sat up and brushed her hair out of her face. "Wait, don't you like my brother?"

I folded my jeans and tucked them under my sweater.

"Cat?" I could feel her eyes burning a hole in my face.

"Yeah, I do."

"Great," she said, beaming.

"Why do you care so much?"

"Honestly, with the risk of you shutting down on me, I just want to see you have a little happiness, and I know Mike could give you that."

"I am happy." Even I could hear the lie in my voice.

"Not surface happy, happy-happy."

I didn't like the conversation anymore, so I turned and held up a ripped tank top with studs on the fringe. "Yes?"

"Definitely." She let the topic go, and I let the high of my presentation sink back in. We needed to get on the road. The four-and-a-half-hour drive to Bristol was just what I needed to clear my head and really let what happened today sink in.

———

The Silver Fox Cottages were just fifteen minutes from the Bristol Motor Speedway and were pretty damn impressive. There were seven little cottages in a horseshoe surrounding a small lake and fire pit in the center. Massive trees provided privacy and shade for those hot summer days.

It was late, but the five of us were wired. Kyle, Chris, and Lizzy were squeezed in the back, and somehow, I lucked out and got to ride up front. Kyle shot me a few pissed-off looks about Lizzy and her need to be the center of attention, and all I did was smirk. I loved the kind of friendship we had.

After we unpacked and the drinks were made, we made our way down to the lake and lit a fire.

"You know what I love?" Kyle grinned at us and poked the fire with a stick. "Even on vacation, we spend it like we're at the Irons' house."

"We know what we like." I shrugged unapologetically. "So, we do what we like everywhere we go." I turned to Charlotte, who was on her phone. "You good?"

"Yeah." She suddenly beamed at me. "What do we have here?"

I twisted to see a bunch of guys wearing board shorts, heading our way with coolers. What was kind of funny was that they all had on bright orange sunglasses.

Match much?

"Who are they?"

"Fresh meat," Lizzy hissed as she yanked down her tank top to give herself more cleavage.

It didn't help.

"Ladies!" The guy holding the cooler granted us a huge smile. "We're in cabins six and seven."

"Were in one and two," Lizzy blurted.

"For the weekend?"

"Yup."

He looked at Charlotte then me. "Lucky us."

Lizzy pushed to her feet and stood a few feet in front of me. I rolled my eyes at Kyle, who was checking out one of the other guy's girlfriends. He loved to play both teams. He called it "Undecided."

"I'm Lizzy."

"Jason." He introduced the others, but my phone alerted me to a text, and I pulled it free.

> Javier: Are you there?

Excitement burst through my veins, and a smile ripped away my frown. My mind scrambled to type a response.

> Catalina: I am. Where are you? Was that you calling me before?

> Javier: Catalina?

> Catalina: Yes, it was me.

> Javier: What's your middle name?

I paused and shook my head because he was back to

being super paranoid. I wondered what kind of trouble he was in now. He may have been my older brother, but I always felt I was the smarter, wiser one. If he was in trouble, I only hoped our father hadn't gotten wind of it.

> Catalina: Sierra.

> Javier: Good.

I waited for a moment and then typed again. I needed more.

> Catalina: Are you okay? Where are you?

> Javier: I need to see you, where are you?

> Catalina: I'm away, won't be home until Sunday night. The key is where it normally is, under the third flowerpot. I'd come home, but we just got here.

> Javier: It's fine, just need a place to crash.

> Catalina: How bad is it this time?

A pause before he replied.

> Javier: Bad. But I'm heading your way, just really need family right now. Thanks, Cat, and I'm sorry.

I didn't care what he'd done right now. I was just relieved to hear from my brother.

An enormous weight lifted off my shoulders, and I felt like I could breathe again. I dropped my phone on the seat and stood with a bounce in my step.

"What's up?" Charlotte grinned at me. She must have sensed my change in mood. "Did my brother text you?"

"Why would Mike text her?" Lizzy cut in and glared at me with probing eyes.

Damn, I forgot she was here.

"No." I ignored Lizzy and lowered my voice so the guys couldn't hear. "I heard back from *my* brother. He's okay, and he's heading to my place tonight."

"Really?" She wrapped her arms around me. "I'm so glad."

The new guys wanted to party, but I really needed to chill out, now that I could, so I said my goodnights early and headed to bed. For the first time in a long while, I was able to put my head on the pillow and fall into a deep, peaceful sleep.

———

"Seriously?" Char spat her toast out when she caught sight of my outfit the next morning. "Where did you get that buckle?"

I smirked as I stole the other half of her toast and poured myself a cup of coffee. "This isn't my first race." I caught my reflection in the glass door. My white Chucks and ripped jean shorts looked good with the white t-shirt. The number four in the center stared back at me. My Jack

Daniel's belt buckle rested right below my bellybutton that peeked out under my t-shirt.

"You look cute." Kyle rubbed his tired eyes. He joined me as he checked his watch. "We should get going, or we might miss..." He trailed off, and I looked at him over the top of my mug.

"Who?" I swallowed.

"A girl I invited."

"Not another Facebook friend?" I groaned. He had a bad habit of dating people from his personal page.

He shrugged, and we all made our way outside. Once Lizzy finally decided to join us, we headed to the track.

Of course, the place was packed, and parking took forever, but once we were through the gates, we all relaxed and hit up the beer truck.

"Wow." I leaned over the railing at the track below us. "Damn, girl, you scored some good seats."

"Perks of some family friends." Charlotte shrugged.

"Mm." I spotted my driver and grinned at how close he was. I closed my eyes and took a deep breath to enjoy the smell of fumes and asphalt. I became obsessed with NASCAR when I arrived in the States. I needed something fast and heart-pounding to help release the adrenaline. My life had finally taken a swing in a positive direction, but the fear of it being ripped out from under me was always right there.

"Stop," I hissed to myself. I didn't need that in my head today.

I felt the heat of someone beside me. A colorful arm

slid into my peripheral vision, and a lightness in my chest fluttered. "Who's your driver?"

I kept my eyes on the track, not wanting to show my excitement right away. He had no problem with staying quiet. I could stay level too. "Kevin Harvick."

"Hmm." Grit laced his voice, which hit straight to the center of my stomach.

"You?"

"Harvick."

A long stretch of time passed before I spoke. "You've been gone a while."

"Yeah."

"You all right?"

Mike turned to face me, his eyes shaded by his ball hat. "I am now."

I bit the inside of my lip and thought. "When you're *there*, are you ever by yourself?"

"Hardly ever."

SEVEN

MIKE

My boots were soaked, mud caked my face, and my clothes were like cement. The team had come upon a group of young kids who were training with the cartel. We had to blend in with the environment to stay out of sight, which meant immersing ourselves in the muddy lake for over an hour. I tried hard to contain my anger. It was sick that boys as young as seven were being taught how to shoot a gun and how to kill.

"How is this shit supposed to help your skin?" Keith muttered next to me.

"The nutrients seep into your pores and help moisturize them," Mark answered but looked up when he

caught us all staring. "What? Mia gave me the rundown."

I continued to stare for a few more seconds then turned to John and a new topic. "So, are we on for the Peak next weekend?"

John tensed when the trees behind me moved. We all raised our guns and scanned the branches.

"Relax, boys." Beast from Team North Rock chuckled as he and his team appeared. "Fancy meeting you guys here."

"You look like shit," Greg grunted and dropped onto the ground with a heavy thud. He always wore a pissed-off look, but I knew it was just that he took his job seriously and was a friggin' good solider.

"It's been a long day," I growled. "About four clicks that way," I pointed west. "there's kids training."

"So fucked up." BT snickered. "All of it is."

"Yeah." Our job was rewarding, but really, the dent we make in the cartel could be patched up only a few hours later. The truth was, for every ten cartel goons we took down, they had another fifty ready to take us on. Not to mention the kids. You never knew who you could trust. One moment you were handing them a piece of candy, and the next they were shooting you in the chest.

I pushed that thought aside. It wasn't something to let in at the moment.

"That's what your sister said this morning." Danny laughed at Mark. They were already in conversation.

The two never shut the hell up when they were together.

"Hey, man." Ryan was North Rock's intel guy. He could find a grain of rice in a barrel of seed. He handed me a piece of paper that contained a hand-drawn map. "I did what you asked. It took a while, but we kept watch and eventually found her. Details later, but one thing, since Elena was taken from the container, I'd say by her appearance, she's now a pretty." I gritted my teeth. I knew being a pretty meant she was to be used for the high rollers. He glanced over the shoulder at his team. "Trigger was right to give you that address." He pointed to the grounds and what they had for cameras. "Seriously high-tech stuff with optical zooms." Shit, they had our military-grade cameras at Salvador's house. "And I'd bet my left nut she's there now, but until they upload her photos to the database, I can't confirm anything. Right now, she's a floater."

"It's a direction, and I appreciate your time on it."

"Anytime, man. Say hi to your folks for me."

"Will do." I shook his hand and went back to my post.

"Where the fuck is Logan?" Steve popped through the trees with Greg.

"Took a call," I shouted. I could tell something happened on their end. We often used North Rock when we had a big case and couldn't spend great amounts of time in Mexico. They were our eyes while *we prepared our next move. We couldn't afford to have any surprises once everything was in place.*

"Hey, guys." North Rock's Mike had a phone to his ear. "A team has been spotted tracking us." I noticed Cole had joined us with the same grim expression.

"We move before we have company."

Before another word was spoken, we slipped into the trees and disappeared into the afternoon sun. Six hours later, we touched down on American soil, and I grabbed my bag, excited I was going to see her smile.

A breeze brought me the scent of her, and once again her heavenly smell smothered my senses and pulled me back from my memory.

Her brows drew together. "How did you know I was going to be here?"

I smirked. "Char."

"What?" A smile tugged at her lips, and the urge to reach out and touch her was intense.

"I told my dad my plans, and Char made sure you guys were going to be here."

"Ah." She laughed softly. "So, you knew you'd be seeing me today?"

"Why do you do you think I told my father?" I grinned shamelessly.

Her smile slipped a little. "You could've called."

"I wanted to," I admitted without missing a beat.

"Why didn't you?" I liked that she was blunt. It meant I knew where I stood with her. No games, just raw truth.

"Maybe I was afraid you'd ask questions I couldn't answer, then you'd shut down on me."

Her lips pressed together, and I felt her mull over what she was going to say. "That's an unfair assumption."

"I guess so, yeah." She was probably right on that one.

She looked back out to the track and tucked a piece of hair behind her ear. "If you like me, Mike, get to know me before deciding how I'm going to react to situations." She glanced up at me. "I can handle a lot more than you think."

I leaned back over the railing and joined her stance. "It's not a matter of *if* you can, Catalina, it's a matter of how much."

Her mouth parted, and her gaze dropped to my lips. The gravitational pull we seemed to create around one another became almost overwhelming.

"Irons, you ready?" John slapped my shoulder as he eyed Catalina. "Oh," he extended his hand, "you must be Catalina. I'm John."

Her eyes lit up, and she smiled warmly. "I am." She shook his hand but quickly glanced at me.

"I've heard a lot about you."

"That so?" Her eyebrow cocked. "So, when do we get to be alone so I can hear all about what you know?" She laughed and reached out for my arm, and the instant she made contact, I felt our magnets fuse together. My arm wrapped around her back, resting my arm on her hip.

"How about tonight?" John winked at me.

"Deal." She nodded. "So, how do you know each other?"

"Army," we answered in unison.

"That's well-rehearsed, boys."

"You get used to it." John shrugged. "We're both in the same unit, if you will, which means we travel and spend entirely too much time together."

"Lucky you." I noticed she leaned into me when she spoke. Catalina was an interesting woman. I liked that she was upfront with her feelings for me to my friends and family. She wasn't embarrassed; she liked me for me. I'd never gotten that from Lizzy. It was odd when someone new came along and showed you the flaws in someone you never thought they had.

"Mike?" a familiar voice called out. "How the hell are ya?"

Catalina's eyes widened as she jerked her head to see who was speaking. "Hey, Kevin." I waved. "I'm doing well, thanks."

Catalina gripped my shirt and twisted around. She looked like she was about to burst.

I laughed and covered her hand with mine. "Hey, I want you to meet my girlfriend, Catalina. She's a huge fan."

Kevin smiled. "Hey!" He then smirked and pointed toward his car. "Why don't you come on down, Catalina, and I'll give you a tour."

"You had me at 'hey,'" She laughed as Kevin called his assistant to come get us.

"I'll see you guys down here." He waved.

"Okay!" She beamed up at me with such excitement I felt some of it seep into me. "Girlfriend, huh?"

"I think we crossed that line when we sprawled out in my thinking spot."

She laughed and lifted her eyebrows playfully. "Touché. Okay, but seriously, you know Kevin?"

"Yes, his father is a friend of my father's, and when I was growing up, Kevin's family would visit from California." I motioned for her to walk and followed her down the stairs and out onto the track where we met Danny Blue, Kevin's assistant.

"Hey, Mike." He shook my hand and handed us some passes. "You must be Catalina."

"I am."

Danny gave a quick tour, and to my shock, Catalina chimed in with some knowledge about Kevin's history. She was no poser. She actually knew facts on the sport, rather than just the gossip a lot of women cared about. I hung back to let her have this moment. I had no objection to watching her enjoy herself. She was incredibly graceful in her movements and spoke clearly when she asked a question. Catalina was highly educated and oozed confidence which, in turn, drew lots of attention, mine included.

As soon as we reached the pit crew, the men started to

flock to her side and tripped all over themselves to help her cross over the fuel line.

"I recognize that accent." One of the men stepped closer, "Coahuila?"

"Born and raised." I could tell she wasn't exactly proud of this, as there was an immediate drop in her level of excitement.

"Yikes, that's a rough area."

"It is."

"Hey, Top, how are you?" He addressed me, and Catalina looked at me, confused.

"Well, thanks."

"Good to see you with ten."

I nodded then followed Danny to our seats just above their pit. We were surrounded by men, and most of them had their eyes on Catalina's sexy legs. Once we sat, I wrapped a protective arm around her, and Danny handed each of us a beer. Just before he left, she snagged the beer cap from the table and handed it to me.

"Thanks." I tucked it in my pocket, pleased she remembered something about me.

"So," she grinned at me, "you do this for all the girls?"

"Nope." I held her gaze to make my point.

"Just the ones you want to impress?"

"Not even then."

"Well, then," her shoulders went up as she beamed harder, "I feel pretty damn lucky."

I chuckled as I sipped my beer.

"Why did he call you Top?"

"It's a nickname for Sergeant First Class."

"Oh, he's in the Army too?"

"He was."

"Why did he say good to see you with ten?"

I pulled my sunglasses free from the collar of my shirt. The sun was hard on my eyes. It was the downside to lighter eyes. I decided to share a little. "I work with explosives. I'm one of the lucky ones who hasn't lost any fingers yet."

"Jesus," she muttered before she took a sip of her drink, "C-4, huh?"

"Kind of." I didn't want to correct her and open a door to more questions.

She crossed her legs and turned to me. "You're a very intriguing man, Mike Irons."

"So are you." I fingered her bare leg, and she reached over and slipped her hand in mine.

"Tell me something else about you."

I rubbed the back of my neck with my free hand, unsure what she'd want to hear. "You make me nervous." I went with the first thing that came to mind.

Her eyes narrowed in on me, and I could tell she tried to understand what I meant. "I don't see you being a nervous man, Mike."

"I work with bombs, I've been shot, and I've been a POW, but you," I leaned forward, shocked at my lack of filter, "you could hurt me in ways I can't even imagine."

Her mouth dropped for a hair of a second, but I

noticed it before she spoke again. "Well, you can't say I didn't warn you."

"What does that mean?" She turned to watch the track, and my hands fought to know what to do. "Do you plan on hurting me, Catalina?"

"No, Mike. My *plan* is never to hurt you."

"If there's something I should know, you can tell me…"

"Where were you shipped out to? Germany? Iran? Where?"

"I can't…"

"So here we are, right back in that loop where we both hold back something because it's the rules, or it's just too risky." She looked back at me and paused before she spoke. "You make me nervous too."

I gently pulled her arm, so she'd come closer, and kissed her hard. Like a fool, I didn't care. I wanted her no matter what her secrets were. *This* would carry us through. I was sure I'd kick my ass later because she still wasn't vetted, but right now, in that moment, I wanted my girlfriend to kiss me.

Her body sagged into me, and I knew things could get out of hand fast if we weren't careful. We both were falling fast. Never would I have thought that meeting this beautiful girl at a bar would lead me here so quickly. Only inches from someone I couldn't get enough of.

"You can't kiss me like that here," she broke the kiss, "not wearing that and tasting…oh, Lord."

I laughed, happy I wasn't alone in the feeling.

The sound of an engine ripped by us, sending her gorgeous hair all around her. She was incredibly pretty without trying. Her smile alone lit fires inside of me and smothered my brain in thick smoke, rendering it useless and scaring me more than anything I had encountered as a Green Beret.

She leaned forward in her chair when the race started, and the delicate shape of her spine was revealed when her shirt lifted. Her hair hung in heavy curls and slid with ease across her smooth shoulders. It took everything inside me not to toss her over my shoulder and go find an empty room.

The race took a turn, and Denny Hamlin crashed into the side of Martin Truex, Jr. and took out some other cars. The race went under a red flag while the paramedics raced to help free the men from the cars. Once they declared they were both okay, we had a good thirty before the track would be clear.

"Hungry?" I stood and stretched. The seats were entirely too small for someone my size.

"I could eat." She attempted to stand when the guy next to her leaned over and offered to buy her a burger. "I'm fine, thanks." She flashed him a quick smile, but when he went to say something, I stepped up and wrapped my arm around her shoulders and sent him a glare. He held up his hands and let his offer go.

"I need you for Jeff," she said and laughed.

"Who's that?"

"My landlord, the greatest sleaze who ever lived."

Oh, yeah, Charlotte and Kyle mentioned him at lunch.

"What does he do?" I used my chest to move her forward through the line.

"He's just an ass who thinks he's God's gift. Sexual slurs and all that. He lives above me."

Huh. Seemed I needed to pay this Jeff guy a visit. "Good to know."

"Mike," she placed her hands flat on my chest as she looked up at me, "it's not that big of a deal. I just ignore him, and he gives up."

"Um-hm," I knew that was bullshit, or her friends wouldn't have brought it up.

When we got our burgers, we found two free stools in the corner of the bar where we could look out and watch the action on the track. She dove into her burger like a champ. Things just kept getting better. I hated when girls ate like they might mess up their make-up or something.

"Charlotte says you kicked ass on the Miller project," I said between bites.

She nodded as she chewed. "Yeah," she smiled to herself, "it was really amazing. I love fashion, so it was a real honor to pitch to such a big fashion designer."

"I bet. Is this something you've always wanted to do?"

Her gaze went back to the track. "No, I just knew I didn't want to follow my parents' footsteps."

"Which is?" I rolled the paper from my burger into a ball and started in on my fries.

"Delivery service kind of thing." She was very vague

when it came to her parents and her past, so I didn't press further. At least not yet.

"Any word from your brother?"

"Yes, he's at my place as we speak." The sexy sparkle that lit up her eyes when she was happy returned.

"Good. When can I meet him?"

"Let me see what his state of mind is like first." She rolled her eyes. "He seems to find trouble."

I found myself wondering if maybe he brought trouble to her place, but that was unfair. I didn't know the guy.

I waited for her to finish before we headed back to our seats. She laughed when she answered her phone.

"Hey, girl." She paused and looked over at me. "Yeah, we're good." She made a strange face before she hung up.

"What's my baby sister have to say now?"

"She's just checking in. I guess Lizzy ditched her and Kyle for one of the guys who's staying at the cottages with us."

I felt that twist in my gut that always came when I spent too much time with Lizzy. She played with my emotions until she was bored, or someone better came along. The damage that had already done to my psyche was still something I tried to internalize. Looking back, I saw I was just a fool in love and missed every damn sign that hit me in the face. That was who I was, though. I loved to see the good in everyone. Oddly enough, when it came to work, I was the polar opposite.

"Oh, my God." She pointed to a man who walked by

looking like he just stepped out of a western. "I never thought I'd see another pair of boots like that." I laughed when I saw he was wearing gold-tipped cobra boots. "Seriously, you'd have to be a very secure man to walk around in a pair of those."

"You've actually seen a man in a pair of those before?" I asked, careful to keep my voice casual.

"Yeah," she shook her head, "and he wasn't Hispanic, so save the stereotype."

"Was he white?"

"Most certainly." She cocked her head, and I felt the mood change. "Why?"

"When did you see him?"

Her expression flickered. "A long time ago."

"Do you remember his name?"

"I-I'm not sure." I could tell she was lying, but I wasn't about to press too hard. The odds of it being Denton were slim to none. "Why?"

"I was just curious."

"Seems kind of strange of you to ask me that."

"Sorry, they're just some crazy boots." I moved my attention back to the track and fought off the thought.

"Okay." She also began to watch, but the air was still charged with questions unanswered.

After the race, John joined us at the gate, and he waved me over away from the girls who were making their way back to the car. He fell into step behind them, and we listened to how the girls were excited that Kevin won.

John turned toward me when he knew they were deep

in conversation. "Logan called, said another video was leaked."

"Shit." I cursed and rubbed my head. We had spent the last three weeks chasing shadows through TJ, and just when we thought we had found Elena, we ran right into an ambush. "How bad is it this time?"

"He wants to make a move soon. He comes in next week so we can discuss it further."

I struggled to hear him over the music from the parking lot. Everyone always partied after a big win. Kevin had crazy mad fans.

I almost bumped into Lizzy, and it took me a moment to see why.

Three guys were standing in front of their car. The girls seemed to know them, but Kyle hung back.

"Who are they?"

"Our cottage roommates." He shook his head, annoyed. "The tall one likes your girl."

That so?

EIGHT

CATALINA

I hopped out of the front seat and glanced at Mike and John as they pulled up next to us. I nodded from them to Charlotte, confused about why they were here.

"Oh, didn't I tell you? They have the middle cottages." She winked and locked her car. "You can thank me later."

"You're something else." I laughed and headed inside to change.

I tossed my belt and kept my jean shorts on. I then swapped my t-shirt for a black halter top. My boobs could use a little help.

"Why do you have to look like you just stepped out of a magazine all the time?" Charlotte bit the cork off the red wine and spat it in the sink. "Come on, we have one last night here, and I'm determined to play with one of those fine fellows out there."

Mike was having a beer with John by the fireplace but spotted me coming over. His gaze made my step waver. Then Lizzy was there to block my path.

Of course.

"Ladies." The guy who had an eye for me wrapped an arm around my shoulders and held up a pack of glow sticks. Mike just stared at me. I kind of liked his protective side, but only because he was also in control of it, which said a lot about a man.

"Who wants to play Murder in the Night?"

"I do!" Lizzy jumped toward him, and I made my move to be next to Mike. He slid his arm around me and pulled me in close. The smell of his body wash made my head spin.

"Pull a card from the bag but don't share what you see. Just do what the instructions say."

He put it in front of me first.

"Catalina." He grinned as I plucked a card out and read it.

'Prey.' Great, so I'm going to be hunted.

Mike went next, then John, and so on.

"Keep what you have a secret," he called as we moved closer to hear the rules. "Okay, so let's see." He pointed to me. "Catalina, will you be okay alone in the woods?"

"She'll be fine." Lizzy dismissed me. "Mike, will you help me?"

Never throat punch a friend.

"John and I have plans," he grunted.

"What? No!" Lizzy whined. "No way are the only two Navy SEALs teamin' up. We won't stand a chance. John," she pouted and didn't hear Mike mutter that he'd been a Green Beret. "Give me Mike."

Maybe just a tit punch.

I sighed and kept my mouth shut.

"No teams! Start on the left side of the property." The guy raised a hand. "It's a singles' game. Girls, you go first, but here are the rules."

Charlotte waved me to follow, but I paused until Mike finally let me go.

We were given glow necklaces. We each had to get to the flag from one side of the property to the other without being murdered.

"If you get shot, you sit by the fire and wait until one of your friends free you by tapping you out on the shoulder. Once there is a collection of 'bodies' by the fire, beware, because at this point you might be able to figure out who the killer is. Trust no one because the killer could pretend to be prey too. Once you make it across the property, you will find a glow stick. Snap it and attach it to the flag and hold it up high, announcing to everyone that *you* survived the game. Game over. But beware, there could be more than one predator waiting in the shadows. The game lasts one hour, people. Trust no one," the guy called as we started to scatter. "Are you the predator or the prey?"

I didn't get a chance to ask what the murder weapon was. "Char?" I tried to keep up with her, but the ground was horribly uneven, and she was set on getting as far away from the cottages as possible. My neon green necklace dangled from my neck as my arms waved around to keep my balance. "You need to slow down."

"Girl, I'm not getting hunted by some predator." She laughed. "I'm too white to be in the woods. Have you ever seen *I Know What You Did Last Summer*? Those stories have to come from somewhere."

"It's a game, Charlotte," I called, but at the same time reined in my inner dick and laughed.

"Right," she reached for a branch to stabilize herself, "that's how a lot of horror flicks start. It's just a game at first, then one of their friends slips into murder mode, and later you find out you killed their father in some DUI accident."

"Seriously, Charlotte, you need some reality TV in your life."

"Ah!" She jumped when she spotted something. "Tell me again why we didn't wait for Mike or John. I could really use his skills right now."

Bang! Bang! Two paintballs shot through the air and hit Charlotte in the shoulder.

"Son of a royal bitch!" She held her arm and whirled around. "I've been hit, by a paintball, apparently!"

Screw this!

"It's never the scrappy Latina who gets hit!" She half laughed.

I dropped to the ground and slid in between a split tree trunk. I tried my best to cover up my lights.

Charlotte muttered all the way out of the woods. "Can someone please get me out of murder jail?"

I smirked at her but froze when someone raced by me, kicking dirt up as they ran.

Yikes! Stay still.

Once the quiet settled around me again, I stood slowly.

I felt around the tree and pressed my body to its trunk and peeked through a split in the bark. I could see John, on the outskirts of the woods, waiting for his move to tap out Charlotte from, as she called it, murder jail.

Okay, so I'll just wait here. That's what the movies teach you, right? The one who stays put doesn't get the ax to the back. Oh, my God, now I'm channeling Charlotte's head.

Suddenly, someone's hands skimmed across my shoulders, but I caught his scent and immediately felt reassured. He unclasped my neon green necklace before his lips made contact with my neck. I leaned my head to the side to give him better access. My entire stomach clenched, and my skin broke out in a fever as his tongue swirled right behind my ear.

"You found me," I whispered.

"I never left you." The heat of his breath skimmed the wet spot he made, and I shuddered with delight. "You just didn't see me."

One of his hands dropped to my hip and slid to the center of my belly before he dipped into my shorts. His cool fingers spread out and held me firmly as he pressed his erection into my back with a hiss.

One thing we were good at was teasing one another. I loved how we were holding out to see who would break first. A test of will and strength.

My head fell back against his chest, and I mentally begged his fingers to travel south. I wiggled my hips and hoped he'd explore further.

My breath caught in my throat when his hand shifted under my panties and started to circle my swollen clit. It had been a while since I'd allowed a man to touch me. I had been so focused on school and work that I couldn't find a good balance, so I gave up.

"Mmm." I let out a throaty whisper as a finger dipped inside me. His fingers were big and strong, and even with only one inside of me, I felt a little stretched. I circled my hips into his erection and felt his other hand clamp down to control my movements. It was the perfect combination of control and dominance.

The coil in my stomach grew tighter, and my lungs shook as my climax built. His knee pushed between my legs and used it as a base to grind his hand better.

"You're my weakness, Catalina," he rasped. I could tell he was just as gone as I was. "Today nearly killed me. I need to touch you." A second finger pushed in, and I bowed my body to try to find more room while he lifted my shirt to rest above my breasts. "I need to be in…" He trailed off, but his fingers kept doing heavenly things. "Shh," he warned, and I felt the muscles twitch in his arms like he sensed something. He became rigid and tuned in to something that was coming toward us.

A moment later, I saw it. One of the guys was just a few feet away.

"Don't move." He scissored his fingers, and I bit down on my lip.

I am so close.

Charlotte and Lizzy appeared in the dark, and Lizzy shamelessly flirted as she tried to fix her hair.

Mike's hand on my hip disappeared and returned with a handgun with a bubble on top. He slid the cool steel across my bare ribs just below my breast and raised it to point at them.

Bang! Bang! Paintballs rushed out and nailed the guy behind them in the shoulder. Suddenly, he clicked my clit, and between the heat of the situation, the vibration of the gun that skimmed my breast, and the sheer thrill of it all, I fell apart, and my screams joined the others as they spread out in different directions.

I wasn't sure if it was the fact that Mike was the murderer in the game or the sexiness of how cool and collected he was about getting me off, but I continued to burst into a billion pieces without a care in the moment.

Once I floated back to Earth, his hands turned my hips so I'd face him. He gently brushed my long bangs out of my face before he dipped down and pressed his lips to mine. His fingers brushed down my sensitive skin to my wrist, where he drew my arms up over my head. Finally, his mouth opened, and his tongue dove inside, taking complete control of my body and mind. He was beast of muscle and could easily overpower me, but instead, he was gentle and careful, but all the while he made it known he was in control.

It was heady. I hadn't experienced anyone like him, and I found myself starting to crave more.

I shouldn't. I really shouldn't.

After my lungs begged me for air, he suddenly pulled back with a groan.

"We need to stop, or I won't be able to."

"I'm not stopping you." My hands went to his massive chest and up around his shoulders to pull his head back down. Again, his mouth took over mine, but I could tell he struggled.

"I want you, Catalina, but not here." His forehead pressed to mine as he squeezed his eyes shut. "We can do better than the woods."

"And I was all 'not today, Satan!'" Charlotte laughed to Kyle.

Christ, were we on the main pathway of the woods? Everyone and their dog had come through.

"Come on." He grabbed my hand and pulled me out in front of my friends.

"Damn, Mike, where the hell did you come from?"

Bang! Bang! Mike shot them both then roared in delight.

"You dickbag!" Char shouted as Kyle ditched her and ran toward the fireplace with red paint dripping from his arm. "You know I hate this predator-prey shit!"

"You'll live. You always do."

"Jackass." She rolled her eyes at me. "Of course, you teamed up with the killer."

"I had a good incentive."

"Yuck, no." She held up a hand and left.

"You brought this on yourself, Char." I laughed and beamed up at Mike.

"You feeling good?"

"Mm-hm," I kissed his jaw and admired his tattoos in the moonlight. He chuckled and pulled me away from my dirty thoughts.

———

As quickly as the weekend came, it left. Lizzy and Charlotte drove in her car, and Kyle and I drove with John and Mike. Lizzy was pissed, but Charlotte was leaving after us, so she got to spend a little longer with the other guys.

Mike's truck was massive. It felt like I was in first class on a private jet with the giant leather seats, the independent TV, climate controls, and tables that folded over the seats so you could work on a laptop or whatever.

"Remind me again why we drove in Charlotte's Ford when we could have been flying with Mike?" Kyle laughed and fiddled with the TV. He stopped at a Kardashian show, and I shook my head. He was such an interesting man.

"John." Mike pointed to the massive cliff ahead of us.

"Time frame," he paused to think, "two hours, thirty-three."

"Fifty, I can do it in under two."

John leaned his elbow to extend his arm to shake his hand.

I squinted in confusion. "What just happened?"

"Free solo." John turned to explain. "It's when you climb," he pointed to the cliff, "without ropes, alone."

"What?" My mouth dropped open. "That's suicide."

"It's about conquering your fears." Mike spoke up. "It's a training tool."

"Yeah, on how to plummet to your death, maybe."

He shook his head like I didn't get it. "It trains you not to move until you know the next move is the correct one."

I leaned back in my seat and tried to look at it from his point of view. Either way, it made my stomach twist into a knot. Heights were a fear I could never look straight in the eye. Mike glanced at me in the rearview mirror when he stopped at a stop light, his eyes crinkled, and once again his charm settled my confusion on what he did for fun.

It was pretty late by the time we dropped John off at his car and Kyle at home. I slipped into the front seat and smirked at the fact that I would need a booster seat to drive this thing.

"Did you enjoy your weekend?" he asked as he eased into traffic.

"I did, and I really liked John. I love how he talks about his twin. You can tell they're close."

"Yeah, they are. She had a bad accident a while back, and we're all glad to know she's recovered fully."

"I'm sorry to hear that. He was lucky to have you guys. Has he always been on the team?" I hoped I wasn't stepping over a line. I was just curious to know how long they'd known one another.

"Other way around, actually." His hands swiped over the wheel when he made a right turn. "The team lost a member during a mission, and when the spot opened up, I was given the position."

"I'm sorry. I didn't mean to bring up a sore topic."

"It's okay." He glanced at me and held my gaze for a beat longer than I thought he would. "I need to be careful with you."

"Why?"

"I've never told anyone that before."

The corner of my mouth lifted. I liked that he shared that with me. Mike was different than the men I'd dated before. He was kind, protective, and shared his feelings.

"I haven't been happy to be home in months." I pointed to my place, and my excitement to see Javier kicked in.

Mike parked and grabbed my bag from behind the seat and met me at the truck door. Jeff stood at the top of the stairs but stayed put when he caught sight of Mike.

"Is that your asshole landlord?" Mike asked when he turned his back to the house.

"Hm-hm." I threaded my bag over my shoulder. "It's really not a big deal."

"It is to me." He reached up, cupped my face, and pressed his lips to mine. It wasn't an inappropriate kiss or a childish moment of marking his territory. It was just a kiss goodbye, and that ripped open a hole inside me that wanted more. "Enjoy your brother, darlin'."

"I'll call you later."

"Sounds good." He rubbed his thumb along my bottom lip before he stepped back and headed to his truck.

I rolled my eyes at Jeff when he glared at me as I hurried downstairs. A box was at my doorstep. I juggled it in my arms and opened the door. I closed it quickly behind me in case Jeff followed.

"Javier?" I dropped my keys and the box on the table and glanced around my empty apartment. "Hello?" Hmm, there wasn't even a note. That was odd. Post-it notes were how we usually communicated, but my pad was untouched.

I pulled my phone free and headed to the fridge for a water bottle while I dialed.

I whirled around as a phone buzzed. It sounded muffled.

"Shit!" I huffed with my hand on my chest.

What the hell?

The call ended and went to voicemail. With a sick feeling, I dialed again, and once again a phone rang. I followed the sound and stopped when I realized it was coming from inside the box.

"Javier?" I called again, hoping he would emerge from thin air. With a steak knife, I broke the seal and flipped the flaps open, and a musty smell found my nose. My brother's beloved Chrome messenger bag was inside. I pulled it out and saw a yellow Post-it taped to the bottom of the box with a phone number. Easing into the seat, I unsnapped the top of the bag and started to pull the contents out on the table. Notebooks, two shirts, ten dollars cash, and my camera he had helped himself to without asking. I paused when I found a folded photo. Smoothing it out, I felt a pinch to the heart. It was my mother the day I was born. I was cradled in her arms, and she had tears streaming down her face while she smiled at me. My tiny fist was wrapped around a string of soft pink pearls that draped around her neck. She looked so happy.

I cleared my throat and set the photo aside. I needed to think.

With the mysterious number typed into my phone and the phone tucked under my chin, I turned on my camera and started to go through his photos as it rang. Javier and some girl, Javier and that girl in a Jeep, them driving through what looked like Texas, and an aerial shot. I squinted to see a car in the background. I used the buttons to enlarge it and felt my stomach bottom out.

"*Hola*, Catalina. I see you found my gift."

No.

I quickly hung up and dropped the phone like it had

burned me. I was on my feet but couldn't feel my legs, my hands grew numb, and my head lost all thoughts.

Breathe, Cat, breathe.

"Think," I whispered and tried to use my own voice to calm my fears. "Fuck!" I kicked the kitchen chair when I knew what I had to do. I needed to call home.

"Catalina?" My mother's worried voice found me after the second ring. "Catalina, is that really you?"

"Mama?" I didn't want to open the door I had shut so many years ago. "Have you heard from Javier lately?"

There was a pause, and I had to check to make sure the call was still connected.

"Catalina, you're scaring me."

That makes two of us.

"Please answer the question."

"Yes, he checked in two days ago and said he was heading your way."

Okay, there was still hope he was all right.

"It's Catalina," my mother called, and I clenched my jaw, not wanting to hear his voice.

"Mama." I needed her attention because I didn't want this. "Has Papa been speaking to Bash?"

There was a long pause before she lowered her voice. "Why would you ask me that?"

I eyed the box. "Because I just got a present from him."

"What?" Her tone turned fearful. "Wait, how did he get your address?"

"Really, Mama? It's what they do."

"What was in it?"

"Javier's belongings and a number taped to the bottom of the box. Bash's number."

"How did you know it was his?"

"I called it."

Silence.

"I think you should come home." I knew she was worried about me because I left and because I knew a lot of things, and that made my father uneasy and me a target. I didn't agree with our family's business, and I never would. My life was mine, and I would never go backward, not when I'd worked so hard to move forward.

"Not happening."

"Please, Cat, I don't know what's going on, and I think you need to be under our protection."

"I have someone who is doing a good job of that now." I couldn't help but hope that stung a little. I never took any money when I left years ago. I only took my clothes and the money I earned myself. Debt wasn't something you ever wanted with them. Debt led to ownership, and ownership led to a lifetime sentence.

I felt the angel on my back shift to tuck her wings in a little tighter, a protective move whenever fear reared its ugly head.

Mama hissed, "I don't think she will," at someone, and my stomach hurt the way it always did when he was around. "Your father wishes to speak with you."

I ended the call.

NINE

MIKE

"Where's your head?" Cole tapped the side of my knee once we were in the air on our way to scope out Salvador's house. We had gotten word from Team North Rock confirming Elena was indeed there at the house, but we needed more information before we could make our move. I knew it would need to be soon. History had taught us that Salvador would stop at nothing to make sure his place was secure, and that meant his own mistress would be expendable. He was completely ruthless.

"Nothing." I leaned back and blew out hard to release some of the heaviness off my chest.

"I didn't ask what was bothering you, I asked where your head is." He eyed me a little harder. Cole was a great leader and always made sure we knew where we needed to be, physically and mentally.

"Could it be that your *tesoro* is clouding your thoughts?" Mark winked at the reference to Catalina as a treasure.

"Oh." Cole grinned and laughed with John, who now decided to listen in. Once they got their jabs in, I went back to staring at the screw that held my harness to the seat. I needed to focus, but I couldn't get past the fact that Catalina hadn't returned any of my calls in over a week.

Cole leaned over and switched my radio to a private chat. "One thing I learned from Savannah is that no matter how much you fight the feeling, it only makes it worse."

"I'm not trying to fight it," I shot back.

His brows pinched together like he was trying to figure out what to say next. "Do you like her?"

"Yeah."

"Then," he shrugged, "get your thoughts in order, but the moment we land, *we* need you, so…"

"I hear ya."

He tapped the outside of my knee again and settled into his seat and switched the channel back to the rest of the guys. I pulled out my clip and started to count the bullets to slowly pull my brain back into the game.

It wasn't long before we touched down and headed to our base camp.

"Okay, Raven Two to team," Mark chirped on the radio, and Keith and I pulled out our Sharpies. "The front, which faces northeast, has three men at the front door and four who circle the front of the properly."

I marked Xs on the laminated blueprints of Salvador's house and waited for John to check in with his notes.

The sun moved across the sky before I finally heard his voice.

"Fox Two to team," I heard John struggle to shift his position in a tree, "we've got a lot of action here in the back. At least six by the door, eighteen by the concrete wall, another twelve who line the back driveway, and if my eyes are correct, six girls who looked to be drugged out of their minds with enough explosives strapped to their chests to take down half the house."

"Shit." I glanced at Keith. He looked as stressed as I did.

Footsteps from behind had us raising our weapons and covering the map.

"Stand down," Cole called. "Radio busted." He tossed the shit radio on the table with a sigh. "What've we got?" He nodded to the map.

"Nothing." Keith rubbed his head. "If we can even make it through the roads without being detected, we'd be killed here." He pointed to the armed perimeter lined with motion sensors.

"What about an airdrop in?"

"See those?" I pointed the roof. "They pick up anything in the air." I squinted to try to clear my headache. "Our drone didn't last a minute in the air before it was shot down, and it's no doubt being dissected as we speak."

"Frank will love to hear that." He studied the map for a few moments before he clicked his radio. "All right, men, plan B. Come back to camp."

"Ten-four," they both acknowledged.

Cole made a few calls while we waited for the guys to return. Keith ripped open a protein bar and looked at me as he chewed.

"What?" I chugged some water.

"The guys are coming to the house until we figure this out."

"Okay." I held the scope of the gun to my eye and scanned the bushes and begged someone to show their head. I was pent up and needed to do something. Catalina flashed in front of me, and I closed my eyes to push it away.

"I was thinking," Keith cut through my thoughts, "maybe we could do a dinner at your parents' place."

"That's fi—" I froze when I met a scope pointed at me.

"What?" Keith reached for his weapon.

"We have company." I waited for a moment, factored in the wind speed, then squeezed the trigger. I saw him fall as another scope came into view, and then another.

"We need to get out of here!"

Keith changed our course, and we raced back toward our pickup place. My boots sank into the mud as I ran, and my feet slipped with every step. Mark shot out in front of me, and John followed. Bullets flew all around us, but somehow none hit us. Maybe someone was looking out for us. I wasn't sure, but I wasn't about to question it either.

"Don't land, just hover!" Cole shouted into his radio to the pilot.

We saw the clearing a few yards ahead. Our pace picked up, and bullets hit off the steel side of the chopper. Sparks bounced in all directions, just missing the fuel tank twice. They were on our heels and closing in fast. This wasn't going to work for long; one of us was going to get hit.

Instantly, I slowed. John wavered in his step when he sensed my change, but I pushed his back so he'd gain an extra bump in speed.

"Go!" I yelled at Mark, and he grabbed John by the scruff of the neck when he jumped inside the chopper.

I got low to the ground and opened fire. I knocked three down and waited for the other four to show. The wind whipped wildly around me as Cole came into view to my left. A man came up with a knife, and I drilled a bullet between his eyes.

The chopper dipped when it took fire from the other side. I raced under the belly and opened fire on two men who were trying to load a rocket launcher as Cole leapt inside.

"Come on!" John leaned out of the chopper and hooked an arm around my shoulder. My feet left the ground, and I felt his grip slip with my weight. Quickly, I grabbed the bar, twisted, and pulled myself into the cabin, but not before I sprayed a layer of bullets just in case.

"Whoo!" Mark slapped my shoulder. "Damn, son! You took out enough to make a dent."

"It's the cartel," Cole hissed. "There is no way to make a dent, but thanks for that. It got pretty close back there."

Keith shook his head at me before he gave me a fist bump. "Thanks for having my back."

"Always."

"Mine too." John nodded.

I closed my eyes and tried to stem my adrenaline.

———

"You're off the clock," Trigger poured me another whiskey, and I felt my blood warm from the alcohol. I ran a frustrated hand through my hair and took the drink in two sips.

"How long are you here for?"

I rolled my wrist to see the time. "Another two days before I can report on their schedule."

"Do you have a twenty on the vic?"

"No, but I did catch them bringing in someone who later left with a camera. Could have been another proof of life."

"Logan seems hellbent on getting this girl out."

"It's his job," I shot back, defending one of my brothers.

Trigger leaned in and studied my face before he lit

his joint. I knew I should leave. I couldn't risk the drug getting into my system. This was, after all, a huge moment to show my skills to Blackstone.

"This one is different." Trigger could read me like a book. He always had, since we were in training together. He wasn't wrong. Logan was consumed with this case. I couldn't blame him, though. The mayor was making a mess of the media, and the girl certainly was in the center of it all. I sometimes wondered if he was just lost in this puzzle and wanted to find his way out. Logan loved a challenge; we all did. That was why we were here.

"It's a big victim with a lot of press after her." Trigger checked his phone, and I wondered where Morgan and Brick were.

"Drugs just crossed the border. I'll meet you outside for payment," he muttered to someone on the other end of the phone. He stood and slid the whiskey bottle in front of me. "The Reaper has a plan for everyone, Irons. While you're still breathing, have a drink." He slapped my shoulder, and then he left. I spun the cap off and went to pour another but decided against it. Drinking wasn't how I dealt with loneliness. Pulling my phone from my pocket and handing the bottle off to the guy next to me, I headed outside.

"Hey, Dad, what are you…" I trailed off when I heard a noise. "Shit, gotta go!" I raced toward a man who held Trigger in a headlock. That gave Trigger

the advantage to kick another guy in the stomach. I knocked the guy who held Trigger out with one swing. We stood back to back, hands up, both puffing air in and out of our lungs. The other two pulled their guns, and we charged them. I slammed mine into the bricks of the bar wall and used all my strength to drive my fist into his intestines. I felt his ribs crack, and then I used my knee to make sure they turned to dust. I had no problem severely injuring or killing someone who deserved it.

After I was content he wasn't moving, I jumped in and stopped another guy from stabbing Trigger while he was on the ground under two other men.

Pound! Pound! Pound! *So many fists flew, and none of it registered to me. Though Trigger and I were raised very differently, we fought the same—to win. Trigger spat blood on the ground and laughed when I rolled over and he saw I was fine. He offered a hand and helped me to my feet.*

"Been awhile since we fought together."

"Yeah." I wiped the corner of my mouth free of blood. "You good?"

"Yeah." He pulled his keys out and headed back to his bike. He stood it upright and pulled out his cap helmet. "Thanks for having my back."

"You look different." Charlotte pulled me from my memory, and I blinked to clear it. "You okay?"

"Just an intense week."

She chewed the inside of her mouth and studied my face before she took a sip of her cocktail.

"What?"

"Just curious why Cole is here." She looked over at him. "I mean, I'm not complaining." She winked, but I could see she was concerned. "But you normally seem a little more stressed when the entire team is in town."

She was observant; I'd give her that.

"Just a change in plans, that's all."

Her finger tapped on the side of her glass. "Have you spoken to Catalina?"

That drew my complete attention to her. "No. I tried calling her a few times, but she never called back."

"She's been jumpy at work and seems a million miles away, like you just were." Charlotte wiggled her nose. "I'm a little worried about her."

"Did you invite her today?"

"Yeah." Charlotte pulled her phone from her purse. "She said she was going to try to make it."

"Burgers are up," Mark called. I shook my head at him. He was right next to Dad with a plate, nearly drooling over the dinner.

"Sometimes I wish I could trade places with Mark," she said and sighed.

"Why? So you can eat whatever and not worry?" I chuckled.

"No." She paused. "So I could know the other side of you."

I turned to look at her and felt her disconnect with me. My heart sank when I reached out for my sister's hand.

"Dad knows, doesn't he?" She dared me to lie.

"Why do you ask that?"

"Because whenever you leave, he won't let his phone out of his sight. He also buries himself in the woods at the cabin and won't act normal again until you call."

"I didn't know that." I sometimes wondered if the job was worth all the pain it brought my family.

"Sometimes not knowing," Cole took a seat across from us, "is better."

"Does Savi agree with that?" she challenged. "Because something tells me she runs that house like a tight ship."

"Yup," Mark laughed and sat next to Cole, "we gave up our balls years ago."

"Savi was thrown into my world without an option," Cole explained. "It's different."

"Does it not bother you that your families never know if you're ever going to come back?"

I shook my head at Charlotte. It wasn't a conversation I wanted to have today. I felt like a wrung-out rag, just needing a day to comprehend what I was going to have to do.

"Sorry, Mike, but shit, sometimes it's hard." Charlotte closed her eyes to stop herself.

"It does." Cole lowered his voice. "It restricts us from having a normal life but know that what we're doing saves lives. Sometimes that outweighs the hard parts of life. It's a sacrifice we make."

Charlotte shrugged, not at all satisfied with Cole's answer. Most weren't.

Mark dropped his head after he finished his meal, like something bothered him. With Mark, you just needed to wait five seconds, because he didn't keep shit inside for long anymore. Now he was like a woman going through menopause with no filter.

"This week sucked. I haven't seen my girl in forever, my boys are missin' me, and I need some fun. We don't do the shit we do and shed it easily." He looked at my dad, who was listening intently.

"I think I know something we can do," he said, and my gaze followed my father as he headed inside. He returned a moment later with two guitars. "Come on, son."

I grabbed my beer and headed to the gazebo. I would never say no to playin' with my pops. Music was what helped us communicate when I couldn't.

Easing into the chair next to him, he fixed a mic stand to point at me and did the same for himself.

"What will you play?" Lizzy called as I ran a hand through my hair then replaced my Hurricanes ball hat.

"Mom?" I looked to her, curious as to what she'd like to hear.

She smiled at me with such love that I knew what she wanted to hear. I looked at Dad and strummed the first two chords, so he knew what we were playing.

Dad's foot tapped to get the beat moving. He came in with the guitar, and I joined him, strumming, until I leaned forward and started to sing *Chicken Fried* by The Zac Brown Band.

Catalina came up the stairs and took a seat next to my sister. She granted me a wave, but I could see she was weighed down by something. Charlotte took her hand and gave it a squeeze before she went back to watching us.

When I got to the line about seeing the love in my woman's eye, I moved my gaze to hers and was gifted with a smile that made my insides squeeze so tight, I struggled to take another breath.

Dad came in on the chorus but mostly made me take lead. He just kept the beat, and I could feel his pride in me. My father was my rock, and moments like this made all the hard parts of the job mean nothing because I got to come home to this…and now *her*.

Once we were finished, I followed her back out to the yard where people were scattering.

"Hey," I leaned down and brushed my lips to hers, "everything okay?"

Her teeth caught her bottom lip, and her eyes looked pained. She cleared her throat and shrugged. "It's just been a long week."

"I called you a few times." I wanted her to know I was thinking about her.

"I know, and I'm sorry for not calling you. I just, um…" She paused, and that painful look she got between her eyes deepened. "Just dealing with some family stuff."

"Your brother?"

"Him and others."

Always so cryptic. "Is your brother okay?"

"No clue." Her hands dropped away from my arms, and I felt the loss. "He's not answering his phone again."

"I'm sorry, Catalina. I know you were looking forward to seeing him."

"I was," she nodded, and her eyes drifted down, "but instead, I was just left with his belongings."

"Oh." That was strange. "Why did he do that?"

"I'm still trying to figure that part out." Her tone told me there was more to it, but I could tell by the way her shoulders sagged forward now wasn't the time to pry.

I pulled her into a hug, and she let me, resting her head on my chest with a sigh. "I missed this," she whispered.

"Me too." I kissed her head and caught my mother's insanely happy smile from the porch. My father pulled her into the house to give us some privacy.

"It's like no one can touch me when I'm in this hole," she whispered.

"Is someone bothering you, Cat? Is it that asshole landlord?"

She quickly shook her head, not moving. "I just meant in general." But I could hear the lie in her voice, and my protective side shot to the surface.

"You're staying with me tonight." It wasn't an option, and she didn't protest.

As much as I wanted to be at Dusk, I couldn't bring

her there, so like we were seventeen, we stayed at my parents' house in my old room. At least it was in the basement of the house, away from others.

My parents had converted the basement into a place where I could have my own space. It was almost like an apartment. A king-sized bed was over in the corner next to a huge window that looked over the lake. Because of the way the house was built on a hill, the basement had big windows. The enormous TV hung in front of the couch, and a little kitchenette was built under the stairs. Mia and Savannah usually used this room when they were in town. They preferred it here rather than Dusk. Fewer men, and my parents loved the kids.

"Should I ask?" Catalina held up a small t-shirt that read "Future Green Beret" with a smirk.

"Aww, that's where that went?" I pulled the little shirt away from her and carefully folded it and placed it on the table. "Cole's daughter is always leaving her clothes everywhere."

"Should I be jealous?" She laughed lightly. "Do I have competition?"

"Oh, yeah." I smiled and pictured the girl's brown eyes that had all of us men putty in her tiny hands. "You really do."

She peeled off her jean jacket and rested it over the chair.

"I think I'm okay with that, but only her."

"Deal." I dragged my eyes down my girl's body and admired the view.

"I have nothing to change into." She rubbed her arms like she wasn't sure what to do. As much as I wanted to tell her she didn't need anything, I wanted her to feel comfortable here, so I pulled out a shirt and handed it to her.

She held it up and smirked. "Do you have more of those?" She pointed to Olivia's shirt. I laughed and pushed off the dresser to smother her in my arms again.

"Come on, I need a moment to feel like I'm home again."

In a pair of sweatpants, I sank into the enormous couch and kicked up my feet on the stone table. Much like my room at Dusk, my basement was styled with a rustic modern feel. I glanced down at my left arm and remembered how Trigger and I snuck out to get tattoos when we had met up in Florida a few years ago. We both got a chain, but for different reasons. His were for his demons that held him back, while mine represented the strength that moved me forward. That was the night I discovered I could do three hundred pushups in under five minutes. Regardless, we got comments from judgy people. I inked to remember, not to repel. I wasn't hard, nor was I a rebel. I was me, and that meant I displayed myself through my art.

Catalina opened the door and stepped out in a pair of panties and a rolled-up t-shirt of mine from when I played rugby in high school.

Shamelessly, I gawked. But when didn't I when she was around?

"Hey," she leaned her hip into the doorway and smiled over at me, "I like this." She nodded toward me.

"Me too." I held out my arm for her to come over. She didn't move. "Come here." Again, she just stared at me. I studied her and tried to read her mind.

"I think I'll get a glass of water." She started to head over, and I twitched when I saw her devil red panties were actually a cheeky cut corset that ran straight up the middle. A sexy little black bow hung from the top.

Instantly, it hit me. She was waiting for me to crack. I played the game without the first kiss, and now she'd flipped the tables on me. Well, game on…

"There are bottles in the fridge." I turned my attention to the TV and fudged watching *Sons of Anarchy*.

"Hey, there, good lookin'."

"Ah!" she screamed but then started to laugh hard. "Mike, why is there a Furby in the fridge?"

"It's Olivia's. Her mother hated it, so it stays between here and another house. He's well-traveled. Although, if you ask Brandon, he'll tell you it's his." I shrugged unapologetically. We were a bunch of children sometimes, but we needed to have fun where we could. "It's a Blackstone thing. Once the horror of seeing its face fades away, you'll get used to him."

"If you say so." She shuddered dramatically and returned it to the fridge, and I used that moment to stare at the panties again. I shifted as I grew twice as hard as normal, and my sweatpants didn't help hide it.

"Excuse me." She appeared at my side and brushed

her legs by mine before she sat next to me. "What are we watching?"

Damn you.

Her nipples pushed through the thin fabric, and she crossed her legs, so they stayed closed right up to her thighs. I went back to flipping the channels when she leaned over me. Her breasts stroked by my erection to grab her water she left conveniently on the table next to me.

"Oh, look," she pointed, "*Sons of Anarchy*. Have you ever seen it?"

"Nope," was all I offered. I was going to break.

"I love it." She flipped her hair out of her face and looked over at me. "It's dirty."

Focus, Mike.

Sure as hell, ten minutes into the show, the main guy was in bed with some woman, and I fought the flinch in my hand to touch her.

"You look tense." She grinned knowingly and batted her long lashes. "Oh." She hopped up when her phone buzzed. She stood with her back to me and laughed.

"Your sister is texting me from upstairs." It buzzed again, and she answered it.

"Hey, girl, I just got your text."

I saw my opportunity and took it.

In two steps, I pressed my front to her back and slid my hands around and dipped my fingers down over the top of her panties and whispered, "Remember when we were in the woods?" I stroked and teased her through the fabric. "How I kissed you here," I kissed her shoulder, "how I sucked here." I moved over to suck where her neck met her shoulder.

"I forget where it is, Char." She tried to think and was quickly forgetting how to breathe.

"Remember the way you moaned when I pressed my erection into your back?" I did just that, and she reached out to stabilize herself. "And when my fingers slipped inside you." I tucked my finger under the fabric and gently brushed over her swollen nub. "Show's back on." I chuckled and stepped back.

She turned around and showed me the phone wasn't even on.

"Thanks for the rub, babe." She beamed at her trickery.

I tossed my head back, having been completely fooled by the power of a woman. Before she had a moment to think, I hauled her over my shoulder and slapped her smooth ass.

She laughed and tried to fight me.

I tossed her on the bed and hovered over her, catching her lips with mine. She willingly let me in, and her hands were in my hair and tugging at the roots.

"I've dreamt of this moment for a while now, Catalina." I kissed the corners of her eyes and watched her face in the flicker of the TV. "I was starting to think maybe someone didn't create a person for me." I swallowed hard and pushed by the rawness that lived inside me. "I thought I was one of those men who was destined to live my life through the happiness of others." She leaned up and gently kissed my lips before she lay back down. "Then one night, I heard this woman on the phone, and when she looked at me, she really looked at me. No fear, no assumptions. She just saw me." I brushed the hair back from her neck, and my feelings for this woman rushed to my heart. "I never thought I would see that woman again. Imagine my surprise when I came face to face with you at my parents' place."

"Fate," she whispered darkly, "or some trick of the universe."

"Trick?" She shook her head for me to let the comment go, but I didn't. "Maybe the universe is testing us, testing to see if we'll make it."

"Catalina," I paused, unsure if I wanted to know the truth right now, "do you want to make it?"

Her lips pressed into a tight line, almost like she was going to cry, and she nodded a few times.

"Then we'll make it." I kissed her hard, and the mood switched from scared as hell to full-blown lust.

I ripped her t-shirt over her head, and she pushed my sweatpants so I could kick them off.

With both hands, I flipped her over and growled at her lace panties. I dragged my fingers from her neck, down her spine, and fingered the little bow before I used my teeth and untied the package in front of me. The two sides separated and released partway, giving me a gorgeous show of her sleek arousal.

"Jesus," I groaned, wanting her so badly but also wanting to savor our first time together.

"Mike," she rolled to her back and spread her legs so I could fit in between her hips, "I love that you're a gentleman at heart, but…"

As I leaned over to kiss her, I quickly slipped inside to catch her off guard.

"Oh!" Her back bowed and pushed her breasts into my chest.

Oh, shit. I clenched my jaw and stopped when I didn't think she could take any more of me.

"Don't stop," she cried but shifted to relieve the ache.

"I will not hurt you, Cat." I didn't move.

"Mike Irons, I will kick your ass somehow if you don't push all the way…" Her head rolled back as she moaned and gripped the sheets. "Yes!"

I didn't stop until she hit my base, and once I was in, I moved to help spread her arousal around to ease the bite of pain she was in. The moment she relaxed and adjusted to my size, I knew I could move freely.

My fists rolled into balls of steel, and my arms flexed by her head as I dragged myself out while I pressed upward to tease her clit. Just before I fell out, I switched directions and repeated this same action and went back in.

Her cheeks pinked and her chest heaved, and her hands clung on to my forearms. I changed the pace and went a little harder and faster, and her head moved back and forth in a silent cry, trying to find her release. Placing my hand flat on her stomach, I gently used my thumb to circle her clit and watched her opening take me to the root over and over again. It was incredibly erotic to watch the woman you were falling for fall to pieces while you were inside of her. It was like a wordless connection that was formed by two bodies fusing as one.

Just when I saw her leap off the edge, I hauled her up in my arms, twisted to sit, and let her ride her orgasm from on top. I locked my arms around her and dove into her neck and joined her bliss.

Lights, sounds, and heat broke over me all at once. If sound and color had a physical feeling, it took me over. Catalina rode me right through her release, which drained me of all my strength. I had never come that hard before, ever. She became slack in my hold, so I leaned back and brought her with me. We were both totally spent.

We should shower, we should talk about the fact that we didn't use a condom, but really, I just needed another moment to relish her.

"Pill." She seemed to hear my thoughts. "Clean too."

I laughed into her hair and kissed her forehead.

"Sorry, I should have been more careful."

"Perfect," she muttered right before her breathing evened out.

"Yeah, you are." I held her tighter and slipped off into the best sleep of my life.

———

The next morning, I dropped Catalina off at home to get ready for work and eyed Jeff as I walked away. What an asshole.

I decided to help my old man out at the cabin. We needed some more time together, and he could use the extra help because winter was coming. Dad was one of the main wood suppliers for the city.

Later that evening, Cole pulled the team away from my parents' dinner table to check in on us.

"We will go over the route tomorrow morning at zero-seven-hundred." Cole checked his watch. "Irons," he directed his attention at me, "you good to go?"

"Yeah." I ran my fingers through my hair and down my scruff, happy I decided to grow my hair out. "I'll prep up when we meet our mark, but until then I will stay like this." Not worth getting spotted in my undercover look.

"We'll be in suits to cover your eagle tat." We both knew it would be a dead giveaway. Cole stopped talking, and his gaze drifted over my shoulder. I turned, hoping to spot Catalina, but instead, Lizzy was on her way toward us.

"Zero-seven-hundred," Cole repeated before the guys all shot off in different directions, leaving me to deal with her.

"Hey, you." Lizzy leaned up on her toes and kissed my cheek. "You've been MIA lately."

"Work," I muttered as I scanned the property.

"She's not here," Lizzy spat. "Just like she wasn't there to cover my shift the other day, like she promised. Now I need to get my hair done at Cha Cha Lomona instead of All Done Up." She huffed out an irritated sigh. "Some people are just not reliable."

"Oh, yeah?" I tried to recall what she said, but I wasn't really listening.

"So?" Her grin brought my attention back to her.

"So?"

Shit, what was she getting at?

"You ready for tomorrow?"

"Tomorrow?"

"The party you told me you'd be my date for at the Brew."

Oh, no…

"You promised, Mike, please."

I wanted to say no, to walk away, to go hunt down Catalina, but I made this promise, and maybe Catalina would show up.

"Text me the details, and I'll pick you up." I pulled out my phone as she cheered. It was the first time I didn't care about doing something with Lizzy.

I said goodnight to my parents, who looked worried about me but would never mention it.

"Get some sleep, Banner." My mother gave me hug. "See you soon, right?"

"Do I ever not come back?" I forced a smile and headed out into the night.

TEN

"Sometimes I wonder why God tests me around women like you," Kyle huffed into his drink.

"Huh?" I wasn't listening. I was still stuck in Thursday's loop of shit. Where the hell was Javier? I just knew a dark storm was festering somewhere, and I wouldn't be able to escape it.

"You in that," he pointed to my red Spanish cocktail dress, "even I find myself checking you out."

"You dabble with both sides, Kyle," I muttered without really thinking. "I would be disappointed if you didn't look."

My dress was tight, short, and it had feathering around the trim at the bottom and lining the V that plunged down between my breasts. The feathery straps hung off my shoulders, and my messy hair flowed all around me. Really, I had no time to think about what I was going to show up in, so I wore what I had from a friend's birthday party a few years back.

"Nice to know I look better than I feel."

"Fooled me." He winked then his gaze flickered over my shoulder, and his mouth dropped open. "Seriously?"

I turned to see Mike with Lizzy on his arm, and my stomach twisted into an uncomfortable knot.

Lizzy had on a white puffy dress that looked like she was at her *quinceañera* rather than a work party. Mike, on the other hand, had on a black dress shirt and dress pants. His dark hair was a little long, so he'd slicked it back. He looked intense as he scanned the room.

Suddenly, my four-inch heels felt like toothpicks and my knees wobbled.

"I need a drink," I grumbled and hurried to the bar just for something to do.

"Damn, girl, I'd take you home tonight," Charlotte joked from behind me. I turned and tried to give her the best smile I could, but of course, she saw through it. "Are you okay?"

"Yeah." I sipped my martini. "Just a long week."

"Yeah, you left early the other day. Are you okay?"

"I wasn't feeling well."

"I'm sorry, honey." She drew me into one of her famous warm hugs, and I held on a little longer than I probably should have.

She leaned back and studied my face the way her brother did. I pushed down my concerns and smiled.

"Your dress," I pointed to her tight black dress, "looks sexy as hell."

"Thanks!" She spun playfully. "I'm waiting for Mike to send me home."

"Huh, yeah." Mike was ridiculously protective of her. It was sweet.

"Speaking of which, is he here?" She looked around and spotted him. "Oh." She seemed just as confused as I was. "He's here with Lizzy?"

"Looks that way." I finished off the rest of my drink, needing another.

"Maybe he didn't know you were going to be here?" She tried to cover for him.

"I'm sure that's it."

"Or she sees that he's found someone new to love, and now she wants him," she muttered, clearly annoyed with her friend.

"Mike," she called, and I turned away.

"I'm just going to go to the restroom." I squeezed her arm and slipped out of the room.

After a five-minute pep talk with myself, I took a deep breath and stepped out of the restroom. A hand wrapped around my wrist and tugged me around a corner and into the empty kitchen.

Before I could think, Mike's lips were on mine, and his hands slid around my waist and down my backside.

"Wait." I stepped back, annoyed he didn't see the problem here. "Why are you here with Lizzy?"

I saw the regret on his face, and his skin flushed with

heat. "Old habits die hard. When she asked, it was a reflex to say yes. I didn't want to come with her, but I did make a promise. It's important to me that my word is kept."

"I respect that, Mike, but if we're together, you need to be with me, not showing up here with her."

"You're right," he stepped closer and raised his hands, "and I'm sorry. I should have explained to her why she needed to find another date. Do you forgive me?"

That was all I needed, and I sank into his arms and let him devour my body. My hands wrapped around his neck and pulled him closer. We were starved for each other. I wished we were alone and didn't have any secrets that could hurt us.

His fingers inched up under my dress and brushed between my legs. I hooked my leg over his hip and felt like I was seventeen again. Young, reckless, and in full-blown heat.

He moved his hands to my hips, and he lifted me up but kept his lips locked on mine as he walked us backward. He sat me down on a long, steel counter and moved in between my legs. Without a word, he tucked my hair behind my ear, and his other hand lifted my jaw. He licked my neck, followed by his lips sucking and nibbling all the sensitive areas.

"Mike," I whispered, finding my voice somehow.

He pressed a finger over my mouth and shook his head. "Just let me have you," he whispered. "I need you."

Something about the tone in his voice told me something big was going on. I grabbed his shoulders and pushed him back to see his face. "What's wrong?"

He closed his eyes and took a long breath, and I tried not to let my eyes roam over how sexy he looked tonight. "I leave tomorrow."

My stomach flinched before it tucked itself into a ball.

"You seem different. It's going to be risky, isn't it?"

"Risky enough." I swore I saw the battle he had inside through his dark eyes. They flickered with something I couldn't understand. "I just want to be with the one person who makes it all worthwhile."

I melted because I understood. Regardless of what life tossed at you, you needed a reason to go on. We were that for each other. How it happened, I was still unsure, but we were.

Without another word, I grabbed his belt and slowly undid his pants to free his massive erection. It sprung free, and he hissed when I wrapped my fist around the base. He took a moment to roll a condom on before he ordered me to lie back. I did, and he slid his hands up the outside of my legs and hooked my panties with his thumbs and pulled them down and tucked them in his pocket.

With both of my ankles in one hand high in the air, he positioned himself at my opening and coated his tip with my arousal.

"Sss," he hissed with pleasure like he tried to control himself. I, on the other hand, was nearly delirious with desire. The heat that poured off his erection made a layer of sweat break out across my entire body.

He let go of my ankles and let them drape around his shoulders as he slid his hands back down my legs and up my stomach to my breasts, which were nearly falling out of the top of my dress.

"You are so beautiful, Catalina," he whispered and nudged a little deeper into me. My back bowed off the table, and my head clouded. "I pictured this going differently, but after I saw you in this dress, and the way my week has been, I can't stop myself."

"Mike—" His name cut off when he pulled me down as he thrust forward to fill me to the max in one swift movement. I gasped, and his head fell to my chest to kiss my breasts.

"Breathe, Catalina," he encouraged me. "Relax so I can get all the way in."

"There's no more room." I nearly cried at the pleasure and pain that bit at my insides. How did I do this before?

He lifted my hips while still over me and inched farther in.

"That's it, my girl," he grunted in the most primal tone that begged my body to explode into a million pieces. "Come on." He gave me more of him. He pulled out and slid back in to coat himself. "Ready?"

I shook my head but found myself saying, "Yes."

"Almost there," he gritted through his clenched jaw. "Christ, you're tight."

"Mike!" I cried, wanting more of the pain. It started to feel unbelievable.

One hand went to my shoulder to push me down and

the other to my hip to help guide me. He leaned back to watch me take the rest of him.

"This is so fucking sexy," he murmured, and finally I felt myself hit his base. He held still so I could adjust. I wiggled and panted, completely at his mercy.

Will it always be this way?

His sounds when I clenched around him had my teeth burrowing into my bottom lip.

"You ready?" he asked softly.

I nodded, fearing I'd lost my voice.

Slowly, he started to draw the length of his erection across my swollen clit, and I closed my eyes with a chuckle. I was drunk on lust and didn't care if Charlotte walked in on us right now. Never had I felt so safe, so sexy, and so full at the same time.

"God, you're so wet," Mike purred like he was calm, but his neck muscles ticked, and I could tell he was holding back his urge to take control.

Three more times, he dragged out the feeling that sent my entire nervous system into overdrive. I was so ready but needed more friction.

I covered my face and moaned. I didn't know if I was coming or going. I felt light as a feather, yet heavy as a rock.

"Take it!" I nearly screamed. "Take control, do what you want."

He granted me a throaty chuckle before he bent me over like a pretzel and folded his body over me to use his weight to hold me down. My legs were over my own shoulders, and his face was to mine.

With a flick of his hips, he thrust into me just enough to shoot me back up to that sweet, blissful space I craved.

"I want to see you come, Catalina." He kissed me softly. "I want to feel you spasm around me and tug at my sanity like the other night."

The muscles tightened in his stomach, and the rest of his body turned to stone as he worked himself in and out. His head fell to the side of my neck, and he grunted like he was close.

"Promise me you'll be here when I get back."

"I promise," I whispered.

I was like jelly, useless, as he ran with me off the edge and dove into mindless bliss. I felt him buck inside me. He was so tight that the littlest movement felt crazy. Every ooze of stress that haunted me from deep within the shadows faded away and let me have this moment.

I came back to his kisses; they ran down my chest into my cleavage. I threaded my hands through my hair and smiled like I had just been royally screwed...oh, wait. I just was.

"You okay?" he whispered and propped himself on his arm. I nodded with a happy sigh, but just as I went to speak, his phone rang, and reality came crashing down around us. He stood, slipped out, and pulled the phone from his pocket.

Something inside of me changed. Maybe it was because the thought of him leaving and not coming back did the scare the hell out of me, or maybe it was because for the first time in my life I realized I needed someone. Needed him.

Shit. The truth wobbled on my tongue, and I knew it was time to share. If he could see past it, we could make it. "Mike," I stopped his hand before he answered it, "I need to talk to you."

His eyes narrowed in on me, but they slipped over to the caller ID, and his face fell. "I'm sorry, Catalina, I *have* to answer this."

I nodded and turned my head away as I pulled my dress down and hopped off the table to find my purse.

"Hey, Logan." There was a long pause, and he turned away from me, and I knew he didn't want me to hear.

I stood there and waited, growing more and more uncomfortable as the call went on. After five minutes of Mike listening to Cole, I decided it was fate's way of showing me it wasn't our moment. Maybe I shouldn't share it before he left. I didn't want to screw with his head.

"Mike," I whispered and pointed to the door, "I'm going to go."

He went to cover the mic of the phone, but Cole must have said something that caught his attention because he stopped and froze. "Oh, shit, really? Well, that changes things, doesn't it?"

I waited for another moment and checked the time on the wall. Charlotte would be looking for me, and Kyle was most likely ready to go home, so I slipped out while his back was to me.

Just as I went outside to check to see if Kyle's car was still in the parking lot, I heard my own phone. I dug it out of the tiny purse and stopped short when I read the caller ID. *Mama.*

"Mama?" I wrapped my free arm around my midsection as her tiny voice broke through the speaker.

"Catalina?" She sounded a million miles away. "Abel is in the parking lot."

What? I whirled around to scan the parking lot. How did they even know I was here? "Go to your place, pack a bag, and come home."

"I am home, Mother," I huffed in response. "What is going on?"

Suddenly, Abel, my ex, was a few feet from me, dressed to impress, as always.

"Mama, you either tell me now what's going on, or you will not be seeing me."

Abel lowered his sunglasses, and I saw the grief deep around his eyes.

"No," I whispered, and I heard my mother break into a sob. "No, Mama, please." My heart split down the center. "No."

"I'm sorry, sweetheart. We just found out."

A sob ripped from my throat. "He can't be dead."

"Please, Catalina, come home. I need you to come home. It isn't safe."

Abel took a few cautious steps toward me. I knew that

look. He wasn't going to play around. He was here to help me get through this, only he wasn't the one I wanted.

My arm dropped, my phone fell to the ground, and the weight of my brother's death rested on my shoulders. Abel reached forward as my knees gave out. He crushed me to his chest, and I broke. I had just lost the one family member who loved me for myself.

Abel walked me to his truck and opened the door. As he shut the door, I looked out and caught Charlotte's worried gaze from where she stood on the steps.

I looked away as my tears flowed. I was about to go back home and felt desperately ashamed.

The truck roared to life while my mind was stuck in limbo, unsure where to navigate from here. All the way to the airport, I did not, would not look at Abel. I was stuck in a nightmare and didn't know how to get out. He directed me through the sea of people with a hand on my back. Normally, I wouldn't allow it, but in the depth of my misery, nothing registered.

"Thirsty?" he asked in Spanish. I shook my head. "Hungry?"

No.

I hardly remembered the trip. We boarded planes, sat in airports, and boarded again. I allowed myself to slip away from the reality that was my life. My mind drifted. I was eleven, sitting in my tree.

"Are you okay?" Javier peered up at me from the ground. I tucked my head into my knees, and when I

didn't answer, he started to climb up to the plank that acted as my treehouse. It was the one place I could go that was hidden from the house, hidden from them.

"You only make him angry when you run off like this." He twisted to sit next to me and wiggled a finger to loosen my grip around my body. He hated when I closed myself off from him, but being eleven and knowing the things my father did was just too much for my young brain to compute.

"She was just scared," I whispered and squeezed my eyes shut when I pictured it. "She just wanted to go home."

"I know." He reached out and tentatively touched my arm. "They're fucking monsters."

"Please, Jav, please take me with you." I started to sob in panic. "If you leave me here, I'll die." I lifted my head to make him see me, so he would know the terror was real. My heart pounded in my chest. "What if he makes me one of them?"

"He won't, Cat." He held my gaze. "You're his daughter. He wouldn't let you get hurt."

I laughed darkly. "Like he wouldn't let his own son get hurt?"

"It's different." He pulled away.

"It's not." I sniffed. "It's only a matter of time. Look at Mama. His own wife has done runs!" I dried my eyes, angry. Tears were useless. "I won't do it. I'd rather die than take any part in it. I want to live

*in the States, go to school, get a job, fall in love,
and have a family. Not work for criminals. I'm a
prisoner in my home. I never asked for this life,
Javier!"*

*"I know." He tried to calm me while scanning the
property line in case Papa showed up. We both knew
I was going to get the belt for what I did. I broke the
number one family rule.*

I helped the girl escape.

*"Look," he drew in a deep breath, "I never planned
on leaving you. I just need to find us a place in the
States. I'll get settled, and I'll come for you."*

*I knew he meant what he said, but him leaving
scared the life out of me. He was the only one who
protected me. The only one I trusted.*

*"Catalina." My father's voice ripped through me,
and I froze to the core. "Down! Now."*

*"Remember the fallen angels are with you, baby
sister." Javier tried to give me strength.*

*He whispered a quick prayer before he helped me
down to the ground where I got the lashing of a
lifetime.*

I hated my father—pure, white hate.

"Catalina?" Abel stood in front of me with my bag
over his shoulder. "Time to go."

Weightless, I followed him onto still another plane,
where I drifted off to an unsettled sleep.

I was a zombie by the time we got off the plane at the

border. Thankfully, Abel's truck wasn't far, and we hit the road in record time.

"Do you need anything before we get to the house?" Abel switched lanes for the exit.

"Nine-millimeter." I barely heard my own voice, but he did and gave me a small smirk. Abel knew how much I hated my father, but he was wrapped up in this world too. When I told him I was leaving, he didn't stop me, but he didn't agree to come either.

I glanced over my shoulder with tears clouding my vision. Now my mind was clearer, I began to think of Mike. I wished I hadn't left the way I did. I was ready to share my life with him, happy to know my dream of love and a family could really be true. Now I knew with cruel clarity that it had all been a façade.

"It's been seven years, Catalina. Do this for your mother. Javier would have wanted this."

"Don't," I snapped and felt hot anger bubble to the surface. "My brother would be devastated if he knew I was in the car with you, driving back to the one place he tried so hard to save me from."

He shook his head and remained quiet because he knew I was right. I stared out the window until I couldn't keep my eyes open anymore. Sleep was bliss.

I jolted awake when the car hit the white-graveled driveway, and my stomach did a violent roll when the house came into sight. The gaudy house was white with gold-trimmed balconies and a four-car garage. The driveway wrapped around the front in a horseshoe with a huge fountain in the middle. At first glance, it was a stunning sight, but if you looked really closely, you could practically see it dripped with blood. So many had lost their lives here, and so many had been stripped of their freedom.

A guy with a semi-automatic rifle opened the door and roughly pulled me from the car. I stumbled to find my footing on the ridiculous white stones and pushed his hands off me.

"You touch me like that again," I spat, "and I will tie your tongue to the end of that rifle and watch your eyes as I pull the trigger!"

And just like that, the old me returned with a vengeance.

"There's my sweet daughter." My father's voice cracked my armor from the top of the massive staircase. "Come." He motioned for me to approach him, instead of him coming to me.

I ignored him and snagged my bag from Abel and walked around the side of the house to where I knew I'd be staying.

My mother stood at the edge of the pond. I knew what I would find; she was just a shell of a woman. So much of me hated her for bringing me into this family. Some would say she didn't have a choice, but if I knew my children would be forced to live in such evil, I would do anything for them. Anything. Better yet, I would have had no children at all.

Her lifeless eyes lifted and settled on me, her mouth

fell, and she started to cry. She wrapped her arms around me, but I couldn't return the affection.

"You came!"

"I didn't have a choice."

"I'm so sorry," she cried.

"You should be."

Her shoulders flinched then she pulled away. I knew my words had reached her, but I also knew they would have little effect on her. Her heart was long past broken; it was hardened to stone.

"You still carry so much hate."

"Can you blame me?" I knew I was being cold, but I just didn't have anything left inside. They had taken my brother from me.

"Was the trip down all right?" She dried her face and tried to gather herself because we wouldn't be alone for long. He hated us alone. I'd seen it in his eyes. He was nervous I might convince Mama to leave. Truth was, I didn't want her to leave. He could have her. She'd made her mind up long ago who was more important to her, and it wasn't her children.

"I'd like to have a shower," I simply replied.

"Yes, of course. You must be tired." She switched modes with a smile and immediately straightened her spine as she walked me toward the main house.

"When is the funeral?"

"Thursday afternoon."

I turned to look at her. "That's pretty soon." Not that I was complaining. I couldn't wait to get out of here.

"Papa thinks it's safer to let his soul rest now rather than later."

"You mean in case Uncle Bash retaliates in front of the rest of the family?"

She gave me a frown, warning me not to speak about Bash.

Whatever.

The ass who yanked me from the car glared at me as Abel walked through the front door. My father slapped his shoulder, giving him praise for returning me in one piece.

"Go get cleaned up, Catalina." He dismissed me. "Dinner will be in thirty."

Not even a trace of sorrow for a lost son could be found on his face.

I went to fire back, but Abel cut me off. "Salvador," he addressed my father, "would you like me to prepare for our company?"

Company?

"Who's coming?" dropped from my mouth. My father shot me a warning to not ask such questions.

"Yes, they arrive Friday, and we will meet in the bar. Be sure their every need is accommodated so they feel," he paused, and the mood darkened, "at ease."

"Of course." Abel nodded but glanced at me before he left.

"Why are you standing there?" my father barked at me. I jumped and headed for my room.

The sheer number of oil paintings that lined the

hallway walls was staggering. It would take one strike of a match to burn this place to the ground. A grin traveled across my lips at that thought. Perhaps that could be my parting gift?

My heels clicked on the tile floor, and if I really listened, I could hear Javier's laughter coming from the entertainment room. Pain ripped through me like a shot to the gut. How was it I was now here without him? How could life take someone as special as my big brother from me? He was the only good thing about this place, my protector.

Breathe, Cat, breathe. With my hand on my stomach, I moved as if drawn by some unknown force across the hallway to the library, where I raised my eyes to see her. Tears ran silently down my cheeks, and her wings blurred into one murky color. I stayed with her as I regained my strength and until I overheard something I tucked away for later. I was always good at being quiet.

By the time I got to the dinner table, my fight was back. I held my head high. I could see that

Abel sensed I had regained my spirit by the smile he gave me, and boy, was he right.

"Hungry?" My father pointed to the bowl of beans.

"No."

"I don't care. Eat." He glared at me.

I didn't move, and he closed his eyes. I fought not to push him further. Yup, his darling daughter was home, and my backbone had grown.

"Eat or be fed," he threatened.

One of the men who stood on the other side of the room took a step toward me, ready to do just that, but I held up a hand to stop him. I reached for the ladle and slowly placed some beans on my plate then reached for the wine, pouring myself a rather large glass. I downed about half of it, feeling the heat of my father's glare.

"Don't be ungrateful, Catalina," he warned.

"That's rich," I snapped back.

Father ignored me, cut into his steak, and started to eat. Mama, who looked to be drugged, sat to his right. I suspected she self-medicated to survive. She had accepted this life, and look what it had brought her. I felt no pity. She had watched my father beat me, watched him force me to cut drugs, watched me learn to pack innocent women full of drugs to cross over the border. The entire time, I'd cry for them, say I was sorry, promised them I would try to help free them when I could. But I could do nothing but bleed for them. He made me do this work until one day a man arrived and wanted *me* to carry the drugs, said he'd pay any amount for me to do it.

My father considered it, and when he told this to Mama, she flipped out. I still wasn't sure what my Mama said or did, but two days later, I was packed and told I was going to live in the States with my aunt. I remembered hugging my mother goodbye as she quickly pushed me into the car where my freedom awaited me.

Later, I found out from Abel that my father had made her wear a bomb vest to prove her loyalty that she would never leave him. He was a fool. Mama was loyal to him to a fault. He should have known she had always put him over us. I knew her life would be easier without me there constantly challenging my father. I didn't care that she sent me away. I had my freedom.

My father started to address the other men at the table and acted like it was a normal workday, and I wanted to vomit. Venom laced with my blood, and the grip on my knife became lethal.

"Who killed my brother?" I kept my eyes on my plate, not ready to see his face. If my father was behind his death, I would kill him myself.

Silence blanketed the room, and the air turned cold. The sound of *Los Tiempos Van Cambiando* by Franky Perez and Los Guardianes Del Bosque was all that could be heard from the study a few doors down.

"I have the right to know." I kept my voice strong and lifted my angry eyes to his. "Was it Bash?"

"Do not utter that filthy dog's name in my house at my dinner table!" My father banged on the table and pointed his steak knife at me. "You are the one, *mija*! You got him killed."

The blow from his words hit so hard I jumped from my chair, and it toppled over. "How can you say that? I'm going to pretend I misheard you, Papa," I hissed, unsure what I was capable of in that moment.

Abel's hand reached back and wrapped around my wrist to hold me in place. I ripped it free and directed my poison in his direction. "So like you, Abel, to defend the enemy and not the girl you once loved."

He looked at my father then slowly stood and placed a hand on my shoulder. He turned me around to move me out of the room.

"You will show up to Javier's funeral on time, and you will behave, Catalina," my father directed, "or you will lose your ticket back to the States." Mama cleared her throat as though to speak, and the snake snarled at her. I did not hear her say a word.

Once we were alone, Abel let me out of his hold, and I tried to shake off my urge to kill.

"You sure know how to piss him off." Abel breathed hard through his words. "Why do you always push him, Catalina? You know he is a dangerous man.

"Don't." I was emotionally finished. "I hate you too. It hurts me to even hear your voice."

He stopped at my bedroom door and sighed heavily. "Catalina, you were the first woman I loved, but we were young, and it's not like I could say no to your father. I owe my life to him. He gave me this position when I had nothing. I am important here."

I knew it was unfair to feel that way. I knew what life was like here, but I found his words weak and unattractive. I wasn't in love with Abel, but I still loved him. He was there for me when Javier left for the States. My father saw Abel only as an opportunity and absorbed him into his sick world. My happiness was never something my father would ever have cared about.

"Goodnight, Abel." I slipped into my room and saw my phone light up on my bed.

> Mike: I'm sorry. I wish I didn't have to take that call. Can I see you tonight? I leave tomorrow a.m.

The screen blurred as a fresh bout of tears came on, and I spent the night curled in a ball, mourning the loss of my brother and the fact that Mike was going to leave me.

ELEVEN

MIKE

"I'm telling you, Mike, she looked like a totally different person when she caught my eye in that parking lot," Charlotte said as she lay across the couch and flipped through the channels. "She wasn't in a panic like she was in trouble. She just fell apart, and that guy took off in his truck. Maybe it was something about her brother?"

I packed my bag and eyed my father by the doorway. He knew what I was about to do, and he was worried as hell. I'd broken every rule by sharing exactly what I did with my father, but I didn't care. If something ever happened to me, I needed him to know the truth.

It had been over a day, and I'd sent countless texts, but I had not heard a word from Catalina. I was worried about what Charlotte had witnessed, and it made my head murky. I knew something was going on, and I couldn't do anything about it. I felt like crap with the timing of Cole's call right after what we had done, but I also had an important job, and I knew every moment mattered when it came to a rescue. Our second team had spotted Elena in Salvador's house, and that meant our mission just got pushed up. They wouldn't leave and risk losing her location until we relieved them. That meant the clock had started. Now I had to leave the country without saying goodbye to the one person I needed to.

"She'll call when she's ready." Charlotte turned back to me when I didn't respond. "What happened between the two of you, anyway?"

"A lot. I have to go." I hugged her goodbye, then I hugged my mother and told her I'd see her soon. My father walked me to my truck.

"Do what you need to do. Keep your head in the game, and Catalina will be here when you return, son." He grabbed my head and pulled it to his, forehead to forehead like we did when I was a kid and I needed his strength to keep going. "Keep your head in the game."

"Okay." I gave him a hug before I left, but I didn't look back. I couldn't look at my father's face when he was this worried; it was too hard.

Once in the chopper, blades beat the air, and I cleared my head and went over every single detail of what I needed to do. I didn't like the idea I wouldn't have my weapon on me, but I knew we'd have eyes on us the entire time.

"Phones." Mark shrugged at me as he held open the steel-lined bag. With one last hopeful glance at the screen, I turned off my phone and dropped it inside. Then he handed us each a new phone, preset just for this mission. "Just days, man, then you can go win your girl back."

"She's not pissed." Cole tossed his phone inside. "She doesn't seem like that kind of girl. I put twenty down it's her brother."

"I second that." Mark sealed the bag.

"Heads in the game, boys." Cole slapped us on the back.

When we landed and the Jeep arrived, we jumped inside, weapons drawn, and headed to our camp about a day's drive away. We'd meet up with North Rock for an update before our mission began.

In Hell I'll Be in Good Company by The Dead South pounded from the speakers as we drove down the dusty side streets. Times like this, the silence wasn't good for our heads, so we let John drive and used his playlist to keep our minds idle.

We took turns sleeping, one at a time, while the others stood watch. John and I rotated at the wheel, so we didn't lose any time on the journey.

Every moment counted.

———

Covered in dirt, face windburned, I tried to dislodge

grains of sand from my gums with my tongue. I unfolded from the Jeep and stretched my legs.

"Heads up." John tossed me a canteen to flush my mouth clean. I spat the cool bliss out and handed it to Mark to do the same.

"Irons." Steve from North Rock waved me over as he emerged from the camp in the woods. "The funeral was yesterday." He pointed to a photo. "Salvador's son was murdered. A lot of people showed up, but what was odd was that Bash's wife was there."

"What?" I shifted and rested my arm on my weapon.

"She stayed in the background, but we noticed her when Salvador stepped away to speak to her."

He handed me a stack of photos, and I started to flip through them to familiarize myself with as many people as I could.

"Mike." Cole pointed to his watch, and I knew it was time. I handed back the photos and rushed to catch our plane. Everything needed to look legit, and we knew when they'd start to watch us.

Three white Ford Explorers were parked at the tarmac when we touched town in Monclova, Coahuila. Cole held up his arm to synchronize our watches. From here on out, we were on a schedule. A timer dictated our every move so we'd stay in sync. There was no room for fuckups.

"Irons." At our destination, Logan motioned for me to follow him into a room where we changed into our business attire. I wasn't that comfortable in a suit, but we needed to play the part of wealthy businessmen, and Army pants and t-shirts wouldn't have cut it.

A Santos Dumont Cartier watch hung off my wrist and matching black cufflinks lay next to it. I didn't like the fact it wasn't our Blackstone GPS watch, but we had a part to play.

"Here," Mark smirked as he walked in and handed me a shoebox, "he'll notice if you aren't the total package."

"Crocodile leather shoes?" I flipped open the box and held up the blue loafers. "There needs to be a line drawn here, Cole."

"Savi said the American wore them. It's some expensive designer, Stefano Ricci or some shit. Whatever, she knows fashion, I don't. Quit bitchin' and put them on."

"Says the guy in army boots," I huffed.

"I'll be squeezing into that shit too." He laughed darkly.

We were so out of our comfort zone, but it would only be for a short time.

I took one last look in the mirror and thought how different I looked. I guessed that was what we were going for.

Cole tossed me a wallet when I went for the door. "Ten grand, cash. Don't lose it but flash it at some point."

I nodded and hopped inside the fully loaded Explorer.

John was our driver, dressed in limo attire, and a local guy we worked with sat in the front passenger seat. If you didn't have a local with you, it sent a red flag. Everyone we dealt with was dirty in some way, and as long as we played that part too, we'd fit in.

The drive to the house took an hour, which meant for an hour I drilled the house plans into my head in case something went wrong. I knew the exits, how many men were where, how many weapons, and how much ammo they all carried, along with the last known spot Elena was seen.

"Remember, you only know the basics," Cole reminded me. We didn't want to let on that we could speak Spanish fluently. The purpose of this meeting was to gain a little more knowledge before we made our final move.

John let the local speak and showed our IDs to the man working the gate. It took a moment, but we got past the first obstacle. Twice more we were stopped and waved on. By the time we got to the house, everyone would know we were there.

Salvador stood at the top of the steps and waited for us to join him. He was a tall man in his late fifties. He'd taken over his father's business when Daniel's team took him out ten years ago. It was one of the greatest victories for Shadows and Blackstone. Salvador loved to flash money and wore more rings than a pimp. His shaggy salt and pepper hair was thin, and his crooked mouth reminded me of the actor John Leguizamo.

"Gentlemen, welcome to my home." He waved us to follow him inside.

Cole shot me a look as he pulled his sunglasses off and

tucked them into his pocket. I couldn't help but laugh inside at the two of us. We were both huge men tucked into business suits pretending to be drug lords. I wondered if Trigger felt just as ridiculous when he went to get Tess back from the house.

"Would you like a drink, Mr. Rutherford?" Salvador held up a bottle of fine tequila to show me the label.

"No, thank you." I shook my head and took a seat on a red velvet chair that was pulled out for me.

"Mr. Kingsley?"

"No, thanks," Cole replied.

"I don't like to drink alone, gentlemen." He eyed us.

"And we don't drink until we've made a deal." Cole's tone was clipped.

"Very well." Salvador took a drink, then he sat down across from us and dramatically folded his legs and lit a smoke. "I hear you'd like to buy some product from me?"

"Yes." Cole pulled out an envelope and handed it to him. "Our usual supplier was taken into custody a while ago, and he suggested we speak with you. We've lost a lot of money and need to make this happen sooner rather than later."

"Ah, yes, Denton." Salvador clucked his tongue. "Such a pity he didn't get the girl."

To the untrained eye, you wouldn't have spotted the shift in Cole's demeanor, but I caught it. The American was our greatest victory to date.

"He really loved her. The little bitch just didn't know it."

Cole's jaw ticked, and I leaned forward to draw his attention to me. "We'll need some women who can bring the drugs over and the money back."

Salvador flicked his ruby ring around his pinky as he thought. "How do you expect to do this?"

"We have three drivers who are signed up for the Baja race. They can bring the girls to the border, and we can bring the cash to a drop-off point near town. We have a guy at the border who has been paid well not to check the panels of the buggies."

"This is good." He seemed impressed. "How much are we talking, here?"

"Four-point-five million, pre-race." I didn't miss a beat. "That is if this is something you'd like to work out with us."

"What the catch?"

"We get to pick the women."

"Pick the women?" A glint of suspicion sparked in his eyes. "Why?"

"We've been using social media to promote these drivers, and we have a girl in every photo. If we stray too far from their usual type, it could send a red flag."

"Yes, I can see this." He held my gaze a moment before he rubbed his lips with both hands. "What kind of women?"

"They must be small-framed, slim legs, and decent breasts." I made a cupping motion with my hands. I felt like a pig, but I needed to sound like one.

"I think I just grew hard thinking about it." He

hooked a leg on the arm of the chair, stretching his sports pants.

"Any of your girls match what we need?"

"I believe we have a few, yes."

"Any tattoos?" I tried a different angle, hoping they'd mention Elena's butterfly on her collarbone.

"One does, yes." He looked at me questioningly.

"I don't want any girl to stand out, that's all. So nothing too elaborate or memorable, then," I covered.

"I'd like to meet the mules before I make any decisions." Cole piped in.

Salvador drew in a long breath of smoke as he eyed Cole hard. "You say Denton told you to come here?"

Shit, we'd spooked him.

"We did say that, yes." Cole nodded. "Denton Barlow."

"If Denton knew you so well, you would have met his woman. What did she look like?"

Cole leaned forward and rested his arms on his thighs. "Green eyes, tight body, and long, dark hair."

"Perhaps. Anyone could have known that."

"She sings and has one hell of a feisty personality. She was taken by the US Army, and Denton managed to get her back."

"Are we here to play who-knows-what, or are we here to make a deal?" I huffed, annoyed. Savi's period of captivity still hurt to think about. "I have a contact within the Devil's Reach if this doesn't work out, so you're in or you're out. Either way, stop fucking with my time."

His eyes widened. I must have hit a nerve because he dropped his leg and plucked at his pants.

"Allen's contract was voided. The DR isn't selling anymore."

I smirked, happy my friend wasn't under their shit control anymore.

"I think it's pretty fair to say that if Trigger wants something to happen, he makes it happen."

"Perhaps."

"We both know you have *pretties.*" I cringed at the word. "If we are going to move that amount of drugs, we need the best you have."

"Sal." A woman draped an arm over the back of his chair and whispered something in his ear.

"And give me something tall. I like my Latinas tall." Cole tried a different take again to see if he could narrow things down even more. Elena was taller than the average Latina.

The woman's eyes snapped over to mine with fear, and I felt her concern with Cole's words.

What do you know, lady?

Salvador cleared his throat before he waved her off, but when she didn't leave, he twisted to glare at her.

"No," she hissed, and the air became charged.

Shit.

He stood, annoyed, but oddly didn't strike her. Instead, he fixed the sleeves on his shirt.

"Shall we do a tour?"

I glanced at Cole, confused at this sudden turn in the

conversation. A nerve in my back started to tick and slowly travel up my spine, alerting me something was about to happen.

"We don't have the time." I stood and fastened a button on my jacket. "Perhaps we chose the wrong brother to make a deal with."

I cut raw with that comment. I knew the bad blood between them, but Cole and I both agreed that if we felt Salvador was going to drop us, then we'd use Bash as a weapon.

Salvador raised his head and looked at me, and the vein in his neck popped out while he thought.

"My wife would like to invite you to dinner."

Cole gave me a knowing nod. If you got invited to dinner, you were in.

"I think we can change some things around." Cole got out the prearranged phone and called John.

"You," he pointed to Cole, "meet the girls, pick who you want, and we'll make a deal."

"Okay," he nodded in agreement.

"You come with me." Salvador motioned for me to follow him. "I want to show you my favorite pieces of art."

Okay...

I was taken on a tour through several rather overdone rooms. Then we headed down a hallway toward a room I knew from my study of the house plans would be the library. I couldn't imagine Salvador ever cracked a book in his life, but the room was still intriguing.

I stopped short when I came to a familiar painting of a black angel. Her wings dipped downward, and the profile of her face seemed to be crying.

"Ah, you like my angel." Salvador sipped the drink he held.

"I feel like I've seen this before," I answered, and I knew where. I pictured Catalina's slender back and my colorful hands skimming down her smooth skin. My stomach was tight with confusion.

"*Sí*," he moved closer as he spoke, "it's a famous depiction by Lewis Devill, one of the greatest cartel lords that ever lived." He pointed to the angel. "There is a story about the fallen. See the way the feathers are ruffled, and the bottoms of the wings have been clipped?" I nodded. "When angels can't fly free, they lose their coloring, their lines become dull, and sadness consumes them. There is a saying in Spanish, which means 'angels littered the ground as prisoners, waiting to be rescued,' and until they realize that won't happen, they sit like this. Frozen in a fragile state."

"And if they're rescued?" I challenged.

"They will not be." His tone was flat as he brushed a finger down the side of the wooden frame. "Lewis used to tattoo his pretties, to remind them they'd never be free." He sighed like he missed the fucking monster. "Sadly, once he died, the tradition ended."

"So, the girls don't have the angels anymore?" I was confused. Why in the hell would Catalina have this on her back? What happened to her that she would have such a sad angel on her skin?

His face tightened, and he looked away. "Only one."

I couldn't help but think maybe it was his wife, by the hate that raced across his face.

"Come, let's go get you a drink." I followed him out to the hallway and back into the bar where he fixed me a whiskey. I didn't want it, but it was evident he didn't like to drink alone.

"Tell me something about you, Mr. Rutherford." He eased onto the stool as Cole joined us with a pale face. A bead of sweat had broken out across his forehead.

"Not much to say, really." I eyed my brother, concerned as hell something bad had happened. "I followed my father's footsteps into the drug world, and here I am now, trying to make sure this deal doesn't fall ap—"

"I told you not to come down!" Salvador interrupted.

"I was looking for Abel," she snapped back, and I felt the hairs on my neck stand up. I turned and nearly let the drink slip through my fingers.

Catalina.

Her eyes widened, and her mouth dropped open, but she quickly recovered with a little nod. Salvador licked his lips in annoyance but then reined in his anger, as he had guests to impress.

"Catalina, come." He held out his hand, but when she didn't react right away, he snapped. "Come here!"

Slowly, her heels clicked across the tiled floor and she stood next to him. Her arms were folded, and her eyes were wild. He placed his finger under her chin and tipped her head back. She turned her head and looked at the floor. I felt the need to smash my glass and jam the edge of it into his throat.

"You'll have to excuse my daughter."

What? No.

"Catalina is visiting from the States and is very tired," he cooed as she looked at the floor. "We had a death in the family. Her brother was killed, and the funeral was yesterday."

I went rigid as her eyes stayed locked on the floor.

"Catalina, don't be rude. Say hello."

She stepped forward in her tight little dress and heels and extended her hand to me. "Nice to meet you," she whispered as I took her icy hand in mine and fought to let go.

"Please, call me Michael." I looked over her head to Salvador. "Lovely. Does she do runs?" I needed to keep my persona up.

"I'd be willing to negotiate." He winked, and my blood pressure shot straight up. Slowly, my gaze fell to hers. So much was written across her face. I was sure my expression showed nothing of her betrayal.

"She doesn't run, nor does she have any part in the family business," her mother snapped from the doorway.

"Yes, well, if these men need Catalina to do a job, then maybe we can work something out."

"I don't make deals with criminals," she said with such hate I felt my own chest tighten.

"Things can be arranged, my angel," he purred over her shoulder, and my arm shot out to tug her toward me. As soon as I did, I realized how it looked, so I took her face in my hand and stared into her eyes like I was checking her out. I shook off the nausea that came over me. I would never manhandle her like this, so I only hoped she understood what I was doing. "She clean?"

She snarled.

"Should be. She has no tracks or cuts."

"I am." She forced her face free from my hold. "Fuck you for asking."

Whoa.

"She has a mouth," Salvador warned in a tone that made her shoulders tense.

"I like that."

"I'm not for sale." She ripped her arm away and took a few steps back.

"If you like that, I'll figure it out." He glanced at Catalina and strummed his fingers over his belt, and her eyes glazed over with fright. He grinned, and I felt Cole move to my side. We both had been tested today, but I was still in shock, so my head wasn't on straight.

"You hit her?" I had to know.

"I have." He licked his lips like he enjoyed the ability to inflict pain on his own daughter, and Catalina, once again, looked away in a state of shellshock. Salvador ended his crude act to pull out his phone and grinned at the caller ID. "Excuse me, gentlemen." He stepped out of the room, and I started to move toward her, but she shook her head slightly and moved her eyes up to a camera on the wall.

"Abel." Salvador snapped his fingers at her, and he quickly joined her side. "Take Catalina for a walk."

"Don't." She pulled her arm out of his hold, and he stepped back immediately as if to show he wasn't going to hurt her. *Interesting.*

Salvador stepped out of the room for another call, and Catalina turned to leave. "Nice to meet you both," she said, but I hooked her arm, and Abel cleared his throat and held back the security guards.

"I'm sorry to hear about your brother." I was desperate for her to look at me, for her to tell me this was a huge misunderstanding, but all I got were cold, lifeless eyes.

"Me too. Thank you," she whispered before she headed out to the hallway. Abel followed, and we were left with the two fat fuckers.

What the hell just happened?

I whirled around to find my brother with his work phone in his hand. He handed it to me. My vision went fuzzy when I saw the photo of Catalina standing next to her mother and Abel in front of a coffin.

"We'll figure this out, Mike."

"I hope you're right," I turned to look at him with my world crumbling around me, "or you might be leaving this place without me."

TWELVE

Abel's face was white and confused as I closed the door. I cupped my mouth as I rushed into my room, in fear someone would hear my sobs. What the hell just happened? Why were Mike and Cole here? How? My insides rolled and stirred like a storm gaining speed as my mind spun out of control.

My secret had just been exposed in the worst way possible, to the one person I wasn't ready to share it with. I was the daughter of Salvador Esteban, son of Alamo Esteban and brother to Sebastian Esteban, a long ancestry of drug lords. Criminals.

My hands shook so hard I dropped them to my knees and squeezed them hard. I heaved in a few deep breaths. Footsteps made their way into my chaos, but my muscles were frozen, and I couldn't get my brain to connect.

"Catalina?" A voice broke through my panic attack. "What happened?" I opened my eyes to find Elena, one of the girls I shared a bathroom with, looking at me in a panicked state of her own. "Come on." She tugged my arm and helped me into the shared bathroom.

Once behind the safety of the restroom walls, I dropped to the floor. Elena dampened a towel and pressed it to my head.

"You look like you might pass out," she whispered, and her kindness broke past my pain. The word had spread quickly that I wasn't like the rest of them when I arrived home a few days ago, but for Elena to be this bold with Salvador's daughter showed me she didn't care who I was.

"You need to pull it together or Salvador will know something is wrong." She shifted to sit next to me on the marble floor. "Are you…" she paused, "are you pregnant?"

"What?" That stopped the storm inside momentarily. "What makes you ask that?"

"You looked so pale and like you might get sick, so I just assumed you were."

"No, God, no." I closed my eyes and shook my head.

Please, someone stop the spinning.

"What happened, then?"

"Nothing." I took a deep breath but couldn't contain my nerves. Everything confused me, sounds, lights, the cool floor. *Ahhh!* I held my head in fear it would spin right off.

"The big guys in the bar?"

"Yeah."

"I heard they're looking for some mules." She leaned back against the wall and covered the bruises that purpled her thighs. "What I wouldn't do get the hell out of this place."

My heart broke all over again, but anger quickly took over. How could I have left these women behind? How could I have never looked back and lived a life that was so much better than this? I felt shame in that moment.

"Have you ever thought about running?" she continued without a care. "Just running without looking back? Or speaking up to one of the border patrol agents?" She sniffed. "I almost did once, but Ana beat me to the punch, and it turned out the agent worked for Salvador… I never saw her again." She paused. "Maybe a bullet to the skull would be better, just end it all."

"You are not alone in that thought, Elena." I used the cool cloth to soothe my sore eyes, and my head pounded behind them.

"Catalina?" Mother knocked on the door, and we both jumped. Elena's fingers dug into my arm, but I gave her a pat to reassure her it was okay. "Catalina, I would like to speak with you now."

"One moment, Mama." I scrambled to my feet, but she opened the door, and her eyes softened when she saw me and the state I was in. Just as I moved my gaze to Elena's, she did too, and I felt the cold smother my insides once again.

"Roman!" she snapped, and one of the house guards

came flying into the room and nearly ripped Elena's arm out of the socket as he pulled her up.

"No!" I shoved him, and suddenly something hard hit my cheek, and I blew backward. My ears rang and my vision blurred, but I made it to my feet and grabbed a glass jewelry box off the counter and smashed it over his head.

He tipped forward but took the blow well. His hand clamped down on the wound, and he drew it forward to see the blood.

"Catalina!" my mother screamed and ran to my side. "Stop, or your father will make you! Your freedom is in jeopardy. Think about it!"

"Freedom," I seethed. "Why should I have freedom when these women don't have theirs?"

"Shh." She tried to calm me, but I couldn't be calmed. "Come with me before your papa takes out his anger on both of you."

I closed my eyes and cursed inside. She was right; this fight would only lead to pain for Elena.

"Roman," my mother said smoothly, "please help Elena back to her room. We have guests, and they will want to see her unmarked."

"Yes, ma'am." He glared at me but helped Elena to her feet and walked her out of the room.

"I think it's time we had a chat, Catalina."

Once in the garden, safely away from any cameras or guards, she walked with me arm-in-arm. My cheek was hot, and I was sure there was a mark, but my mother seemed to be able to look past it, like normal.

"I never wanted you to be a part of this." She kept her gaze forward.

"I don't believe you."

"You are my daughter."

"You let him hurt me."

The sound of the pebbles under our shoes filled the silence while we both let the hurt in. What little sun was left lit the tears that threatened her eyes and showed her pain.

"I've lost one child this week. I won't lose another."

"Then make it right and leave." What I wouldn't do to have a mother again, someone to love me the way I deserved.

The crickets chirped high, and the frogs took the bass in the night's melody. From a distance, the place was beautiful. The joke was on those who thought so.

"I caught your father in bed with your *tía*." Mama swallowed hard, and the muscles in her arm tightened.

"Bash's wife?" I nearly stumbled.

"When I caught them in our bed, I lost all control, but also gained leverage." A sliver of a smile tugged at the corner of her lips. "I threatened to tell and leave."

"Oh, Mama, I'm sorry." My heart ached again for her. I never could understand why she loved Papa, but to see a backbone appear in my mother was rather thrilling. "What did he do?"

"He panicked and threatened to kill me. In spite of

her, your father still loves me. Even as he loves her." She fiddled with the button on her blouse, and sadness replaced her smile. "Remember the man who asked your father to buy you?" I nodded and fought to keep my tongue silent. "It was that night I found them, and that was the night I realized what I had."

"What do you mean?"

"I had something to use to get you freedom, *mija*." She kept going. "The only way to save you was to threaten him. We both know Bash has more power than Sal does, and all it would take would have been one phone call from me, and this would all be gone."

I secretly wondered if she was giving me the ace I needed to tear down the kingdom.

"After I collected my thoughts, I approached him in his library and laid out my decision. That I would stay and continue to rule next to him if he agreed to let you leave the family business unharmed. I know you hate me," she whispered, "hate the life you were born into, hate that we do such unspeakable acts. I traded my life for yours, Catalina."

I searched for the right words, but nothing came but a heavy weight on my heart. I'd thought she was a weak woman who only loved one man and didn't care about her children, but all along she had stayed in chains so I could be free.

I stopped our walk and stood in front of her. "Mama, I'm so sorry."

Her warm hands gently cupped my cheeks. "I'm not.

You got to live and be free. I'm so proud of you, Catalina. You made a life for yourself on your own with no money or help from us. That's truly admirable."

I had always wanted a relationship with a mother like others had, and I was jealous of those who did. I was so wrong to hate her all these years. I was sorry for so many things.

When one of the guards moved closer to the railing to watch us, she urged me to continue walking.

"You must promise me one thing."

"Okay," I whispered.

"You must never let your father know *I* told you."

Again, by the way she said the word *I*, I felt like she was telling me something else. I nodded then groaned when my father appeared out of nowhere.

"What happened to your face?" he snapped and glared at my mother.

"Roman," she answered for me, "lost his temper again."

"What did you do?" He addressed his question to me, but I unlinked from my mother's arm and moved past him.

"I asked you a question, Catalina."

"I know."

"Get ready for dinner. We need to make our guests comfortable."

I rolled my eyes just to piss him off further and headed inside.

We entertained guests in the west wing of the

mansion, where my father kept his most expensive items to make himself appear larger than he was. The windows were floor to ceiling high, a small stage stood off to the side, and five over-the-top gold candelabras lined the length of the glass table. Needless to say, it was ugly.

"What happened to your cheek?" Abel shook his head and stepped up to me to examine my blue, swollen face. There was a time when his touch meant the world to me, but now he was merely a friend.

"It's nothing."

"It's not nothing, Catalina." He followed me as we entered the dining room, where Mike and Cole stood by the bar admiring the view of the gardens.

"Who did that to you?"

Mike whirled around when he heard Abel's voice, and his expression darkened when he caught Abel's topic of conversation. When Mike started to move, Cole caught him by the arm just as my father joined us.

"Good, you have drinks." My father took his seat at the head of the table and glared at me to sit. Abel's hand landed on my lower back, and so did Mike's gaze.

It's not what you think.

I sank into the chair across from Mike and dropped my napkin on my lap so my hands could shake in private.

Mama joined us shortly afterward and greeted the table in her normal way, only this time I smiled back. It would take baby steps, but now that I knew the truth, I was more than willing to work on our relationship.

The staff set our meal in front of us and stepped back to wait for the next order my father would bark at them.

"Lovely house you have." Cole tried to make small talk, and when I looked up, Mike was staring at me. My mother's brows pinched when she caught it too, but she remained quiet.

I tuned out my father's normal bullshit story on how the house came to be in his. He always failed to mention that it was actually Bash who was given the house, but later, due to a mishap between the brothers, Bash moved out. They hadn't spoken since, and now I wondered if it had something to do with my aunt and my father. The brothers had been in a constant feud for years and killed anyone who stepped in their way.

"I'm sorry to hear about the death of your son." Mike addressed my mother. The blood drained straight down to my feet and took my stomach with it.

"Thank you," she replied carefully, with a look at her husband, then took a sip of water to moisten her mouth.

"You live in the States, Catalina? How sad to be so far away when it happened. When did you find out?"

I shot him a small warning not to do this here, but he dismissed it.

"Um, it was right after a party for work. I had gone outside to look for a friend, and that's when I spotted Abel." I nodded toward him. "My mother had sent him to pick me up. She called me with the news."

Mike's lips pressed together like it wasn't enough for him.

"Is your work okay with you leaving so quickly? What about your friends?"

I shifted, annoyed. He was gambling with both of our fates. "Well, Mr. Rutherford, I wasn't thinking about them. I was thinking about the fact that my brother was now dead, and I had to come back to the last place on Earth I'd ever wanted to return to."

"Catalina," my father snapped, and I swung my gaze in his direction.

"I'm sorry, Father, did that just earn me the belt, or will I just get another crack to the cheek from your dogs?"

His chubby face turned three shades of red as his blood pressure rose. Sweat broke out along the collar of his dress shirt, and the grip on his fork tightened. I'm sure he would have liked to stab me with it. *Yeah, I'm not scared of you anymore.*

"Excuse my friend for upsetting your family," Cole interjected with a hard look at Mike. "We appreciate your hospitality, but we are here on business, after all."

"Bring the girls in." Salvador snapped his fingers, and one by one they filed in, each wearing a skimpy outfit.

Elena caught my eye, and I gave her a look to stay strong. She shrugged and dropped her head. Cole caught my look at her, and he glanced at her and then back at me. He then used his elbow and signaled something to Mike that had him gazing in my direction again.

What did I miss?

"This one," my father roughly grabbed Elena by the

arm and swung her around to show off her backside, "is one of my favorites."

"Stop!" I jumped to my feet. "She's not an animal, Father."

"My apologies." My father let her go and quickly turned to his company. "My daughter doesn't agree with the family business, not like her brother. I understand that you could be interested in her as well. Perhaps this could be arranged," he threatened as he looked furiously at me.

"Javier hated everything about his house," I hissed, "but mostly we hated *you*."

"Enough, Catalina. Go now." His warning had me pushing back into the chair. "Your freedom has an expiration date."

"So does yours." I tossed my napkin on the table and ran from the room.

THIRTEEN

MIKE

I slammed the truck door behind me and ran a hand over my aching head. My entire body felt as though it was turning itself inside out.

"Irons." Cole's tone was all business as he ordered the guys to give us a minute.

"Logan, I just need a second to get my head on straight."

"I know it was hard to leave, but…"

"But what?" I rubbed my face and tried to keep my mouth from stepping over a line. "If Savannah was in that house, you would have burnt that place to the ground by now."

"Yeah, I would have." He made me look over. "But you're forgetting the basement full of innocent people." He stepped closer. "We have a chance to get both Catalina and Elena out safely without any casualties." He paused and cleared his throat. "We were ordered to shoot first and ask questions later when we saved Savannah, but this is different. I know you know that. You're just in shock, so give yourself the night to breathe, and we'll recap tomorrow." He stopped before he left to go call Frank with an update. "We'll get her back, Mike, but it seems to me she has a way out. Sal and she are oil and water, and she could be a loose cannon around any actual buyer. You're in shock—shit, so am I. That nearly tossed me off my game, but this is a game-changer. You saw what happened at the table. She knows Elena. She might be able to help us."

"She's one of *them*." I was pissed at that. "She's a fucking Esteban!"

"No, she's not." Cole stepped closer, sensing my internal meltdown. "She told you that at dinner. You just couldn't hear her. She might have their blood, but she isn't any part of that family."

"So you could love Savi, even if she had direct roots to the cartel? You could still love her?" My eyes burned.

"I loved Savannah before I even met her." His face hardened. "If she left me for a member of the cartel, I wouldn't stop loving that woman." He sighed. "You don't see it, Mike, because you hurt right now. But, brother, you love Catalina. Let the sting wear off before you make your mind up because I can promise you that battle," he pointed to his head and heart, "is not going to be pretty."

I covered my face and wanted to scream in frustration. I was so confused and hurt. "Would you let her stay at the safe house?" That stopped him in his tracks. "Would you let the woman I love be in the one place you guard with your heart and soul?"

I wanted a fight, and he saw it, and to my surprise, he didn't give it to me. Instead, he landed his hand on my shoulder and squeezed as he spoke.

"Mike, you're the smartest person I've come across yet. You always think and rethink before you make any move. You've saved our Blackstone asses on countless occasions. If you love this woman and if *you* trust this woman, I would figure out a way for you to be happy."

I broke and was beyond thankful it was only Cole who witnessed it. This was uncharted territory for me, and I had zero clue how to navigate it.

When I turned the corner on my way to get changed, John was sitting on the hood of the truck, holding his weapon like he was ready to go fight. I snagged my bag off the ground and started to walk away when he jumped off and grabbed my shoulder.

"Whatever you need." John held my gaze, unsure where my head was, and so was I. "Whatever you're thinking, I'm in."

"Thanks." John always had my back, and we were equally crazy and got that about each other.

Dusk was buzzing when I swung open the front door. Cole had ordered the guys to hurry up with the transforming the off-road buggies to fit eighteen bricks of cocaine on each side. Normally, we'd be doing most of this work at Shadows, but Daniel was in the middle of a huge renovation, so Dusk was the main headquarters for now.

"Sir?" Crawford stopped me at the kitchen. "I was wondering if you could teach me how to deal with explosives."

"Don't get blown up," I muttered but stopped myself when I realized he was asking for help. "Look, I will. Let me just through this job, and I'll give you some tips."

"Okay." He grabbed an apple. "Sir?"

"Yeah?" I dug some Advil from the drawer.

"Lopez was telling a story the other night about how you disarmed an entire room that the Blackstone team was locked in. He said shots were fired, and one of the walls was on fire."

"What's the question, Crawford?"

Mark came in and started to drink from the bottle of orange juice. He looked as drained as I. The word about Catalina had spread through Blackstone quickly, and we all tried to process it.

"That's a lot to deal with at once, sir. Doesn't that scare the shit out of you?"

I swallowed the lump that wedged itself in my throat and blinked back the pain from my migraine. "No," I answered truthfully, "that doesn't scare me."

Mark looked over and gave me a grim look.

The next day, I tried hard to pay attention to the mission details, but the more I tried to focus, the more I let thoughts of Catalina pull my head away. I'd picture her face when she spotted me, and the way Salvador loathed her, and how Elena seemed to have a connection with her.

"Mike," Cole snapped my attention back to him, "John will be with Elena, Mark and Keith will pose as drivers number three and four with whoever else they give us. We pick up the drugs and girls here." He pointed to the end of the Baja race. "We have fifteen minutes to load each vehicle, then we drive from here to here." He slid his hand across the map. "John, you will cross the border first. Once he checks in, Mark, you go, and so on and so on. We'll have North Rock as our eyes, here, here, and here. I spoke to Steve this morning, and they understand the plan and are ready to move when we are."

I felt a sense of relief knowing North Rock was still close to the compound. We were playing with fire, and at any point, the prison guards could allow Denton to have his phone rights back, and we'd be finished.

"We move out in two days." Cole glanced at me. "No one moves unless I say otherwise. Dismissed."

"Mark?" I snagged his arm. "Is she home?"

"No," he shook his head, "not yet."

I pulled out my phone and called my sister.

"Hey, big bro, nice to hear from ya." Once again, that little spot in my chest heaved when I went to mention her name.

"Has, ah…" I choked on my own words. "Has Catalina touched base with you lately?"

"No. I'm worried about her too, but I'm sure she'll be

back soon. By the way, Kyle and Lizzy got into it last night at the Brew, and it was hysterical…"

"Charlotte," I snapped, "sorry, but…"

"What's wrong, Mike? Are you okay? Is Cat okay? Have you heard anything?"

I pinched the bridge of my nose. "No, but when you talk to her, when she shows up, will you let me know?"

"Of course. But, Mike?" I paused before I hung up. "Whatever is going on, just know she loves you. I'm sure it was that brother of hers got into trouble or something. I have honestly never seen her this happy before."

"Just let me know." I hit *end*.

The next night came and went, and I paced a pathway through the hardwood floor in my room. When I couldn't take the silence anymore, I grabbed my keys and headed out to my truck and tore off down the road.

The old, winding road that led to his shop was cloaked in fog, much like my brain was. Flashes of Catalina popped up in front of me, and my patience was like a rubber band, stretched too far. I grabbed the coffees I had picked up in town and kicked the door closed behind me.

"I didn't know you were back yet." The crow's feet around my father's eyes rose but fell when he caught my mood. "Are the boys okay?"

I nodded, unsure of how to start this conversation.

"Mike?"

"Catalina," I choked out. "She's not…" I couldn't even say the words.

My father took a few unsure steps toward me and then wrapped his arms around my neck and pulled me to his shoulder.

"Her father is the man we've been hunting for years." I tried to hold my emotions down. "I love her, Dad, but how can I deal with her, knowing this?"

"We'll figure this out, son." He sniffed. "Come on inside and help me understand it all."

By the time I filled my father in, he was as blown away as I was.

"I mean, she did mention a little about her family to your mother, but not much." His flannel coat was full of wood chips and pine needles. He brushed away the ones at the bottom while he mulled his thoughts. "You can't be mad at her for who her family is, son. That's not fair."

"Why?" Hate filled my veins again, not for her, but for her father.

"Mike, your own mother doesn't know where you travel off to." He closed his eyes. "You both carry secrets, some worse than others. How was she to know that she was going to meet someone who chased the cartel? The odds of that are extremely thin."

"So what?" I tried another tack. "We'd get married, and they'd show up at the wedding?"

He gave me an understanding smile, and I knew he was right. Still, I needed to get the shit out.

"Just because you were dealt two parents who care about you and a loving sister doesn't mean others get the same." He shrugged. "Look at Mark. You wouldn't judge him for the horrible things his mother did, right? No, because you love him like a brother. Seems to me Catalina left that life to make a better one. She's not strapping drugs to those women. Sounds like she's making friends with them. Son, see past this," he rubbed my American flag tattoo, "and see that not all people who are laced with the enemy are bad."

I closed my eyes and took a long breath and let it out as much as I could.

"I'm nervous, Dad."

"That's because you love her. Any time the heart's involved, the stakes get higher."

"She hasn't come home yet." I tried to rub some tension out of my neck, "what if her father doesn't let her leave?"

"There's always a chance of that happening, especially if she gets mouthy with her father again." I noticed he seemed entertained by the idea.

"She's got fire." I glanced at him.

"I rather like that."

"Yeah," I leaned back, "me too."

Again, we sat and thought. The loons on the lake sang a sad tune, and I tried to control my next thought, but before I could say anything else, his eyes suddenly moved to mine, and I saw it. "What about asking…"

"I thought about it too."

"Well?"

"Cole wouldn't like it."

"Son," he leaned forward in his chair, "sometimes it's

okay to bend the lines between good and bad when your intentions are in the right place."

We sat next to the warm cast iron fireplace and finished off our coffees before I went behind my brothers' backs and made a call. I wasn't proud of it but figured they'd do the same.

I went for a long walk in the woods and gave things a good once-over in my head before I pulled my phone out and hit dial.

"Hey." Trigger sounded like he was on his bike.

"Good time?"

"Yeah."

I took a deep breath and tried to figure out where to start. "I've got a problem."

———

Dad convinced me to have dinner at home that night. Mom could tell something was up, and Charlotte hovered around me a little more than normal.

"Hey." She handed me her plate to wash and started to dry the one I handed her. "Any chance the reason you're so quiet is because Catalina dumped you?"

"What?" I shook the fog. "No."

"What the hell happened between you two, and where is she?" She looked worried. "She's going to lose her intern spot soon as well." I didn't answer; I couldn't. I wouldn't put that secret on her. "Mike," she reached for my arm, "is she okay?"

I held her gaze, and her face fell.

"Mike? You are kind of scaring me."

"Don't ask me questions like that right now."

"What does that mean?"

"Charlotte," I pressed my palms into the counter and dropped my head, trying to cool my emotions, "I can't answer that right now."

"Okay." She nodded, but I could see a million questions on the tip of her tongue. We went back to the silence and finished cleaning up.

Later that evening, while my family watched TV, I headed down to the water's edge. I couldn't help but glance between the boards where I first got a taste of the woman I fell head over heels for. With my feet hanging over the edge of the dock, I waited with my phone in my hand for what my friend had found out.

FOURTEEN

Catalina

"Where is she?" I found Abel in the kitchen the next morning.

"Who?" He bit into an apple, spraying juice through the rays of sunshine.

"Elena," I whispered. "I need to speak with her."

"Catalina," he started, but when I shot him a pleading look, he closed his eyes and cursed. "She's getting prepped with the other girls."

"He's sending her, then?" Though I knew Abel would never hurt me, I knew his loyalty was to my father.

"What's going on in there?" He pointed to my head.

"When do they leave?"

"Tomorrow."

"What are the chances the girls will be returned safely?"

"About the same of you loving your father again."

I glared at his example. That wasn't funny. "Abel," I looked at him, "does it not bother you that they leave and don't come back?"

"It bothers me that you left and never came back."

The squeeze in my chest returned. "You could have left."

"Yeah?" He grinned darkly. "Your father would never have allowed it."

"If you really loved me, you would have fought for me, not fallen into line with the rest of those monsters."

We would never be on the same page. He stepped forward and handed me a card with a number on it. "Think what you want about me, I know I watched the girl I loved drive off to a different life without so much as a glance over her shoulder." He held my gaze a beat longer than I would have liked. "Despite our past, if you get into trouble here or over there, call me."

I kissed his cheek as a thank you and tucked the card in my pocket before I left in search for Elena.

"Arms up!" Roman's demand drew me to the top of the staircase that led downstairs. Removing my heels, I hurried down the polished marble and peeked around to see the entire room coated in white powder. A package must have broken. I caught Elena's terrified eyes and nodded for her to make her way in my direction. There were fifteen pretties who lived in this house, and thirty who lived at Bash's. Only five were leaving with Mike, so I needed to know if the others were leaving with someone else or not.

"What are you doing here?" Her eyes were wild and fearful. "He'll kill you."

"Elena, do you trust the girls who are going with you?"

"Yes," she nodded, "I really do."

I glanced over her shoulder to make sure Roman was still busy. "Do exactly what they say, and don't try to escape."

"I can't tell them not to run, Catalina. This is our only chance to get out of here."

I took her face in my hands. "Elena, your freedom is with them."

"What?"

"I know you have no reason to trust me."

"I do." The way her eyes softened around the edges, I knew she was telling the truth.

"I will see you on the other side if you just listen to everything they tell you to do."

Her chin started to quiver, but I shook my head. She needed to keep her state of terror at the surface so she didn't send a red flag to Roman or anyone else.

"Do you understand me?"

"Yes."

I dropped my hands away and smiled. "Okay, if you trust them, share it."

"You need to give her wings back."

"Huh?"

She smiled through some tears. "Your angel." She sniffed. "You're not a prisoner anymore, Catalina. You're free."

I tossed myself in her arms and hugged her hard. "We will both be free soon."

"Where's Elena?" Roman barked, and we both jumped.

"Can you give this to any one of the men? Try, if you can, to give it to the biggest one with lots of tattoos." I handed her an envelope, and she tucked it in under one of the bricks of cocaine. "Thank you."

Though I didn't bring anything with me when I came here, when I returned to my room, my mother had a new suitcase on the bed, full of clothes. She folded a sweater and placed it on top before she sensed my presence.

"You need to leave." She wouldn't look at me. "It's much too dangerous to be here."

"You didn't need to do this, Mama." I stepped into the room and closed the door.

"Yes, I did." Her voice was low. "You're my daughter. It's the least I can do."

Moving onto the bed, I saw by her worried face something was about to happen, so she wanted to make sure I wasn't in the crossfire.

"What's going on?"

"I never thought he'd do it," she muttered to herself.

"How can the person you lay with most every night destroy you so deeply?"

Coldness washed over my skin, and my heart quickened. "Did Papa hurt Javier?"

Her face snapped up to mine, and I saw the look in her eyes.

No.

She reached for my hand, but I stepped back, not wanting the comfort. Pain ripped through my heart. Blood rushed to my ears and drowned me a swell of white noise.

"Javier wanted to mend fences with the family, without knowing the true family secrets. When your father got wind he was at Bash's, he sent..." She trailed off as the pain switched to anger.

"Sent who?" Mama's face looked pained, and I drew in my lips and bolted out of the room, down the hallway, and down the stairs.

"Catalina, no!" Mama screamed after me.

"Abel!" I whirled around in the entryway, knowing he was never far. "Where are you, Abel?"

"Catalina, don't open this up. You will not be allowed to leave."

"I don't care anymore!" I was finished, finished with it all. "Ah!" How could he kill his own son?

"Catalina," my father snapped at me from a doorway, and I saw red. If you could taste what pain was like, I could in that moment. It swirled my taste buds like a soda popping at the tiny nerves. "We have a visitor." His nostrils flared at me and dared me to act out again. "Perhaps you could have your conversation outside."

Just when I went to attack, a man stepped out with an intense look. He ran a hand through his long mohawk, and I took in his entire appearance.

He looked like Lucifer's son.

He stole my words and made me step backward, needing that extra space. "You must be Catalina," the man said with a deep, gritty tone. "Why don't you come and join us?"

What?

My mother had begged me to obey, and I found my feet moving without my consent.

"Behave," my father hissed, and my hand twitched to tear his chest apart and claw out his useless heart.

"Your time is coming, Father," I used my best American accent just to dig the knife a little deeper, "and I really hope I'm there for it."

His hand reached out, but our guest cleared his throat, and my father switched back to his host mode.

"Catalina, this is Trigger. He runs a motorcycle club in LA."

I extended my arm, and it shook while I waited for him to take it, then dropped it as he didn't reciprocate. He just kept his intense gaze on me. Slowly, his head tilted to one side then the other as if to crack his neck, and then he ran a finger across his top lip and down his beard.

"I'm happy to hear you are thinking of joining forces

with us again." My father tried to fill the silence. "We've missed the Devil's Reach. Speaking of which, how is your father?"

That made him break his gaze with me, and his pupils dilated. "Dead."

"Oh, shit," Salvador huffed. "My condolences for your loss."

"Not necessary, no loss."

My father seemed razzed by this man, and I saw an opportunity.

"Devil's Reach?" I pointed to his vest. "Any affiliation with the Stripe Backs?"

"No," he nearly hissed.

"Well, that's good," I twisted my head to see my father, "because my father tried to do business with them a few months ago." My father's eyes widened, and I smiled sweetly. "Remember, I have ears too."

"That so?" Trigger shifted his intense green eyes to stare at Papa. "Unlike my father, loyalty is what's most important to me in a business deal."

"I was under the impression you weren't looking to work with us anymore."

"Mmm," Trigger mused over my father, who shot me a look of death. It didn't go unnoticed that my father's hands were shaking.

Who the hell was this guy?

Trigger's phone rang, and he pulled it out. "I need to take this." He stepped out of the room, and I felt the mood shift.

"You stupid little *culo*," my father hissed, and his jaw started to tick, "if you screw up this opportunity for me, I will kill you myself."

I shut down.

He was ready for a swing, but he pushed me to the floor and leaned down and slapped me across the face.

"You think you can touch me? You need a reminder of who is the king of this house." He went to hit me again, but Trigger had returned. He reached out and held his arm back without effort. Then he took a step toward my father and pointed a finger in his face.

"If Denton gets word that your girls are black and blue, he'll look elsewhere for help."

My father's face reflected a series of emotions, but the one that came across most was confusion. His brows pinched, and his mouth slacked open.

"Denton and I have an understanding," Trigger snarled, inches from his face.

"She's not a runner, she's my daughter. She's not even in the family business, so bruises don't matter."

"Not when I tell the story," Trigger threatened, and my father took a step back.

Damn, that was really impressive.

"Sal?" Roman held up a hand, knowing it was a bad time. "A word?"

To my shock, my father agreed. He answered his phone and stopped to have a conversation at the door of the room.

"Do you know who I am?" Trigger directed his attention back to me.

"No," I shook my head, confused, "should I?"

Trigger leaned down, and the leather on his cut made a noise against his muscles. His long fingers skimmed the mohawk out of his eyes so he could see me better. He lowered his voice. "We share the same friend." The smell of pot found my senses.

I squinted and tried to understand how someone like Trigger could know the same person as I did.

"Catalina, it's time to go." My mother stood next to my father. He must have sent her in. "Let's go."

I nodded, but Trigger leaned in closer. "Go home so he can stop worrying." I frowned for him to elaborate. "Mike.

The air was sucked from my lungs before my mother tugged me out of the room. *What?* I didn't have time to process what Trigger had said before I was dragged from the house.

"I love you so much, Mama." I hugged my mother as I stood near the truck and buried my head in her neck, needing a moment to relish the feeling. "Thank you."

Her shoulders shook, and I knew this might be the last time I'd get to hug someone who truly loved me back.

"I love you, Catalina. I always have and always will." She brushed my tears away before she kissed my forehead once more. "Make sure she gets home, Abel." My blood rushed to the surface as he slipped into the driver's seat.

"He's not the one to be angry at." She tried to calm me. "Let me deal with your father my way." She lifted an eyebrow, and it was amazing to see that side of my mother. She was actually insanely strong and had my father by the balls.

Closing the door, she kissed my hand one last time before the truck roared to life and I watched her grow smaller in the mirror.

I waited until we stopped for gas to pull my suitcase out of the back of the truck when Abel went inside to pay. Everything was cash with my family, no paper trail.

"Where are you going?" He sounded tired and not up for a fight.

"You promised me once you would always take care of me."

"Okay." He looked annoyed.

I stared at him, too tired now with everything that had happened to show the depth of my anger. "Did you kill Javier? Or just deliver him to my father?"

His mouth dropped open, and shame spread through his eyes. "Catalina…"

"Oh, my God!" I shouted, finished with this shit. "Just answer the damn question!"

He sniffed and looked away for a moment, and when his eyes returned, I saw how weathered he was. His soul seemed battered, and the lines around his mouth deepened. Abel was part of my family, and for once in my life, I saw it that way.

I bit on my lip to stop my chin from quivering, and

he mirrored my actions. We were both at a standstill, and it tore at me.

"Just be honest." I needed to know.

"I…" he cleared his throat, "delivered him."

My heart bled. I couldn't imagine how confused my brother must have been when a boy he grew up with, his dear friend who was in love with his sister, betrayed him. I stepped back and shook my head when he went to touch me.

"I have to," I closed my eyes, and my tears spilled over, "draw a line here."

"Catalina, please," he begged, but all the happy memories I had of us turned to smoke in the air and faded into the wind. "I'm sorry."

"I believe you, Abel." It took all my willpower, but I looked up at his panicked eyes. "You need to leave, now."

"No."

I shrugged. "You gave up the right to help me when you…" I couldn't do it anymore. I grasped the handle of my suitcase, and I left my first love in the parking lot of gas station.

So classy.

Twenty minutes into my journey to the next town, I heard the roar of a bike. I stepped off to the side and covered my face for a possible dust cloud heading my way.

To my surprise, the engine dropped a few gears, and I suddenly felt nervous not having a weapon on me.

Trigger, of all people, slowed his bike and stopped

next to me. I looked down at his dusty boots and wondered what to say.

"What the fuck are you doing, girl?"

I dropped my suitcase and glared at him. "I'm going home." My tone held no nonsense.

His mouth curved up like he was impressed, then he pressed a button on his helmet. "Brick, tell Morgan to bring the van up front. We have a passenger."

Wait, what?

FIFTEEN

5 minutes ago

MIKE

I was under a truck and full of oil when my phone buzzed in my pocket. I awkwardly tapped my earpiece and waited for it to connect.

"Irons."

"I just left," Trigger grunted, sounding pissed.

I pushed myself out from under the truck.

"And?"

"I just lost my tail." He paused. "She's okay. But, shit, that place isn't for her."

My head thumped, and I closed my eyes.

"Look, man, something is brewing in that house. I can feel it. Catalina knows something, and the way she talks to her father tells me it's not anything small."

"Okay, thanks, man."

"I made sure to mention Denton, and I can say he believes you for now. They were strappin' the girls when I arrived. Your Catalina is smart. She outed her father on trying to make a deal with the Stripe Backs."

"Really?" Again, every time my heart hurt for her, confusion followed and took its place. "Was she hurt at all?" I couldn't help myself. I needed to know.

"Don't ask questions like that." He cleared his throat, knowing I wouldn't let the topic go. "They were rough with her, but nothing she can't handle." He chuckled. "She reminds me of Tess a little."

"Yeah." I half smirked. She did have some hidden talents, like knowing how to shoot large weaponry.

"Just get your ass to her this weekend and be done with it. Something tells me if you leave her there much longer, she'll make shit happen herself." I could hear the warning in his tone.

"Thanks, man." I hung up and headed toward Keith's office. Logan had been using it since we got back from Salvador's house.

"Damn," Cole cursed as I opened the door.

"Everything okay?"

"Salvador has been calling the prison trying to get a call through to Denton. I think they might back out."

"They won't." I knew it was risky to share, but it was Cole, one of my brothers. He'd be angry, but he'd understand.

"How do you know that?"

"Trigger just left there." I held up my phone. "Said he gave our alibi some credibility."

"How's Catalina?"

I took a careful step forward. "Okay for now." I studied his face. He wasn't making eye contact. "You're not mad?"

"Who do you think called him?"

That made my mouth open. "You called Trigger?"

"I did." He finally glanced at me.

"But that's a gray area, and you don't go into the gray."

"Savannah showed me that a gray area exists whenever the heart is involved."

"Thanks."

He nodded and went back to his paperwork, but just when I got to the door, he called out my name. "Irons?"

"Yeah?"

"Not a word."

"Not to anyone."

His phone rang, and he looked back at me. "It's time."

We got word to ship out, and all communication with the outside world was gone until we returned to US soil.

———

Cole, John, Mark, and Keith were dressed in racing suits littered in sponsorship logos with their numbers on their back. I had on an all-black suit that had RockStar in bright yellow letters. From a distance, we played the part of the famous drivers who dominated the Baja race, Rob MacCachern, Luke McMillin, and Ryan Arciero, to name a few, exactly what we needed to look like. The actual drivers were somewhat aware of what we were doing, and all had agreed to sign an NDA allowing us to use trucks and trailers that looked just like theirs.

PCI race radios allowed us to slap fifteen-foot stickers on the sides of our trucks as well as the inside on the center of the steering wheels. Their swag littered the back seats. We did whatever it took to make this look authentic. We may have an in with the border, but that was assuming he'd be there when we made it through. You never assumed life would be easy. That was when mistakes happened.

Instead of heading to the start of the track, we took a detour and slipped by the public and made our way to the finish line at La Paz. The drivers couldn't be in two places at once. We'd meet the girls and start back to the beginning while the real racers stayed behind and partied.

What took Justin Morgan sixteen hours and twenty-three minutes to drive during the race took us almost two days due to side streets and not drawing attention to ourselves from the local PD.

"Maybe next time we don't pick such flashy looking trucks," Mark piped over the radio behind me.

"What would you suggest?" Keith challenged. The fact he was entertaining Mark just proved how bored he must be.

"Well," Mark grunted as he switched the gear into

second, "I'm in a lime green truck in the middle of the desert. Maybe we could pick colors that would blend in?"

"Spoken like a true soldier," I chimed in.

"Oo-rah." Mark chuckled, and the silence took back over as we made our way through the thick terrain.

"I see the meet-up spot." John spoke quickly, as he was the leader of the pack. "There are two more trucks than we anticipated."

"Roll with it for now," Cole ordered.

My gun sat next to me, and I flexed my fingers in different patterns going over what lineup with my tattoos meant what. I was a creature of habit and liked knowing I was completely prepared. Though I felt naked without my camo and I wished I was in a Humvee with all my gear in the right spot, this would have to do.

Eight men stood with long rifles, three with handguns, and four more surrounded the trucks. The cartel never did anything half-assed. My guess would be there were at least seven snipers up on the mountains too. They were all dressed in jeans, plaid shirts, and boots. They sure fit the stereotype well.

"Anyone feel that?" Keith whispered and referred to the fact something seemed off.

"I guess I missed the memo on the longhorn belt buckles." Mark laughed darkly.

"Stay focused," I muttered calmly as we came to a stop.

Salvador hopped out of the black SUV and pulled on a pair of sunglasses. The front side of his half-buttoned shirt flipped up in the breeze and showed us his gold-plated Glock tucked in his pants. I felt like I was in a Baz Luhrmann movie with all the bling these men wore. Even the gold in their teeth caught the sun.

"You made it." Salvador shook my hand and then Cole's. "Let's get you loaded up."

I dropped the duffle bag with a quarter of the money at his feet and kept my head down as the dust rose around it. My eyes hidden behind my shades, I scanned the windows and tried to figure out where the girls were.

John walked the men over with the drugs to fill the trophy trucks' fuel cells and spare tires.

"Where are the girls?" Cole joined me.

"They're here. They're each strapped with nine thousand, so running isn't an option for them." He grinned and nodded at Roman to open the door to another SUV.

One by one, they stepped out of the truck, wrists bound, dressed in tight dresses and heels. Elena looked around and almost seemed relieved when she saw me. I couldn't believe we finally found our victim after all this time.

My stomach sank when Cat wasn't one of them. Not that I expected her to be there, but a part of me almost hoped so in my need to know she was okay.

Mark appeared and snapped his gum like he was totally at ease.

"We're expected to check in at checkpoint two by sundown." He blew a bubble, and the scent of watermelon filled the air. "You have the money, we have the drugs, hand over the women so we can go."

"And you are?" Salvador hissed, annoyed that Mark tried to take lead.

"I'm the one who will be returning your girls when we're finished." Mark turned to me and shook his head. "Does Denton know about this guy?"

"All right," Salvador called out, "one man per girl." I whirled around, confused. He pointed to Elena. "Two for her."

"We never agreed to extra bodies," I yelled.

He jumped up on the step of the SUV. "We're all full of surprises, aren't we?"

"We can't get them across the border. We'll stand out."

"Figure it out." He ducked into the car and slammed the door.

"Change in plans." Cole's smooth voice came over the radio as we headed back to our trucks. "When we get to checkpoint two, we'll figure our new guests."

"Ten-four," I responded and helped Elena into John's truck. "Your mother is waiting for you at the border," I whispered, and her eyes bulged. She started to speak, but I shook my head and peeled back the monster patch to show her my Army flag that represented my unit. I never did anything without proof of who I was. Even my dog tags were neatly tucked under my gear. If I needed proof of who I was at the border, that would be my ticket out. It was a risk I was willing to take.

"Catalina," Elena whispered and moved her gaze over my shoulder before they came back to me.

"What about her?" I tried not to sound too eager. "Is she okay?"

"Here." She handed me a folded envelope.

I tucked it in my pocket.

"Hey," she grabbed my arm, "they each have two guns, hip and ankle. They were told to shoot first. We're disposable."

"No," I covered my hand over hers, "you're not."

"Irons." John nodded toward our approaching company.

"Okay." I hurried to strap her into the truck before the other man joined us. "Whatever you hear on this ride, you ignore it. Got it?"

"Okay." She started to cry with relief, but I shook my head.

"We're not out of the woods yet. Hold it together until after we cross the border."

She nodded but a few still leaked over.

"Do whatever he says." I pointed to John. "Thank you." I squeezed her hand, beyond thankful for the tip. "I'll see you at the second checkpoint."

She nodded when her escort jumped in the back and eyed us both suspiciously. It took all my power not to drive a bullet in his head.

"Good to go. You have a full load." I slapped the top of the truck's hood and wiggled my finger to let John know they were trigger happy. His eyes shifted over to mine, and he gave a very slight nod that he'd understood.

"What's your name?" I asked the girl who had her arms bound by a zip tie.

"Marianna." She sniffed and watched as I took out my pocketknife. The shit in the back protested, but I stuck a gun in his face, beyond finished with this shit.

"Can't have her hands bound."

"The border is two days away."

"Yeah," I hissed, "and the imprint will be there for two weeks if we don't remove them now."

He shook his head but knew I was right. Carefully, I cut the plastic with my blade and broke her hands free.

Her wild eyes found mine, and I tried to show her I wasn't the enemy, but given her past treatment, when she drew herself into a ball, I wasn't surprised. I could tell she was nervous in her dirty shirt. Why they didn't give her something cleaner was beyond me. I reached in the back and pulled a PCI race radio shirt free from the canvas swag bag and offered it to her. With trembling fingers, she pulled it over her head and seemed to relax a little with the bulk of it.

I tossed one at John's window for Elena to put on too. The more we looked like we belonged in the racing world, the better.

As I watched John help Elena, I couldn't help but let my mind slip over to Catalina.

Frank would have my head on a stick if he found out my girl had any part in the Esteban family. We failed to mention that part when we returned home last and debriefed. He was still a little uneasy with Cole and Savannah. Not to mention, Frank's own daughter was married to Mark. Yes, Blackstone had created their own little family, and it webbed nicely through the Army itself.

"Yeah, you be scared, little rabbit." One guy started in on the girl about to get into Cole's truck.

Just as I went to confront him, Cole hopped out and stood in his path.

"Look, man," he commanded, "I don't care what you do with the girls any other time of the year, but if they look anything but well-rested when we cross that border, I'll personally take you out myself. We have orders from Denton, and if you want to fuck it up, that's on you and Salvador. Until then," he stepped closer, "keep your hands off!"

"*Sí, amigo*." The asshole smiled and chewed on the end of a toothpick. "We'll play on the way home."

Cole's jaw ticked as he swung around to look at me. I knew he was as pissed as I was. These men were savages and would more than likely rape and beat the girls if we weren't careful. We had a job to do, though, and we couldn't allow ourselves to show any weakness.

"Okay, you," Mark took his girl by the shoulder and moved her toward his truck, "are with me." One guy looked confused but followed Mark to his truck. I was guessing he barely spoke English.

Mark gave me a reassuring smile before he started his engine and we all fell into line.

It wasn't until two hours into the ride that the girl next to me shifted. She was obviously uncomfortable. I peeled my eyes off Mark's truck to glance briefly in her direction.

"Are you going to hurt me?" She sniffed.

"No."

"They always say that."

"I have no interest in hurting you."

I glanced at the man in the back. He was passed out cold. I threw the girl an extra blanket. I remembered Savannah mentioned that when she was wrapped in the blanket in the car after being rescued, it eased her nerves and gave her something to hold herself together with. For some reason, that always stuck with me, and sure enough, after I handed it over, I noticed the girl seemed to relax a bit more.

"Marianna, right?" I asked in a low tone, and she waited for a beat before she answered.

"*Sí.*"

"Okay, Marianna, how long have you been with Salvador?"

"Since my sixteenth birthday," she paused, "so, four years."

I looked over at her sadly. These poor girls were taken when they were babies. Their lives hadn't even started yet, and they were forced to become slaves in their own country.

"Where's your family?"

"Last I knew, Texas. We didn't last long on the freedom soil before I was taken back."

"You want to go find them?"

Her face flashed a number of emotions, but mostly it was uncertainty and distrust.

"You don't work for Denton, do you?" She bit her lip and waited for my answer.

I gave her a quick glance before I went back to watching Mark's truck.

"Weatherman." A gruff voice blasted over the race radio. I knew who it was based off my research. Bob Steinberger was the voice of desert racing and a hero, to say the least. I turned down the volume and glanced at the asshole in the back, but he didn't seem to notice.

We didn't hit the first checkpoint for another hour. We let the girls out to use the restroom and to eat a quick bite. I knew we were all desperately trying to figure out how we were going to ditch these men before the border. Then we still had to try to cross it without catching the eye of the other cartel who watched the border for Salvador.

I set my timer as we jumped back in the truck to continue. We all needed to be in sync at all times.

Checkpoint two was all I could hear from my radio. Everyone called in with their status. Mark used Morse code to let us know he had a plan. Cole let us know he did too. Thankfully, a plan was forming. No thanks to me, though. I was stuck in a loop. I eyed the shit's cell phone and forced away the idea of calling my sister to see if Catalina was home. That was a forbidden line I would never cross in my world. The fact my head even went there scared the hell out of me.

Suddenly, we came to a setof lights, and I felt my stomach sink. The local PD would set up checkpoints, and if you weren't ready, things could go south quickly.

"Pretend you're asleep," I whispered to Marianna, who wasted no time doing what she was told.

The cop moved to my window and shined a flashlight over our faces. He squinted at Marinna's bulky shirt that was raised up on the side but seemed more interested in her short shorts than the fact that she was carrying a party's worth of cocaine.

He pointed to the PCI sticker in the center of the steering wheel.

"Stickers?"

I pulled out a handful and gave them to him.

"Money?"

"No." I shook my head and held up a stack of magazines. "Porn?"

The officer made a face but nodded as I handed them over a few *Hustlers* from a black bag.

"You're pretty." He nodded at her and went back to speaking Spanish. I guessed he now assumed I didn't speak it. "I think you should come with me."

"Not a chance." I jumped in, and the cop grinned in surprise at my perfect Spanish. "Can we go?"

He waited for a beat and licked his lips. They loved

the power they had over people, but I was not in the mood on this night.

"You like girls, huh?" I felt my mood shift from calm to just plain pissed off, but I knew to be careful.

"*Sí*." He laughed like a seventeen-year-old boy who just got his first BJ.

"There's a party full of girls, in a blue minivan coming up behind us. Oh, yeah. Young too."

"The younger the better."

My hands flexed on the steering wheel. "So, can we go?"

"*Sí*." He gave me a wink and waved us on.

"Porn and stickers," I chirped into the radio, so the others knew what to expect, "and the girls."

Checkpoint two was finally reached, and we could all get some rest. I was tense from the drive and from the constant scenarios I ran through my head. The cartel with us leaned forward and zipped-tied Marianna's wrists together then led her to a spot and pushed her to the ground. One by one, the girls were brought over, and they sat next to her, each with their hands tied. They looked like sacks of grain leaning together. We could not show any kindness to them, as we all had roles to play. Instead, I found a spot under a tree and leaned my head back.

Shit, my head hurt.

SIXTEEN

CATALINA

My eyes begged to close, but my brain stayed alert. This was way outside of my comfort zone, and we had been driving for hours. The hum of the motorbikes in front of us didn't help my exhaustion. Morgan, my driver, was a really interesting man, with a long beard and a shaved head. Rings were tattooed around his head, looking like the rings around Saturn.

He smiled, and with his knee against the steering wheel, he twisted the cap off a beer and handed it to me.

"Thanks." I sipped the cold brew, happy to have something to moisten my dry mouth.

"Not gonna lie, I didn't picture myself sitting in a van with Salvador's daughter."

"I didn't think I'd be in a van with a motorcycle gang,

so…" I held my beer high in lieu of a 'cheers' and smiled at him.

He laughed and turned the radio on to a dull volume. "I'm just glad we made it over the border without any trouble."

I turned my attention to the world slipping by us. "They're not going to go after me yet," I sighed, "but when they do, I'll be one step ahead of them."

"I like the way you think, Catalina."

Good.

We listened to five songs before I finished my beer and was handed another.

Sure, why not.

"So, tell me about your club."

"Like?"

"I don't know, just tell me something about it." When he didn't respond, I glanced over and found him watching me out of the corner of his eye.

"Look, I get it, I'm connected to the cartel," I hated this topic, "but do you think they give two shits if I know something about an MC crew in California?"

"You really know nothing about Trigger, do you?"

"No, I don't. He's scary as shit, and I kind of wanted to shed a layer of skin when I met him, but…" I shrugged.

He rubbed his long beard and fiddled with the end of it while he thought.

"We had a problem a while ago, and we're all fuckin' edgy right now. Okay?" He reached for another beer.

"When we get there, listen to Trigger. If anyone says different, listen to Trigger."

"All right, I get it."

"Also, do not let a guy named Mud talk you into getting a tattoo. Mike would have our heads."

I laughed again, and it felt good. "I highly doubt Mike will care what happens."

He huffed out a laugh. "Why do you think Trigger was there at the house? You think he was looking to make a deal with Sal?"

"Yeah, of course. Isn't that what he does?"

He turned to look at me again. "Fuck, no. He went because Mike asked him to."

"What? Huh…I thought…" I leaned forward in my seat to study his face.

"Trigger just got us free of a drug deal with the cartels. The last thing I thought he'd be doing the day before yesterday was telling us to suit up for a trip down south."

"Why?" I sounded like an ass, but I needed to know.

Morgan glanced over at me. "Because Trig and Mike are tight. Mike was all messed up about you, and he was headin' into one shit-ass situation with his head screwed up. He needed to know you were okay. He needed someone he trusted to put eyes on you."

"I need to call him."

"No can do."

"Why?"

"Because he's heading toward the border now with five trucks packed full of cocaine and girls."

"There's no way to reach him?"

"Nope." He tossed the beer bottle on the floor.

"So, what I am supposed to do now?"

"Now," he flipped on his blinker and headed down a dusty road, "you stay with us until your boy arrives."

Holy shit. I eased back into my seat and let that sink in. I guessed Mike was full of surprises too.

The words 'Dirty Demons' blinked in my face when my eyes fluttered open hours later, and my stomach rolled from all the beer that tried to filter through my kidneys. Morgan opened my door and helped me unfold from the seat.

"Where are we?"

"Cali," was all he offered.

Okay.

Once inside, a beat found my ears and neon purple tubing led the way into a strip joint. *Seriously?* Were we really sticking with the stereotype, here, people? Or maybe they wanted a place to take me that stayed under the radar?

I slipped into a booth, and Morgan plopped in beside me while Trigger and some guy named Rail sat across from me.

Three cages had women dancing in them, and one huge stage had four girls doing a terrible dance to *Save A Horse, Ride A Cowboy* by Big & Rich.

To say I was nervous was an understatement. At the same time, I felt they must be testing me, so I tried to muster up my strength to go along with whatever happened.

These guys were intense. They barely spoke, and I couldn't help noticing that people in the strip club shot them glances now and then.

Again, I moved my hands under the table to hide the shakes, and my knee took over and thumped my heel into the floor. I was happy the music was loud.

Morgan was the first to break the intensity when he dropped his head and tried to cover his laughter. Even Trigger, who I guessed rarely broke into a smile, used his whiskey to conceal his smirk.

"Fuck the hell right off," Rail suddenly snapped. "What are the odds you'd marry the chick?"

"He never had a chance. Tess marked Trigger before he even realized it." Morgan let his laughter out now. He was in a full-out belly laugh. "But, really, the video is gold."

What? I looked at all of them in amazement, not sure what to think.

"No one marked me." Trigger pointed.

"Right." Rail rolled his eyes then looked at me. "What these guys tell you about me, it's all a lie."

"Oh, so you're not good in bed?" I asked, deadpan. "Good to know."

Morgan laughed harder, and Trigger let out a little grunt of amusement.

"Baby girl, I'm a legend around here."

"Anyone who's connected to that song must be a legend." I snickered. The tension was quickly draining from my body as I downed the water Morgan had gotten me. "White country music at its finest." I gave a lame thumbs up.

"A trip in a van with Morgan, and we have another feisty chick on our hands." Rail tossed his hands up. "Super."

Trigger picked up his phone and made a call, but I could tell it went straight to a voicemail. I hoped it was to Mike. I felt torn now that I knew he was behind all this. I could still see the look of disappointment and shock on his face when he first found me at the house.

"You better be able to back up that tongue of yours, sweetheart." Rail grinned playfully, and his words struck a chord.

"You forget," I leaned over the table, "where I was brought up."

There, the elephant in the room had been brought to light.

You're welcome.

"Oh, please." He waved a hand. "You ever kill a man?"

"Not yet."

Trigger looked up from his phone, and my gaze held his. "If you're planning on killing someone, you better understand the toll it takes on your soul," he grunted.

"Oh, it'll do wonders." The way I said it caused a few eyebrows to lift, and Morgan glanced a question at me but went back to his drink. We all settled and just listened to the music. My mind drifted, and I thought about the suitcase my mother had packed for me. I had opened it in the van and found she had stuffed a few thousand in there for me, and for the first time in my life, I was willing to use it. "Do you mind if I step outside for a moment?"

Tigger flicked his head at Morgan, and he quickly moved so I could leave. I had been in a private battle since I arrived. I needed to relieve myself from all the beer and water I had. As I made my way around the tables, one girl snickered, and a couple of cage dancers shot me dirty looks. I had a pretty thick skin and didn't care what people thought of me, but there was still a part of me that was raw and exposed when it came to who I was.

My secret was out, and it hurt. People judged me and made assumptions when they knew. All I'd done for the past seven years was try to rebuild myself into the woman I wanted to be, without the stigma of my family name. I was strong, loving, and loyal. I was a good person.

And now…

After I left the restroom, I went outside. The van window was open just enough for me to get my arm inside and unlock the door, but as I went for my suitcase, a huge arm pushed it back down.

"Going somewhere?"

I closed my eyes and internally cursed. "I just need to get out of here. I appreciate what you have done, but you don't need to babysit me."

"I wasn't." Trigger lit a joint and leaned back to blow

the smoke away from my face. "But I made a promise to my friend that I'd look out for you."

"Honestly, Trigger, I don't think he wants that anymore."

"I disagree."

"Then we agree to disagree." I reached for the handle, and once again he stopped me.

"We can do this all night, Catalina."

"Fine." I folded my arms, and I could swear I saw him smirk. "Can I ask you something?"

"Depends."

"Did you bring me here because you were afraid of me knowing where you live? Because of who I am?"

He pointed over his shoulder to a rundown one-story building with blacked-out windows. "Clubhouse is right there, and this is my strip joint. I didn't take you to the clubhouse because Mike wouldn't have wanted me to."

"Why?"

"Lots of assholes."

Wait.

"Wait, you said he wouldn't want me to. Does that mean he doesn't know I'm with you?"

Trigger sucked in another long breath. "I spoke to Mike five minutes before I came across you in the desert. When I called him back, he'd already left."

I shook my head and let the fact that Mike struggled mentally about where I was hit the center of my stomach. Sinking against the door, I felt the weight of the world take me in its hold.

"Ahlam Shahraban," I whispered, and Trigger stepped closer.

"What about him?"

"My father has a meeting with him, and he didn't know I was in the library. They'll be looking to make a deal. The route will be through Baja to Hawaii."

"Hawaii?"

"Some guy from Dubai is looking to take over the west coast to feed his drugs through California. He wants the Stripe Backs to be the middlemen."

"Is that so?" He sniffed once, and I thought he was going to leave, but he took a seat next to me.

"I wrote the name down. It's in my bag. I'll make sure I give it to you before I leave."

"That was a big risk…listening."

I shrugged. "When people don't think you're a threat, they get sloppy. I hadn't been back in seven years, but being in that house for only a week, I got pretty well caught up on all the shit they're into."

He nodded and tugged at the end of his beard. I sat in silence so he could mull the information over. I stared at the van and the line of bikes and wondered if the locals came here or if they knew better.

"The biggest part of a motorcycle club is trust and loyalty," he murmured roughly. "Initially, I trusted you because Mike did." He peered down at me. "Now you've handed me something that could protect my club, and for that, you've earned my trust on your own."

I really needed to hear that. "Thanks." I tried for a smile, but my body was still in knots.

Morgan and Rail joined us a few moments later, and they told me I was going to a hotel. They refused to let me pay when we checked in. I really wanted to protest. I had money, after all, but I was really tired and just let them guide me into the suite.

Rail was told to stay in the living room tonight, and I intended to head for the shower, but the bed looked so good, I never made it. The last thing I remembered thinking was I had a guy named *Rail* on my couch. Who would have thought? My eyes were so heavy, I just let them close.

"Hey." Mike's voice broke through the music of the Brew, his charming smile aimed at me.

"I didn't know you were coming in." I handed a guy a beer before I turned back to the most handsome man who ever lived.

"I got home early and wanted to see you." He snagged my waist and pulled me into his arms. I didn't care I was at work. Nothing was better than this Irons's hug. Well, any Irons's hug. I even made Charlotte give them all the time now.

He leaned back and tucked a piece of hair behind my ear. "You know, I picture your face at least three

times a day, and my imagination still can't capture
just how beautiful you really are."
I blushed and felt my heart quicken. "And yet you
stand here and have not kissed me yet."
"But if I kiss you, I'd close my eyes, and then you'd be
gone."
"Not gone." I leaned in and pressed my lips to his for
a moment then moved my hands to his chest to settle
over his heart. "Never, never gone."

I jolted awake and felt my tear-soaked pillow against my swollen eyes.

My head started that terrible loop right where it had left off last night. How could something so wonderful be taken from me so quickly? Was it karma's sick game to punish me for being born into the wrong family?

I tossed the blankets off, showered, and flopped open my suitcase. I felt around until I found a clean bra and panties, then slipped on a pair of ripped jeans and a tight AC/DC t-shirt. I felt a little better. As I was about to close the case, I felt something hit my fingertips. My mother's famous little black leather bag was tucked into the side pocket. Ever so slowly, I unzipped it and glanced inside.

No woman should feel scared or alone. Use this wisely as I have. xo M.

A handgun lay next to a burner phone, and a sharp ring with a metal shard on the end was hidden neatly inside. I looked up at the ceiling and let out a long breath.

I wished I could take back all those years of hating her so unjustly. I was young and thoughtless and angry. To know she had given her life for mine brought tears to my eyes.

Once everything was back in its place, I rolled my belongings out into the room and spotted Rail at the table.

"Morning, Cat." He grinned through a mouthful of pancakes. "Hungry?"

"I am."

"Good," he handed me the syrup, "I hate women who don't eat. Oh, and don't freak out, please, because our prospect, Kane, is here."

Kane?

I whirled around to find a man cleaning blood off his hands with a rag.

Holy shit.

A full-on human skull was tattooed on his stomach. The eyes were his pierced nipples, and his chest was, well, I didn't know, as I was too focused on the blood that still stained his face.

"Morning," he said with studied nonchalance as he reached for a shirt from the chair next to me. I cringed in shock.

I looked back at Rail, confused. Had he just witnessed what I had?

"We had a run-in with an SB prospect." Rail tilted his head at my fork. "You want me to wipe Charlie off your fork?"

"I'm good," I held up a hand, then slid the fork with a droplet of blood over and grabbed myself a new one.

Don't throw up, don't throw up.

"I've never been more turned on." He wiggled his eyebrows at me when another man walked through the door. "That's Zay, Trig's half-blood."

Okay…I may need a road map, here, people.

"Tray, I need you to deal with it. Me and Kane are heading there now." Zay waved at Rail as he and Kane left together. Rail chuckled then checked his phone like this was the norm.

In through the nose and out the mouth, Cat. You can handle this.

"Eat up because we need to move."

I dove into the heavy stack of pancakes and nearly moaned at the flavor. I was starving.

"Where are we going?"

"Gus's."

Who?

SEVENTEEN

Mike

The edges of the paper were now bent, and the middle was wrinkled, but I couldn't stop reading the note.

Mike,

I know I wasn't honest about my past, but it's my past. I never thought you would collide with it. Everyone comes from somewhere, Mike, good and bad, but the actions we choose are what define us. I left and never looked back. I may have been born an Esteban, but I'm a Mendez now, and for once in my life, I'm proud of who I am. Of who I have become.

The look on your face, when you saw me in the house, will forever haunt me. I will not apologize for being me, but I am so sorry I hurt you. I never meant to fall in love with you, Mike, but I have, and I can only hope that time will heal the tear in the center of my heart.
Goodbye,
Cat (Juliet)

My thumb brushed over the word Juliet, and I squeezed my eyes shut. We were in our own version of that story, and I hated it. In her own way, she tried to tell me. I just didn't want to see or hear it. I didn't care because I had fallen too.

Her hands covered her forehead as she paced the dock, annoyed that Lizzy was on her way back. We had just found a moment alone, and she was once again trying to warn me of something I didn't want to see.

"You don't get it, Mike. We're like a modern version of Romeo and Juliet…"

"They ended up together in the end," I tried to counter.

"Death separates, and with my blood, I'm not going where you are."

I dropped my arms and moved in front of her.
Brushing her hair off her face, I cupped her cheeks.
"If you believe in us, we can make this happen."

"You good?" Cole peered down at me, concerned, and drew me from my thoughts. I nodded, and he offered a hand to help me up. "You in there?" He was referring to my head.

"Yeah," I lied, but I would always do my job.

We gathered our stuff and started the next leg of our journey, the border. We still had five guys we had to deal with before we crossed it.

"So, what will happen to us?" Marianna spoke softly as she watched out the window. "I mean, we will not be free just because we will be in California."

Her haunting words couldn't be truer. You were never really free from the cartels. If they wanted you, they got you.

"Be quiet!" I responded with pretend harshness when the sleeping man behind her twitched his eyebrows. "You will do as you're told." She looked at me with under-standing and let it go. We both watched him until he began to snore again.

"You know what that one does to me at night?" She used her chin to point at the sleeping cartel member. A haunted expression I'd seen before on Savanah's face when she spoke of her ordeal, appeared in her eyes. "He told me I looked better to him with bruises. He has broken my bones and hurt me in so many ways. He is a pig, but he never broke me." Her expression shifted to hate as she turned to the window, her finger pressed against the glass where a bug had been squished. "I did drug runs for a year, and he did so much damage." Her fingers peeled back her jean skirt to show me a long scar. "I'll follow your directions. I will do whatever I am asked, but you must help us when we are in the US, or we will simply be brought back to this."

Why was the world so screwed up? When did pain and suffering take over and compassion fade into the wind? It was an endless battle that wouldn't stop in my life or the next, but if we didn't try to fix it, who would?

"Nine minutes to the border," Cole crackled over the radio.

"Truck one, stop and knock 'em cold."

Silence fell over the airwaves, but finally, John spoke up. "Copy that, pulling over."

Just as we rounded the corner, I cleared my throat. "We have company, Marianna," I lied. "I need you to stare straight ahead and not move at all. Can you do that? I need you to promise."

"Yes." She sat a little straighter, and I kept one hand on the wheel and watched as we grew closer. When the roar of the engine idled down, the man behind me woke with a startle.

"What's happening?" His voice was still slurred with sleep.

"Green light," I chirped over the radio and slammed

my truck into park. Marianna's head did not move as I twisted suddenly and pulled the man's arm forward to slap handcuffs around his wrists. His eyes went wild, and he tried to fight me, but I was ready and knocked him out with the butt of my gun. When his body went slack, I jumped out of the truck and hauled his ass to the ground. I bound his legs to his arms with him on his belly.

Cole joined me and dropped his own piece of shit down by mine, and then John did the same. Mark, who returned with a fat lip and a big smile, nodded at his two on the ground. All six were knocked out cold.

If Trigger had been here, this problem would have been wrapped up in minutes, but we couldn't think that way, so we called in the two guys at North Rock to come and deal with them. We could only hope the cartel wouldn't beat them to the punch.

The walk back to the truck took effort, and my anger grew with each step.

"Irons?" Cole called as I grabbed a bag from the back of the trailer and headed over to the men.

"Mike?" Mark followed me back. "What's happening, man? We're losing time, here."

"They feed on fear, so fear is what they'll get."

He kept his mouth shut while I went to work, doing what I did best. A few times, Cole cleared his throat, but my brothers knew I needed this, so they kept their distance. We all broke at some point.

Seventeen minutes later, my masterpiece was built.

"Shit," Mark huffed behind me, "that's intense."

I kicked the man who had driven with me and woke him from his fog. He groaned and cursed before he opened his eyes in confusion.

"What the hell?"

"I wouldn't move if I were you." I kept my voice deep and calm.

He called out to the other men. One stirred slightly, then a couple more.

Six water bottles filled with an amber liquid circled the men. Six wires were attached to the tops, which then fed in between each of their legs to a square piece of wood they all lay on. A landmine sat near it so they could all clearly witness what fate had in store for them.

"One of you moves," I grunted, "you all blow." I spoke in clear Spanish so there could be no misunderstanding.

"Salvador will kill you for this. Kiss your freedom goodbye," the second man hissed.

I smiled at him.

"He'll kill the women too," he spat and twisted to look at Marianna.

In a flash, I had my weapon pointed at his head.

"This," Cole stepped into my line of sight and pointed to my makeshift bomb, "is a much more fitting death for him, don't you think?"

He was right, but I needed an extra minute to allow my hatred for him and his kind to sink into his head.

In one movement, I lowered my weapon and headed back to my truck.

"Move on to the border like we planned, checkpoint three." Cole slapped my shoulder and signaled for John and the rest to move out. They were to be the first to cross. Elena was with John, and she was the one we'd been sent to get, so she needed to cross first. Her mother Martina had the list of names we so desperately needed. Her intel would change the way we dealt with the cartel, so we needed Elena safe and sound.

Whack! I was hit with something from behind and a puff of white exploded around me.

"Who are you?" Marianna yelled. I jumped out of the way, then went for the broken coke bag she held. What the hell, had she completely lost her mind?

"Stop, Marianna! What the heck are you doing? We have to get going. What does it matter who we are? We're the ones who are trying to get you out of this hellhole." I spat on the ground to try to rid myself of the tinny flavor that now laced with my saliva.

"Back to what?" She shook her head. "My life ended the day I was taken. I will never go back. They will always find us."

"What the hell, then?" I tossed my arms in the air, unable to understand her. Every damn moment we stood here were moments lost getting across the border.

She headed toward the bound cartel. "You might want to hurry." She pointed to the road. "They have eyes everywhere."

Seriously?

"Marianna, you said anything was better than them."

"I'm staying. I can look out for myself." She didn't move.

Fuck!

"Mike, where the hell are you? Get your truck moving." Cole sounded pissed.

"Logan, my ride went batshit crazy. She's staying here."

"Fine, leave her. We don't have any more time. Pull out and catch up."

I hated to leave someone we'd tried so hard to help, but at the end of the day, we were sent here on a mission, and Marianna wasn't part of it.

I headed back to the driver's side and hopped inside. I watched her the mirror. She just stood there while I drove off, and I watched until she was only a speck.

"Best of luck, then," I muttered and hit the gas to pick up speed. I was over it.

Assassin by Muse pumped through the speakers when I felt it. My adrenaline pulsed to the beat, and I became hyperaware of my surroundings.

Shit! I had never done cocaine, so the fact that it was forced into my system was a battle all in itself.

The dust rose and curled into a blinding cloud in the distance behind me. One of the cartel members must have tried to escape and set the bomb off.

Holy shit, Marianna.

There was nothing I could do but head north as fast as I could and make contact with Lopez. I knew the explosion would draw attention. Sure enough, several Jeeps flew by me in the opposite direction. As I continued, I could taste the border with each click on the odometer.

"Lopez?" I tried my radio every few minutes. "Lopez, can you copy this?"

Silence.

"Lopez's radio is shit," Cole came through. "I'm at the border. Take lane number four. That's our guy. I have a visual, and we have the green light to cross. I'll reach out when we're over."

"Copy that," I answered.

I rubbed my head, and some white powder floated down from my hair.

Shit!

Using my free hand, I peeled off my t-shirt and pulled out a new one. I finger-combed my hair and used a little of my water and my old shirt clean the rest up. Once I could focus again, I pressed the gas pedal to the floor, but it wasn't long before sweat lined the collar of my clean shirt, and my heart sped up as I grew closer.

Twenty-eight painful minutes later, I slowed my pace and dropped to the speed limit and started to scan every single vehicle on my horizon.

Lane four caught my attention, and I eased my way over to claim a place in line. With my heartbeat in my throat, I pressed two fingers to the button on my neck.

"Lopez, do you copy?"

"'Bout time you showed." His relief was evident, and I was able to breathe.

"Has Logan made contact with you yet?"

"That's a negative on the boss connecting with me."

Shit!

Slowly, I felt them, a set of eyes two lanes over. I prayed it wasn't one of Salvador's men, but it made sense they would be watching the border.

I looked up ahead where Mark was five cars deep. There was no way we could move if we needed to.

"Lopez."

"I see them. Do you have a Plan B? 'Cause I don't."

"Plan B would be a worse nightmare."

"Copy that, brother." Mark laughed darkly, which made me smirk. I couldn't count how many times our missions went to shit, and we'd had to improvise.

A border agent started to direct the cars in different lanes to speed up the process. The cars in between Mark and me were moved to lane five, and thankfully, we stayed together. I caught a glimpse of Mark's girl as she peered out the window. She looked drained and white. That was good; we needed them tired. We needed to look exhausted. After all, we just had finished a long, grueling race, and we had been on an epic journey through the desert, I reminded myself.

"Made it through. I'll meet you at the next checkpoint," Cole's voice chirped over the radio.

A wave of relief broke through me. Elena was over, the main purpose of the trip.

Suddenly, two drug dogs sniffed their way over and around my wheels, and their handlers started to poke around. Mark adjusted his mirror so he could see what was happening.

I checked myself out carefully and caught a little powder in the grooves of my watch. Using the rest of my water, I dumped it over my head and arms to free myself of any evidence.

My brain spun, and it took all my effort to keep it still. Thankfully, I only ingested a little of the drug.

I reached back, while keeping my face forward, and snagged the cartel's phone from the back seat. I pretended to watch the screen. I needed to appear relaxed and calm.

With my head bent down, I watched as they moved up the body of the truck to my window.

"Where are you coming from?" The agent held his hand out for my ID.

"La Paz."

He squinted up at me. "Why?"

I was driving a billboard for off-road racing, but I knew they wanted to hear it from me. I kept my voice respectful and friendly.

"Just raced the Baja."

He nodded as he looked at his phone. "How'd you do?"

"Placed third." I grinned. He must have Googled me.

"Stay in this lane." He handed me back my ID. He called off his dogs and moved to another lane.

I sagged into the seat and lifted a small, friendly wave toward Mark's truck as he moved forward. I knew he would have been sweatin' it along with me.

The sun beat down, and I was thankful for the AC that blasted my face. I normally ran hot, so days like this nearly killed me. I missed my cool mountains.

There was activity ahead just as Mark's truck was about to arrive at the gate. *Shit, they changed agents.*

Mark was up next, and I had no clue what would happen now. The new agent waved him up, Mark handed him the paperwork, and everything went still for me. I felt like I was punched in the stomach when he was directed to drive over to secondary holding.

Here we go. I was up.

"ID, proof of where you stayed, and vehicle registration."

I handed him what he asked for and glanced over to Mark, who stepped down from his truck.

"Are you two," he nodded at Mark, "traveling together?"

We were obviously both racers but had been ordered not to say we were together. However, I wasn't going to leave without Mark.

"We both raced the Baja, but we aren't exactly together."

His head leaned to the side like he tried to read my mind. "Welcome to secondary holding."

I nodded once and followed directions to park and exit my truck.

The girl stood like stone while Mark answered the questions, and two men who were obviously cartel talked with the guard. These guys must just work with the border. I could see they were confused, as they'd probably been instructed that cartel members were traveling with the trucks they were to watch for.

"Do you understand why you were pulled from the lane?" The agent watched my expressions.

"Yes, sir, I understand, and I welcome you to look around." As he moved toward Mark, I moved a little closer to the girl.

"Darlin'," I whispered in a warm tone, and she stayed with her eyes locked to the ground, "you need to breathe. You're sending a red flag right now. You understand?"

Her lips opened, and air escaped.

There she is.

"They are monsters. They are everywhere."

"Yes," I smiled at her, "but you are with us, remember. Baja racers. You must relax."

"You," the agent pointed at her, "come with me."

The girl looked up at me with such terror I wanted to grab her hand and run.

"She doesn't go anywhere without one of us." I stepped forward, and Mark joined me.

The agent smirked, loving that he had control over the situation. "I don't think so."

"I want a female agent to escort her over." Mark held up a hand. "We have rights."

The agent prattled something over his radio and waited for a response. Mark glanced at me, and we both knew what we'd have to do next. We'd have to identify ourselves, but we weren't there yet, and the repercussions of doing that would be hard to come back from. Plus, the girl would be put into holding, and it would take weeks to get her out if we could even get to her before the Salvador did.

Another agent approached and started to yell in frustration at the agent who, he complained, wasn't moving us along fast enough. He pointed to the girl, and she stepped a little closer to me.

"What are—" The agent pointed at her, when suddenly a giant wave of energy blew by us, nearly knocking us off our feet. The roar of a fireball shot straight into the sky, and then alarms and lights started to go off in all directions. Instantly, I grabbed the girl and used my body as a shield to protect her from what might happen next.

"All units to lane three. I repeat, all units report to lane three!" The supervisor looked directly at me and yelled, "Hurry! Go, get out of here!"

We didn't waste any time, and I made sure the girl got into Mark's truck as we turned our engines over.

"Go!" I commanded, and we tore out of there.

Agents waved the already cleared trucks through a small break they'd cleared to rush us out faster. Once we were a few yards away, I eased back into my seat and took a breath.

"Holy shit!" Mark laughed into my ear. "Someone somewhere was looking out for us, brother! I think that was our guy."

I squeezed a bottle of water at my face and fought to

clear my head. When I tossed it on the floor, I spotted the phone. I fumbled to remember the numbers through my murky head.

"Who the fuck is this?" Trigger barked over the line, confused by the number.

"We barely made it, but we crossed."

There was a brief pause before he spoke again. "I think it would be best if you made a detour, to me."

My stomach bottomed out. "Why?"

"Because I'm sitting here with your girl."

What?

EIGHTEEN

The lake was like glass. I watched a dragonfly as it dipped its wing to the surface to send tiny ripples outward, and the sky wobbled in its wake.

Trigger sat next to me on the top of the picnic table. His silence was comforting, but in time I grew nervous. He must have checked his phone roughly six times in the thirty minutes we'd been here.

"When I was eight," I said quietly, not wanting to disturb our moment, "I used to follow a little path down to this quarry. It was my happy place. Javier and I used to play mud fights, and once it dried, and we could barely move, we'd jump in the water and wash off." I smiled at the memory. We had some fun times despite everything going on around us. "One time, after we were coated head to toe, we heard voices, so we hid behind this huge bolder. If my father caught on to what we were doing, he'd probably fill the quarry or something. God forbid we act like kids. We spotted our father with a man. The man was begging for his life. My father pushed him to his knees and shot him. Just like that. My brother tried to cover my eyes, but I saw everything. Blood from that man mixed with the water we had played in. Our favorite place in the world was tainted by our own father just like that."

"Why are you telling me this?" Trigger asked gruffly.

"I guess I just had a feeling something is coming."

"Are you always this paranoid?"

"I was born paranoid."

He laughed, and as odd as it was to hear someone as scary looking as Trigger laugh, it made me join in. "You're funny." He sucked back on his joint before he offered it to me.

I shrugged. *Screw it.* I held the little white stick between my fingers and inhaled. Two-point-five seconds later, I was hit with a relaxing rush.

"Better?" He smirked.

"Well, guess I'll be relaxed now when you off me. So, yeah, better."

"You know if North Carolina doesn't work out, you can always squat at the DR."

I knew he was kidding, and he tried to be kind, but my stomach twisted into a hard knot. "Be careful what you offer." I leaned back and let the sun warm my face. A truck's engine roared, and my lake companion moved as his phone buzzed.

"Yeah," was all he said before he flicked his head for me to follow him.

"Where are we going, anyway?"

"Just keep up, Catalina."

I tried to keep up with his long legs, but my shoes weren't made for a hike in the woods.

"You promised you weren't going to kill me." I half laughed.

"I'm not."

"I beg," I slipped, and he caught my elbow before I took off down the hill, "to differ."

A truck arrived as we hit a clearing. A sad-looking piece of property, if there ever was one.

"Who's that?" *Company?*

The door flew open, and my heart leapt into my throat. My emotions welled up, and I wasn't sure what to do with myself.

"Hey, man, thanks." Mike shook hands with Trigger then moved his attention over to me.

I chewed on my bottom lip. I wasn't ready to see him yet. I wasn't ready to say goodbye in person.

He reached into his pocket and pulled out a paper and held it up. "You're breaking up with me in a letter?"

I fought to hold my breath.

"I need a beer," Trigger muttered before he disappeared to the front of a trailer.

Once we were alone, he took a few steps closer, and the hurt on his face sent a sharp pain through my chest.

"Are you okay?" His gaze raked over me as he muttered, "You're okay."

I started to laugh like a crazy person. He had no idea what the hell I'd been through this week. "Trust me, Mike, I'm far from okay."

He closed his eyes and acted like he wanted to say more.

"So, now what?" I asked. We had so much to say to one another, but neither of us knew where to start.

"Now?" Mike grunted. "Now, we go visit my friends."

"What?" I didn't want to see anyone.

He stepped closer and towered over me. "These people are important to me, and they made sure you got home all right. I owe them a lot more than a hello." I nodded and followed him; he was right.

A blonde bombshell stepped out of the trailer holding a plate full of raw meat. She was dressed in jean shorts and a leather top that made her boobs look huge. She shot me a smile then dragged her eyes up the length of my body. I could feel the heat.

"Mmm, I wouldn't kick her out of bed. Dibs."

Mike muttered something I couldn't make out, then took my hand to pull me closer. We were not okay, but I welcomed his touch.

Rail whistled and took a step toward me. "Well, well, well. Mr. *Army* has finally come to get his Latina hottie. Don't worry, I took good care of her."

"Thanks, man." Mike leaned forward and shook his hand.

Once he stepped back, I got a good look at the rest of them. It took me a moment to realize they were more of Trigger's club.

"Trigger." Mike waved him over, and I felt my hands go cold.

"How was it?"

"Rough." Mike ran a hand through his hair.

"You shake your tail?"

"Hope so, though two were left at the border after a truck exploded."

"Yours?" Trigger tugged at his beard.

"Yeah, plan B."

"Nothing like a ball of fire to scatter the rats." Trigger handed us each a beer. I swore all these guys did was drink and get high.

"Spend the night here, and we'll get you off in the morning."

"Thanks." Mike pulled out a phone and turned to me. "I need to make some calls. Here, sit," he ordered, pulling out a chair.

I grew frustrated. "I'd like to go home now," I called after him, and the place went quiet. I scanned the eyes that looked at me.

What?

Mike marched back to me with a face that told me not to push right now. "You should have thought of that before you took a trip back home."

What? Oh, hell no!

"No one asked you to save me, Mike."

Mike licked his lips like he was trying to calm himself. "I wasn't there to save you," he hissed through a clenched jaw.

I know.

"I was perfectly capable of looking after myself. I was on my way home when your friend," she looked at Trigger, "picked me up."

"Right, and your friend Abel was probably on his way back to tell Daddy exactly where he left you," Trigger interjected.

"You have no idea what my family would do." I addressed myself to Mike. "You have no idea what my past was like."

"Right. That's because you never shared your past," Mike spat back.

I crossed my arms and felt my bones burn with fury. "That's calling the kettle black."

The anger and sexual tension charged the air around us. I stood my ground, and so did he. We'd never fought like this before, so it was new to both of us.

"Um, Catalina, is it?" The girl came to my side, wrapped an ivy tattooed arm around my shoulders, and directed me away from Mike, who had a death stare on me. "You look like you could use something a lot stronger than this." She eased the beer from my hand. I couldn't help but study the artwork that graced her skin.

"Nice tat."

She smiled and led me inside the old trailer. "Damn, did Mike ever find himself a girl after my own heart." She laughed and held up a bottle of tequila. "You'll fit in fine around here."

Great...

"I'm Tess, by the way. If you need anything, come to me. The guys are useless." She handed me a shot and held out her hand for me to lick the salt. I licked the stem of her thumb and watched as her eyes flared with arousal. My head tipped back and let the hot amber burn down to the pit of my stomach. "You really should think of relocating to the west coast."

"I just might." I smirked, amused she was amused. We did another shot when Rail came in like hell on wheels and knocked a bowl of watermelon down my front.

"Oh, shit!" he cursed. "I'm fucking sorry, doll."

"It's okay." I batted his hands away from my chest with a laugh. Rail reminded me of a giant kid. He meant well but was so jacked up inside he was a mess.

"Come on. I'll find you something to put on. I have left the odd thing here."

Tess tossed her phone on the dresser before she started to go through the top drawer.

"Here you go." She tossed a few items on the bed. "I'll give you a minute to get cleaned up."

"Thanks." I waited for her to leave before I stripped down.

I held up the short jeans shorts and eyed the ripped halter top that was mostly held together with safety pins.

It wasn't something I would wear, but it was cute, and I was pleased to discover it fit me like a glove. I examined the back of it in the mirror. The way the pins trailed down the center of my back, it gave my angel a metal spine.

I liked it. I slipped back on my flats and headed outside since I couldn't hide out inside anymore.

"Mike!" A guy tossed his beer can in the rusty garbage bin. "I'm officially stealing your girlfriend."

"That so, Brick?" A redhead punched his shoulder hard. "I'll remember that."

He laughed, and Mike turned around with his ear to the phone. His eyes widened at my outfit, and he looked like he might take me right here in front of everyone.

"Give it a rest, boys," Tess snapped. "Rail spilled shit down her front."

"Hey, Catalina," Rail tucked his hands in his pockets and grinned like the charmer he was, "ever rode on a bike before?"

"No," Mike bit out in a voice that made me jump.

"Rail," Trigger warned as his hand ran up Tess's thigh without a lick of shame.

"Don't mind him, Cat." Tess rolled her eyes at Rail. "He has the mentality of a seventeen-year-old with a morning woody."

"Never bothered you before." Rail winked at her.

"And it still doesn't, baby." Tess played along until Brick groaned.

"There's too much vagina here." Brick reached for

another beer and tossed me one before he popped his open.

More booze? The tequila was already kicking in.

"Then why deny me at night, Brick?" Rail kicked his knee, and I shook my head and tried to keep up with their crude banter.

Finally, when the sun had set and I had a decent buzz on, Mike joined the group around the trash can fire.

I hated that we had so much to talk about, but he didn't seem like he wanted to.

"You good to head back tomorrow?" Trigger handed Mike a beer.

"Not sure yet." He sighed like there was more to the story then he was letting on. "Lopez was followed right into John Wayne Airport. He's lost them now, but he needs to get to Long Beach to catch his ride back to…" He trailed off. "Just gotta hang tight until we get the green light."

"Gus would've wanted you to stay. The trailer is yours unless you want the club."

"No," he cut him off, "no way am I leading any shit to your home."

"We love shit," Rail piped in.

"Yeah, well, this is not your shit to clean up."

I felt my back rise slightly. I couldn't help but take that comment personally.

"Whose fault is that?" I challenged, and Mike glared at me. Mike had moments when I could tell he could hurt someone, but he'd never used that look on me.

"Denton Barlow, to start."

I couldn't help my reaction, and they all caught it. "How do you know Denton, Mike?"

A blanket of silence draped over everyone. Mike leaned forward and tilted his head like he could see inside my mind. "No, how do *you* know Denton?"

"Family friend."

NINETEEN

MIKE

The pop of the fire was all that could be heard as her words sank into my gut. Shit, her involvement just kept layering on. Sure, her father worked with Denton, but a family friend was a different level of madness.

"Catalina." I stood, but when she didn't move, I tried again. "Please, Catalina, it's time to talk." She unfolded her legs, and I took her hand and led her down to the little cabin by the water. Once we were far enough away from the guys, I let her go and wondered where the hell to start.

"You hid a huge secret from me!"

Her shoulders tensed. "So do you, all the time."

"You know I can't talk about my work. I'm sorry, but

it has to be that way. But, Catalina, you could be killed. Your father has a lot of power."

Her arms dropped to her sides, and her eyes momentarily looked to the ground. "You don't have to worry, I have protection. A deal was made for my freedom. No one will touch me."

"The kind of protection that leaves you on the side of the road?"

Her head snapped up at that.

"Feel free to answer some questions now, Mike." I hated that her tone twisted into dark sarcasm. The direction of our conversation was taking the wrong turn.

"So, now what, Catalina?"

She half laughed. "I warned you we came from very different worlds. Worlds that when they collide, someone gets hurt, and look where we are. So..." She shrugged like her mind was made up.

"So?" I spread my feet and stood like I would if I were about to use force with someone. I was ready for a fight, a fight to figure out how we could make this work.

"Mike, why am I here?"

"Because when I saw you in that house, I've never..." I felt the words stick in my throat.

"Never?"

"Never been more scared in my entire life! The woman I loved was in the one place I had just mentally prepared to die in if I had to. I'd said goodbye to my family in case I never came back. So, when I got there and walked into the home of a major cartel lord and I saw *you*, a part of me panicked. I never panic!"

"Imagine how I felt," she nearly shouted. "I'd just been told my brother was killed. I had to return to the one place I hated beyond anything in this world, to attend his funeral and to figure out who killed him. Then I walk into a room to find you dressed like a GQ model. I had no idea what on Earth you were doing. No clue, Mike! If my father got a whiff that I had feelings for someone who did what I think you do, he would have taken you out on the spot. *That's panic!*"

Her neck flushed as we both took a moment to breathe.

"God," she covered her face with a sigh, "I feel like I'm back at the strip club."

"What?" *When the hell was she at a strip club?*

"Mike. Do you trust me at all anymore? Can you get past where I came from, who I was?"

Yes.

"It's complicated, Catalina." I wanted to explain it wasn't only me who needed to trust her. The people I worked for did too.

"Okay," she whispered.

I grabbed her waist as she went to walk by me and held her in place so she couldn't leave. There was no way I would let her walk out of my life, not after risking what I did to bring her home.

"You have my word, Catalina." I brushed the back of my hand over her cheek. "I will figure this out."

"That's the sad part." She turned into my touch. "It should only matter what *you* think."

"No, not when part of my job is fighting people like your family, it's not."

Her eyes softened, and she gave me a little nod of understanding, but we both knew it would take more than a few days to fix a mess like we were in. My mind went to Frank, and I knew I would have a shit show on my hands when he heard about Catalina and her involvement in this situation.

"Do you still love me?" Tears rimmed her eyes, and my heart broke. Why couldn't she see it? "Because if you don't, please just let me go. I don't think I can take any more."

"Come here." I swooped down and captured her mouth with mine, and she immediately sagged into me. We had both been waiting this entire time for each other's touch. I palmed her breast and pressed her up against the wall of the cabin. She fiddled with the fly on my jeans and freed me from the fabric. My heavy erection dove into her hands and begged to be handled. She greedily obliged.

Using one hand, I pushed her shorts down. I used the other to hook her body to mine so I could whirl her around and sit her on the railing. Her legs wrapped around my waist, and her lips were back on me, on my neck, collarbone, and ear. I growled when she nipped at my skin. Everything inside burst, and all I cared about was spending the rest of my life with this woman.

Her plump breasts were the perfect place for my tongue to swirl and explore. She moaned and threw her head back, so her hair spilled all around her. The smell of jasmine had my brain firing off in many different directions. I couldn't hold back anymore and lined up my tip with her slick opening. Without waiting, I dove in, and she bowed backward. Only my arms stopped her from falling into the water.

"Jesus, Mike!" She moaned and pressed her head into my neck.

"Sorry." I took her chin in my hand so she'd look at me. "I can't control myself when you're like this. Knowing how warm and tight you are," I kissed her lips, "knowing I may not have gotten you back if fate hadn't dropped you right in front of me. I need to be inside you, make sure you're still mine."

She wiggled her hips then stopped as she digested my words.

"We have a lot of figuring out to do before you should say that."

"You could be Denton's ex-wife, and I'd still want you."

She let out a long breath. It looked as though she wanted to say something, but I couldn't risk losing her to a bad thought, so I dragged my erection across her sensitive spot and watched as she tuned in to it and me.

Every muscle in my body flexed when I plunged inside and got lost in her. No one said love was easy, and someone was out to test us, but we could still connect physically, and I'd hang on to that for as long as possible.

When we were both exhausted and thoroughly satisfied, we went up the back way, and I slipped Catalina into bed in the trailer before I went to say goodnight to the rest of the guys.

"You look satisfied." Rail lit a cigarette and smirked. "Nothing like make-up sex to soothe the soul."

"How would you know?" Brick kicked the beer out of his hand.

"He reads, remember?" Tess laughed. "Literary sex is hot."

"Two words. Olivia and Caleb."

"You finished?" Tess leaned forward in her chair.

"You called it 'deliciously dark,'" Rail laughed. "Nothing like a little underground sex to help the tube sock slip on faster."

"Wow." Brick shook his head but eyed Minnie when she came up with another case of beer. Something about the two of them seemed off, and, by the looks of it, she was the one with the problem.

"I'm going to bed. Thanks again, guys. I really appreciated everything." I waved off the guys and made my way to the trailer. I hated to sleep in someone else's bed. Normally, I'd opt for the woods, but I wanted to hold Catalina, so bed it was. I wrapped my arms around her, pulled her close, and nuzzled my head into her warm neck before sleep took over.

———

The sun showed it was well past morning when a bang on the door had me unfolding from Catalina and trudging to the door.

"Yeah?" I squinted at Trigger, who held up two coffees and a bottle of whiskey.

"We should talk."

I pulled on a t-shirt and set a coffee next to Catalina. She was still out cold. She lay on her stomach, and the angel on her naked back beckoned me, but I wouldn't make my friend wait.

Trigger was halfway through a joint when I sat down and sipped the hot brew. "Sleep okay?"

I shrugged. "Felt like Gus was creepin' some of the time."

Trigger smirked, amused with my ability to bring up Gus in a way for him to handle it. "He did love good porn."

"I hope I did him well."

We both chuckled.

"I got to know your girl a little while she was with us," he started as he spun off the cap and took a swing of whiskey. "She's got a fire inside."

"That she does." I smiled, glad he'd taken the time.

"She's paranoid that people will always see her as the enemy." He eyed me. "Do you?"

"Of course not. No," I rubbed my head, "but it makes things complicated."

"What does Logan have to say about it?"

I leaned my tired arms on the table and hunched forward. "He's good, but he's not the one I'm worried about."

"Frank?"

"Yeah."

"Look," he moved beside me and leaned to look out at the dusty property, "last night she gave me a name and some information on a guy who is moving into my territory."

"Really?"

"Yeah." He nodded. "I asked around, and it turned out she was right. She saved my club from being blind-sided," he paused, "again."

"I don't want to use my girlfriend as a source."

"I'm not askin' that, but she did right by me, showed trust and loyalty, and in return, she seemed to ease up and relax. Maybe if you give her a chance to make it right, things will slowly fall into place."

Maybe.

"I don't know." I hated that I was so confused inside. My phone rang, and I pulled it from my pocket.

> Mark: Elena is settled in at Dusk. Frank wants a house meeting tomorrow. Wants to meet Catalina but in Washington first.

Here we go.

"Time to go." I pushed from the table and stood next to Trigger. "I can't thank you enough for what you did for me."

He lit a joint and smoked a bit before he replied, "My debt to you is far from over."

"I disagree."

He peered up at me and squinted. "Everglades."

I closed my eyes and grunted in agreement. That wasn't a good time for either of us.

"Like I said, brother, far from paid. If you get into trouble, call me."

I nodded and took the hand he offered me. Trigger didn't do contact, so I knew he tried to drive his point home.

After he left, I woke Catalina, and we hit the road.

We dropped the truck off then made quick work to the Long Beach airport. Once the plane was in the air, I pulled my bag off the chair in front of me and handed Catalina a stack of paperwork.

"What's this?" She thumbed the papers.

"Frank wants to meet you."

"Okay." She waited for me to go on. "Who is Frank?"

"Catalina, I work for a group called Blackstone. Frank oversees us from Washington, and he wants to meet you, which means you need to sign a few non-disclosure papers."

"Given what's happened and who I'm about to meet, can you share a little more?"

She was deep enough now. I guessed it wouldn't hurt.

"We're a special ops team that handles kidnappings of high-profile people and their families. Mainly when it involves the Mexican cartel. We're like shadows. We slip in unseen and slip out with our rescue. It's very dangerous, hence us not sharing anything with anyone."

She studied my face. "You shared it with your father." She wasn't asking, but I knew she knew.

I nodded. "I had to tell someone. If anything happened to me, I couldn't put my parents through the lies that would be my cover story. They deserve better than that."

"Okay." She sucked in a deep breath and seemed to be happy with what I offered her. Catalina was good with heavy, intense things, and I admired that about her.

"Am I going to see where you live?"

"No," I sighed, "but this is protocol, so are you okay to look through this with me?"

I spent the next hour going over everything with her, and by the end of it, she looked more confused than she did when we started.

"I know it's a lot, but it's protection."

"From me, right?" I could hear the hurt in her voice. "The sad part about all of this is that I spent my whole life trying to be different than them. I fought against evil and welcomed the light. I educated myself, have my own place, and love my job. Then my brother gets killed, and his death tipped the scale, and everything I worked so hard for just slid off. Now I'm the one you look at with uncertainty. How am I supposed to fix that?"

I covered her hand with mine. "Time."

"Or something else," she whispered and picked up her book.

TWENTY

Catalina

The red light above the door had been on for the past hour and a half. I was growing more than a little annoyed. It was a long damn journey to make it here, and I had been given a banana to hold me over until after the meeting.

A banana, seriously? Where was Mark when I needed him?

I pushed off the chair and peeked my head outside the door to see if the coast was clear. With a quick glance over my shoulder, I ventured out into the hallway. At least the air was cooler. I was happy I had chosen the appropriate outfit for this trip, particularly as the airplane bathroom had me bent like a pretzel when in dire need. *It was a good trick to store in the old pleasure box inside my head.* I mentally smacked myself because I hoped I would never have to travel any great distance in that thing.

My flats helped conceal my presence as I whisked past two open offices and down another hallway where I could smell food. My stomach growled, and I tossed all care to the wind. I stopped at the door and peeked in. Food. Sweet, heavenly food lined one wall, and a chef was rolling something white onto a dish.

Screw it.

Then I spotted him in the corner, and my anger flashed as I hurried to stand next to the table.

"Wow." I folded my arms and glanced at his heaping plate of food. "You saw them hand me that banana," I hissed, "then to sit me in that 1970, Jeffrey Dahmer-looking room to watch my life dwindle without so much as a cup of coffee!" I glared and felt *hanger* take over as he tried to hold back his boyish grin. "Listen to me, Mark Lopez, you of all people know a Latino appetite is not something to mess with."

He laughed his infectious laugh and shot me one of his "I will win you over because I'm cute" smiles.

"Nice to meet a girl who likes to eat." He pulled a chunk of meat off a rib bone and sucked it from his fingers.

"Don't try charming me." I stuck a finger in his face, and he laughed harder. "Give me a chicken wing, or I will get scrappy."

"Ohhhh," his eyebrows shot up with entertainment, "I don't know, I kind of wanna witness that."

I snatched the chicken wing off his plate and sat at the table next to him. I pulled the tiny sliver of chicken free and swallowed it before my tongue could appreciate the taste.

"Major Lopez." A soldier in camo appeared from nowhere and stood at attention at his side. "You asked for me to pull out whatever I found." He handed him a file. "Blue is the USA side, and red is Mexican."

"Great." Mark flipped it open on his lap and nodded. I glanced at it and saw where they were homing in on. "Dismissed."

The officer gave me a polite nod then left, taking the corners sharply. I had to smile at that.

Mark tipped his tray in the trash and brushed his hands free of crumbs before he handed me a card. "If I had known you were starving, I would have found you, then ate in front of you."

"Jackass." I laughed but gladly took the meal card.

"They should be done any minute now. I'll let Mike know you're here."

"You're way off, you know?" I spoke lightly as he walked toward the door.

"Huh?"

"Your map," I pointed to the file tucked under his arm, "it's inaccurate." I moved to the fridge, and he followed. "My father would never allow his men through that part of the desert. That's forbidden territory." I had no illusions about what I was doing. I shrugged and let my mouth run. "What your soldier pulled is exactly what they want you to see. They purposely show that route being used, and they allow visuals there. Those are not actually their men. They're castaways."

"Castaways?" Mark questioned.

"They are men who have done the family wrong, but instead of killing them, they use them to throw off the scent of the real route." I snagged an apple and bit into the crisp flavor. I wanted to moan, but my stomach demanded I swallow and share in the happiness.

"May I have a chicken avocado salad, please?" I beamed at the chef, and he nodded and smiled at me. I went back to my story. "It's quite brilliant if you think about it. You set up a false route using expendable people. If they are caught, they only ever have a very small amount of drugs on them. They would never talk. My father has spies everywhere. He would kill them, and he would also kill their family. Salvador Esteban is a very smart man, but he's got nothing on his brother. If you want to make a dent in the cartel, you go after his brother Sebastian. Uncle Bash. Now, there's your true nightmare."

"Why?" Mark followed me back to the table and sat across from me. "How's he worse? Drugs or human trafficking?"

"Take your pick." I shrugged.

"Shit, seriously? We've never had a lead that has ever led to Bash, to your uncle."

I popped a fork full of greens in my mouth and lifted an eyebrow. "Exactly. He's smarter."

Mark's eyes were fixed on me as he concentrated. His expression was as if I had unlocked something inside.

"What?"

"I just don't think…I just realized…" He trailed off. "We've been making connections for years with mules, offering them deals for freedom, for information. And now here we are with a woman who was born and raised in that world. You've uncovered something huge for us. We would have continued to waste endless manpower and money chasing ghosts."

"I'm glad to help." I stood and moved to get a brownie the chef just put out when he blocked my path.

"Catalina, you should be careful who you share what with."

Seriously?

I moved around him, but he stopped me again. "Mark, did I mention I'm scrappy?"

"Huh?"

"I'm hungry, and you are literally standing in my way."

"Look, just stay here, and I will be right back."

"I have zero desire to go anywhere, but you *are* the one blocking my food."

He hesitated with a concerned look and decided to let me pass.

Once my stomach was full and I'd downed my body weight in water, I felt I could think clearly again. Mark hadn't returned, but a boyish looking soldier stared at me from a few tables over. I felt like that was a requirement to be super cute at this Army headquarters. I didn't mind the eye candy at all.

"Sorry," he blushed, "it's not often we have civilians here."

"It's cool." I went back to playing with my water bottle.

"You look bored."

"That's an understatement." I dripped with sarcasm.

He glanced at his watch then at the badge hanging around my neck. "Where's your group?"

"In some meeting for over two and a half hours now."

He slid over a few chairs. "Have they shown you the shooting ranges?"

As much as that sounded like exactly what I needed, I didn't want to test my luck in this place. "I was told to wait here, so…" I shrugged.

"Well, then…" He moved over to my table and waited for me to invite him to sit. I waved a hand, and he sat perfectly straight and held out his hand. "My shift just ended. I would be happy to keep you company until your people arrive. Name's Corporal Davie."

"Catalina." I glanced around. "Sure, that would be nice."

He grinned as he set his paperwork aside and removed his hat. He was extremely polite and well-mannered, a lost art these days.

"Tell me something about yourself, Davie. What do you do here in the Army?"

"I'm a diver now." He laughed.

"Sounds like there's a story there."

He scratched his face as he thought. "I had a problem with the water once upon a time, and a good man saw that, despite my problem, I could still perform."

"So, that's what you like to do now?"

"Not really, but they needed one, so I took one for the team."

"There's that word again." I fiddled with my fork and poked at a cranberry. "Everyone has a team, but that's where the story ends."

"What do you mean?"

"Nothing." I shook my head.

He frowned, and I could tell I sent a red flag. "Who are you here with?"

"Mike Irons and the Blackstone team."

His face fell, but he recovered well.

"Oh," he stumbled, "so that means you're the…"

"Yes, the daughter." I wanted to cry because even three thousand miles away, my father still could affect my life, and I was so tired of it.

"Ms. Mendez?" I jumped at the solider who appeared at my side. "Frank would like to speak with you now."

"Nice to meet you, Catalina." Davie offered me a smile, but it didn't touch his eyes.

Apparently, I was a wolf in sheep's clothing.

Finally, someone appeared and informed me he was there to escort me to meet the boss. The soldier knocked on Frank's door and waited for a command to enter.

"Go ahead, miss." He opened the door and waited for

me to step inside. I noticed Mike first then Mark and John. Then Cole came in after me.

"Thanks, Sloane." A man nodded as he listened to someone on the phone. "I'll let John know to be there." He hung up and turned to greet me. "Hello, Catalina. I'm Frank Brandon." He looked like a poster boy for the US Army. He offered me a hand.

"Nice to meet you." I couldn't help but study his perfect crew cut and meticulously ironed t-shirt, tucked into a pair of camo pants.

"Please take a seat." He pulled out a chair next to Mike, and my stomach slowly crept up into my throat. Frank took a seat across from me, and I felt Mike's hand move to my thigh to stop my trembling.

"I'm sure this is a little strange for you, Catalina, but I do appreciate your coming here to meet with me."

"I didn't realize I had much of a choice," I muttered, annoyed he asked me to come here and then made me wait nearly three hours.

"Of course, you do, Catalina." He wore a confused expression, as though what I said was the farthest thing from his mind. "You agreeing to come, it says a lot, and I appreciate it."

"I didn't do it for you." I felt Mike's hand tighten as a warning to be nice.

"I know." Frank's eyes shifted over to Mike's for a moment. "Do you mind if I ask you some questions?"

I shook my head. "No."

He pulled out a map of the US and Mexico and

spread it in front of me. "You shared something huge with Lopez. Could you please show me the route your father actually does use when he sends his drugs across the border?" He placed a blue Expo marker in front of me.

I licked my dry mouth and hesitated, realizing this was suddenly very big. It was one thing to talk to Mark, but what I was about to do just became real. I knew I could never come back from this decision, sacrificing my father and all the family to the US Army. It was a huge decision. I looked at Frank and knew he understood. His eyes told me he wasn't going to rush me. Molten steel poured down my throat and suffocated my insides. I knew my freedom and that of so many people would never happen unless I helped to end it. Javier's death would be avenged, and my father and uncle would not get away with murder anymore. Bottom line was, I needed to show them I wasn't a threat.

I internally glanced at my braver side, who gave me a nod to continue. With that, I leaned forward and pressed the blue marker to the map and drew three trails I knew he used.

"This one," I pointed to the center trail, "is patrolled by Alamo Juan. He's slowly being bought off by Uncle Bash, I mean Sebastian, so you won't find my father's mules there much longer. This one," I moved my finger to the far left one, "will be out of commission soon too, because a new client has moved in and will be running drugs from Hawaii. Not to say that my father..." I stopped for a moment and looked at Frank. "If you don't mind, I will not use the word 'father' again. Not to say that *Sal,*" I used my mother's term for him, "won't just move it over to the right a bit." I reached over and fingered the black marker and circled the stopping points. "But like I told Mark, if you want to make a dent in the cartel, you take out Sebastian."

"Any suggestions on how to do this?"

I chewed on the inside of my lip. "Yes."

"How?" The room was so quiet you could hear a pin drop—or my wild heartbeat.

"What if I told you I could get you inside the house *and* get my father and my uncle in one place for you to take them both out?"

Frank leaned back in his chair and tilted his head as he studied me again.

"I would ask what you want in exchange." He glanced at Mike, but his face was like stone.

"I want trust."

He turned back to me, confused. "Trust?"

"Yes, I want to be the person I was, who I became when I moved to the US seven years ago. I worked very hard to become Catalina Mendez, and that was taken from me when my brother was murdered by them."

A small smile spread across Frank's face and soon was mirrored on Mark's and John's.

"You have my trust already," Mark piped in, and it warmed my heart.

"Mine too," Mike pulled my attention to him, "but are you really willing to take down your own family?"

"Yes and no." I turned back to Frank. "One other condition."

"I'm listening."

"You must not hurt my mother. She has no part in this. She told me the family secrets and how she bought my freedom, at the expense of her own. I owe her my life, so if I could finally help her obtain some form of freedom in this world, I must try. Perhaps you could get her in a witness protection program or whatever you guys do?"

"Seems fair." Mike leaned forward.

"Agreed." Frank spread out another map, but this time it was the blueprints to the house. "But tell me, how do you plan to get two rivals, like those brothers are, together in one spot?"

"You leave that to me. I have some ideas, and I will let you know soon."

TWENTY-ONE

Mike

"That was a hard one." My father handed me a beer and sat in the gazebo across from me. I turned to face him and leaned my hip on the door frame.

"Yeah, it was. I knew deep down it might have to come to her helping us. I couldn't show Frank how terrified I was for her. I couldn't have him ever question my loyalty to Blackstone. If he thought I was so far gone on her that it would affect my head, he would never have let me continue to be a part of this mission. Things are sure tricky at times."

"Sounds that way. Catalina is a strong woman, son. She will make her own decisions. She has proved that. How's Trigger?"

"He's good. Still tore up from his uncle's passing, but he's got Tess, and she's good for him."

"Good." He tipped the beer back and drank the neck of the bottle. "Just like Catalina."

I searched the property until I found her with Charlotte and Kyle down on the sand, deep in conversation. Her small, curvy frame was under a burnt orange sundress, and her hair was swept up in a messy bun. Somehow, she must have felt me watching her, and her head moved slowly to find me.

Once our eyes met, I felt a punch to the gut and a tug on the heartstrings.

"I know you love her, Mike," he said behind me. "The question is how much."

Catalina gave me a shy smile. Her bronze skin shimmered in the afternoon sun.

She was that kind of pretty any woman would wish for, all-natural. She didn't have to try at all, and to me, she was the most beautiful woman in the world.

"If she was an active member of the Esteban family, I would still love her." I admitted the truth. My father would never judge me for loving the enemy.

"You can't help who you love, son. Keith is a perfect example of that. Most people would have thought he was nuts running after Lexi, running into the gang like that. Lexi was full of hate and pain then, but he knew who she was underneath it all, and now look. Lexi has dropped her guard and is one big sweetheart."

"And they've created a mini Keith." I smiled when I

thought of their little guy's face and how much his parents loved him.

"Imagine a little Mike."

My heart lifted, and pride burst through my chest. "Or a little Catalina?"

"Or both." He laughed lightly behind me. "If you love her, Mike, you do the right thing by her and make sure she knows it."

I nodded and looked back at the one person who taught me to be the man I am. He taught me to be honest, respectful, kind, and loving. Most of all, he showed me how important it was to have a stable, loving family. That you would fight to the very end for the ones you loved.

He came up to my side and held out something. "I know this is old fashioned, but I think the sentiment behind it would mean more to her than anything brought in a store." He handed me a red box and flipped it open with his thumb. A single round diamond sat in the center of a gold band.

"Gram's ring?" I shook my head, unable to take it.

He nodded. "When your grandmother passed, she told me to give this to you when I knew you were ready. Fifty-two years of love is inside this diamond. The type of relationship they had can't be traded. No, sir, there's no better luck than that."

I ran my fingers over my lips while I thought about how this would show Catalina how much I trusted her, by giving her a family heirloom.

"Thanks, Pops," I pulled him into a hug and held on to him for a beat longer.

"Go big or go small, just make her yours so Frank will see what I do. She's not going anywhere."

I slipped the box in my pocket and removed my vibrating phone.

Mark: Remember how you were a dick and foreshadowed with the Furby of death?

Mike: Quite vividly, actually.

Mark: Mia is pregnant…again.

A laugh ripped out from my throat. Wait until Savannah and Olivia heard about this one.

Mike: So happy for you, brother.

Mark: I'm going to get my band!

Mike: If only you knew how to sing.

Mark: That's why they have Uncle Mike.

Mike: This is true. Seriously, though, congratulations.

Mark: Thanks, man. We'll have to
celebrate after all this shit is finished.
See you in two days.

I headed across the grass and leaned over the dock to admire the woman I could see having endless children with.

Charlotte told a joke, which made Kyle laugh so hard he nearly fell off his chair. Catalina tossed her head back and looked so carefree. I wanted to keep this picture in my head. I wanted to get back to this place, no matter where the journey would take us.

"Mike?"

I turned my head to find Lizzy behind me. Her hands were tucked into her pockets, and she looked uneasy. She waved off the man she came with, and I shook my head at her constant need for attention. She really did need to grow up.

"Hey."

"You love her?" She nodded toward Catalina.

"Yeah, I do." I turned to see her better.

Her face scrunched like my words stung her, and her shoulders tensed and stayed up. It was time she heard how it was going to be for now on.

"I waited for you, Lizzy, but you never saw me until I found someone else."

"I was stupid."

I shrugged in agreement. "Yeah, at times, you were."

"Ouch."

"Yeah, ouch, Lizzy. I was in love with you for years, and you knew it, yet you paraded man after man around me. Shit, I even caught you in bed with one of them."

She dropped her head in shame and moved to lean against the railing of the dock. "Do you love her like you loved me?" she asked softly.

"No." I felt the freedom that came with this much-needed conversation. "It's very different."

"How?"

"Because she reciprocates it, therefore it's grown into something strong."

She nodded while her eyes were locked on her shoes. "Are you going to marry her?"

"If it was up to me, we'd be married already."

"Wow," her tone was low, "you sound very sure of yourself."

I smirked and watched her date flirt with Catalina. What a winner he was.

"I'm sorry I hurt you, Mike." She finally looked at me, and I saw her remorse. "I'm sorry I didn't see you until it was too late. I think I'm just not ready for what you want."

"Agreed." I nodded. "Will you be nicer to her now that you know she won't be going anywhere?"

She sighed and laughed a little. "No promises. She just bothers me. She's perfect and knows it."

I glared at her, unhappy with her comment. *Grow the hell up, Lizzy.*

"You really can't see past your own nose." Her face dropped. "If you want to be in my life, Lizzy, you need to grow up."

"Wow." She laughed loudly and drew the others' attention, and they turned in our direction. "Well, I guess that's that."

"Yeah." I pushed off the railing. "I guess it is."

Taking two steps at a time, I made my way down to the sand, kicked off my sandals, and stood behind Catalina. Tucking my hand under her chin, I leaned her head back and bent to kiss her lips.

"Hey, you." She grinned at me. "Everything okay?"

"Yes," I kissed her one more time, "everything is great."

She glanced at Charlotte, who held up a finger to Kyle.

"Hey, big brother? Would you grab my phone from your bathroom?"

"Sure." I rubbed Catalina's shoulder, just because I needed to touch her. Her head leaned against my stomach, and I wanted to moan with need. I wanted this woman every moment of every day.

I made my way inside and headed for the bathroom. My sister's phone was on the counter. Just as I snatched it up, I heard the little frigger's voice whistle. I jumped, and her phone went flying into the toilet.

"Hey, there, good lookin'."

"Son of a bitch!" I cringed and fished the phone from

the bowl, glad it was in a waterproof case. I hated that damn Furby!

Laughter filled the beach, and I hurried out to find them nearly in tears. I tossed her phone at her and she caught it with a shriek.

"It's wet, Mike!"

"There's a voice message." I snickered and waited for her to lift it to her face.

"It's from Dan." She wiggled her eyebrows at Catalina.

"It fell in the toilet, Char," I interrupted and watched her face fall into twisted disgust. Her mouth dropped open, and she tried to dry her wet, pissy hands on her legs.

"That's disgusting!" Charlotte shouted.

"Don't prank me. They always backfire," I warned and playfully glared at Catalina, who apparently couldn't stop laughing at all of us. "You think that was funny?"

"It was her idea!" Kyle pointed in glee.

"Oh," my face twisted in delight, "is that so?"

Catalina backed up with her hands in the air.

"Mark asked me to do it." Tears lined her eyes. "You know you can't say no to his smile."

"He is a charmer," Charlotte hissed with a grin.

"Charmer, huh?"

"Mike, be nice." I had her backing up the ramp to the grass. "Remember your parents are here. You don't want me to tell your mother on you."

"Banner?" My mother called from the patio on cue. "Are you behaving?"

"Not at all, Mom," I called back and grinned as if to ask, *now what?*

"Mrs. Irons," Catalina pressed her lips together, "your son is going to attack me for something Mark asked me to do."

"As long as I get grandbabies, I'm all for the attack."

Catalina's hand shot over her mouth as she laughed. "Mr. Irons?"

"I'm with his mother on this one, sweetheart."

"The parents have spoken." I took another step closer, and she made a face then twisted on her heel and full-out sprinted across the yard.

"Aw, baby, you're forgetting what I do for a living," I called, then I slipped into predator mode and shot off after her.

I rounded the house on the opposite side and waited behind a bush, watching her frantically look for a place to hide.

She decided on the little toolshed, so I hurried around the back and peeked in the window. She was out of breath but started to laugh at something. I opened the door and pressed myself to her back and nipped at her neck while she screamed.

She suddenly spun around and grabbed my face to kiss me hard. I hooked her waist with my arm and sat her on the flipped over dory.

I pulled at her bathing suit bottoms until I was free to roam her soft skin with my fingers.

She was turned on and wiggled when I coated my finger with her excitement.

"So, a little chase gets you turned on?"

"Mmm," she moaned. "It's the look you get right before I run that does it." Her hand covered mine, and she showed me how she wanted it.

"What look?"

Her hips rolled around my fingers. "You look hungry for me."

I nibbled on her earlobe. "I am hungry for you, Catalina."

"Mike," she huffed into my neck, "you need to be inside of me now."

Shit.

"I don't have a condom."

"Don't care," she nearly cried and clawed at my shoulders.

I pushed down my pants and almost jumped at her tight grip as I moved to line up.

"We seem to have sex in some unique places." I chuckled and pushed into her as the tight walls stretched around me. I pushed in further.

Home.

"Yes!" She leaned back and bowed her spine into the sexy curve I craved to see every time we made love.

My hand landed on her hip, and the other dragged up the center of her stomach. I flicked my hips and shot her forward. Her breasts bounced, and I nearly crumbled at the sight.

She wasn't just the woman I loved; she was the woman who saved me from my childhood nightmares. Catalina could look past my appearance and see me for who I was. I would spend the rest of my life reminding her that she was the most important person in the world to me.

"Mike," she screamed when I changed the angle and hit her walls with my assault. "Oh, my God, yes!"

Just as she leaped over the edge, I joined her and pumped out all that I had inside of me. Her hands found my face again and stopped me when I went in for a kiss.

"I love you, Mike," she held my wild gaze, "so much."

"I love you, Catalina."

Later that night, with the Furby in hand, I raced down the hallway and into Keith's office while he was in the kitchen. I rushed around the room looking for the perfect place to hide the little shit.

"Hi!" A little voice had me whirling around red-handed.

"Hey, baby B." I smiled down at my nephew. He had his blanket in one hand and a lollipop in the other, both taking their turns in his mouth.

"Thus mine." He pointed to the Furby.

I looked down at the nasty little toy and hatched a plan.

"Okay, B, go find Daddy," I picked him up and headed out of Keith's office. I unfolded the cuddle bug from my hip and placed him on his feet and gave him a nudge toward his father, who balanced an armful of papers.

"Dad-dy!" He tried to run to him. Just as he did, he held up the toy, and it screamed, "Fire in the hole!"

The papers went flying, and Keith jumped with a string of curses.

Lexi came racing around the corner and laughed at her husband, who looked fit to kill.

"Irons!" he boomed and scooped up his little boy with a laugh. I stayed behind the wall and listened to him try to interrogate his son. "Did Uncle Mike tell you to do this?"

"Yes." The little crap outed me to his father. "My toy!"

"I will get you a toy, but this one is going to haunt your uncle's dreams tonight."

"Boys and their toys." Lexi chuckled at her family.

I rolled off the wall and laughed all the way back to my room. I needed to get changed because Daniel was in town, and we were about to start training.

TWENTY-TWO

CATALINA

"I'm so glad you're good at your job, Cat." Charlotte sipped her coffee at her desk across the room from me. "Anyone else would have been let go."

"I know." I pressed my lips into a line and wondered if she was jealous I didn't lose my job after I just up and left. "Are you mad?"

"Mad?" She shook her head, confused. "I get to sit six feet from my one of my best friends and I hope soon to be sister-in-law. I would have been devastated if you got canned."

"I second that." Kyle popped his head in the door. "This place would be super boring without you."

"Hey!" She tossed a handful of paperclips at him, and they hit the wall and flew everywhere.

"Like I said." He laughed when he caught a few and beamed in delight at Charlotte as she rolled her eyes.

"Just making sure." I moved over to help myself to a second cup of coffee. "I didn't mean to leave, but when I got the news about my brother, well, things just…"

"We're sorry, Cat, really, we are." Kyle came in for a hug, and I gladly accepted it. I had such wonderful friends in my life, though I couldn't share my entire past with them. That was for their own protection and part of my deal with Frank.

My past was my past, and my future was much brighter. Besides, who wanted to live the in that past, anyway?

———

The next two weeks flew by, thanks to Nicole Miller signing on with our ad agency. She'd insisted I take lead on the account, and I chose Charlotte as my number two. I had never had more fun than I did when creating an advertisement and a launch party for her brand-new line. One no one else had even seen yet.

A bottle of champagne sat on my desk, thanks to my loving boyfriend who knew how big of a deal it was that I got lead on this project.

I popped the cork and joined my friends in the conference room for a late dinner.

"Steak and champagne?" Kyle snatched the glass from my hand. "My kind of date."

Just as we were finishing up, I caught sight of someone chatting with security. The guard handed him a visitor pass, and I instantly felt my stomach turn the bubbles of champagne into the perfect storm.

"Who is that cowboy?" Charlotte smirked at me when she caught me watching him. "A friend?"

"Something like that." I slowly pushed to my feet as he stood by the door, uneasy.

"Catalina," Abel removed his black cowboy hat and ran a shaky hand through his hair, "I need to speak with you."

He looked terrible, which sent my nerves through the roof. Something was wrong; I could feel it deep in my gut.

"Charlotte," I whispered, and by my warning tone she realized I wasn't playing around, "call your brother."

Out of the corner of my eye, I saw Kyle slide her bag across the table, and she quickly retrieved her phone.

I walked over to him so he would step away from Charlotte and Kyle. "What is it, Abel?" I asked, keeping my voice level.

"Can we speak alone?"

"He's not picking up," Char said, her voice worried.

"Keep trying," I heard Kyle say.

I pushed past the mental block of not wanting to hear the news Abel brought me. He could barely look at me when we faced each other in the hallway. I led him into another room and closed the heavy glass door behind me. Kyle had his eyes locked on me through the window, and

Charlotte kept trying to call Mike. I folded my arms and waited for his blow to hit.

"Let me guess. My father has retracted my freedom card?"

Abel's troubled eyes shot to mine, and what I saw there was something much worse.

"Abel? You're scaring me."

"I know I'm the last person you want to see right now…"

"I think that's a fair assumption."

He shut his eyes, and when he opened them again, I could see the pain that flickered inside him. "The *secret* got out." The words barely passed over his lips. "Bash retaliated."

I reached for the steel door handle as I processed what he'd said. A shockwave ripped through my core, and I knew another hit was about to come.

"Your father was the target, but when they came for him, he escaped. Your father's men fought them off, but this is not over. Bash will not stop at anything to take down your father now he knows."

"My mother?"

"Salvador used your mother as a shield. She took three bullets to the chest. She went down fast, didn't feel any pain."

Boom! The shockwave weakened my knees.

"No," I cried, and my two friends flew to my side.

"What just happened?" Kyle was in Abel's face. "What

did you say? Do you know who her boyfriend is? He can make one…"

"No," I quickly cut Kyle off. He couldn't know who Mike was. No one could! Hot tears blurred out the world for a moment, and I had to struggle to keep myself together. I was at work; anyone could walk by.

"Shit," Charlotte hissed, inches from my face. "Pick up your phone!" She looked at me, confused and scared. "I can't get him."

I covered my face and tried to think through the storm that brewed inside me. Once I could suck a full breath in, I knew what I needed to do. Somehow, I willed myself to stand and drew myself up to my full height.

"Abel, give me the afternoon, and I'll call you when I'm ready." He hesitated but nodded, and I waited until he left before I turned to my friends. "I have to go. There's a problem."

"Catalina," Char grabbed my arm, "this whole thing is really scary. What is going on?"

I tossed my arms around her neck and hugged her hard. "I know, and I'm very sorry, Charlotte, but please listen. Can you take me to your father?"

"What? Why?" She looked intently at my face, and when I didn't answer, she shook her head. "Sure."

Charlotte's mouth was in a constant frown, and her eyes shifted from the road to me like clockwork. She hated that I had shut down on her on the way, but I knew she had enough experience with her brother's job that she understood not to keep asking questions. I knew I would break if I wasn't careful.

"You look pale." She tried to get me to talk. "Are you going to be sick?"

I shook my head and drew my knees to my chest and buried my head. My mother's face popped through my armor, and I let out a small sob.

"Oh, God, honey!" Charlotte reached for my arm and gave it a squeeze. She tried her phone again, and Mike's voice message filled the car.

"You've reached Mike Irons. Leave a message, and I'll call back when I can."

"Mike, when your sister texts and calls more times in one day than ever before, there's a reason! Call me back!"

When she peeled off the main road and drove for three minutes on gravel, I felt like my stomach was going to betray me.

"That's his cabin. Go knock. This time of day, he'll be inside." She brushed a tear from my cheek. "I'll keep trying my brother."

With shaky legs, I unfolded from the front seat and headed to the wooden door. The heavy smell of pine laced the air and filled my nostrils with its comforting scent.

"Mr. Irons?" I knocked on the cabin door and waited for him to look up from his leather-bound book.

"Catalina?" He smiled warmly and invited me inside. "Please call me Ray. What a lovely surprise."

"Sadly," I swallowed hard and tried to control my emotions, "this isn't a friendly visit."

"No?"

"Ray, I need your help."

Ray looked like I just asked him to help me move a dead body after I told him what happened with my mother and uncle. I knew it was a lot to throw at him, but Mike always said his father was great in stressful situations. So here I was, the girlfriend of his son, and I just dropped the big one at his doorstep.

"I'm trying to do this right, but I can't get hold of Mike, and I don't know how to contact Frank. Look," I paused and took a big leap by stepping over a line, "I know you know, and now you know I know, so can you give me any suggestions on who to call?"

His bushy eyebrows finally smoothed out as something hit his memory.

"After Mike joined Blackstone, he gave me this." He moved to pull a dusty jar out from behind the canned pickles and showed me the label. "He said if he or I was ever in trouble, I should call this number."

He handed me the paper with a name and a number scribbled in pen. I pulled my phone free and dialed the number.

"Ray?" I stopped him at the doorway. "Would you stay?"

He smiled and took his seat by the fireplace and picked his book back up, licked his finger, and started to scan the words.

Thank you.

"Hello?" a smooth voice answered.

"Hi-hello," I stumbled, unsure where I should start. "I'm Catalina Mendez."

"Hello, Catalina. I've heard a lot about you." There was a pause, and I could hear someone yelling in the background. "Not to sound unfriendly, but how did you get this number?"

I glanced at Ray and knew Mike would get in trouble if I told the truth.

"Mike told me if he was ever to get into trouble to call this number."

"I'm sorry, Miss Mendez, but Mike isn't in trouble. I can see him from where I stand."

I closed my eyes, so happy to know he was safe. "I know, Mr. Logan, but I am."

I was put on hold while Daniel patched Frank into the call and let me spend the next hour going over every single detail of my plan. I did everything by the book... well, *almost* everything.

"I've raised two children, Catalina," Ray licked his finger again before he flipped the page, "and I can spot the look of someone about to do something really stupid."

"Yeah." I dried my tears and felt another surge of emotion head to the surface.

"So, now, do I need to worry about another?"

I leaned up and gave him a hug. "I can protect him, if I get there first."

His eyes closed, and the lines in his face deepened with concern. "I'll give you a twenty-minute head start."

I thanked him again as Charlotte and I left. She pulled me into her arms when she stopped to drop me off on the main street. She had been warned by her father not to question what was happening, but her tears tore at me when I left her there and hopped into the passenger seat of Abel's truck.

"Drive."

"Where?"

"I'm going to my father's."

"I don't think that's the right move, Catalina." His face was shocked.

"You either take me, or I fly back alone."

He thought for a moment then shoved his truck in drive. "Dammit."

The journey back into Mexico took its toll on my strength. We flew part of the way and drove the rest. I couldn't keep my eyes open, no matter how hard I tried. Abel tried everything he could to make sure I was comfortable on the journey.

Yeah, guilt can be a real bitch, can't it?

I hated him for what he'd done, and I was curious what else he knew about my mother's death. Once we crossed the border, found his personal truck, and hit the road again, I finally acknowledged his existence.

"Tell me what you know, and none of the bullshit like you did with my brother."

His jaw clenched like he was pissed at my comment, then he tightened his cowboy hat on his head.

"I'm not proud of what happened with Javier," he

hissed, "and, of all people, you should know that when the boss calls on you to do something, you do it."

"Even to kill your best friend?"

"Javier knew what he had done. He knew when I arrived that he had to own up. I did not kill him. I just took him home."

Anger replaced my sorrow, and I balled up my fists with my urge to hit him.

"Oh, so that makes it okay?"

"No." He held my gaze longer than he should while driving. "None of it is okay, Catalina. Your mother was like a mother to me too, and to watch your father cower behind her lifeless body nearly tore me to pieces. I left to find you, to tell you in person. My number will be up too when I set foot back in that house."

"Then why not just call me? You have my number."

"Because, woman!" he snapped and tossed his hat on the dash. "I love you! You deserved more than a phone call!"

The air suddenly sucked out of the truck in one quick motion.

"I've loved you forever. Nothing I've done would ever change that."

"I didn't know," I whispered after a few seconds of silence, "that you still felt for me that way."

"I never stopped." He played with the steering wheel cover. "That's why I came back. You needed to know the truth."

"Thank you, Abel. I do appreciate that."

He nodded, and when the silence became too much, he turned up the radio, so the haunting stillness went away. We both said our piece, and we each knew where the other stood. He was in love with me, and I was hopelessly in love with someone else now. He tried to do the right thing for once, and for that, I would try to hold on to my memories of the love I had for him in the past.

I leaned my head into the window and let my scattered emotions try to find their place inside my chest.

Abel was waved past the three checkpoints without being stopped, and we pulled into the driveway without any security present. The vibe was completely different—eerie, almost—from the last time I was here.

"Something is not right here. Come on." He started to walk up the stairs, and I followed, although a part of me felt like I was being led into a trap.

The house was empty and cold, and a shiver found my lower back and scurried up my spine like a rat in trouble.

Wait, was I the rat?

I'd flipped.

Did they know?

I shook it off and swung my huge purse around to my front and started to pluck items from the shelf.

"What are you doing?" Abel peered down at me. "Do you need money?"

"It's not about money, it's about having something that was my mother's." I tucked two photos in my purse and moved toward the library. My mother was a reader, and I wanted to grab a couple of her favorites.

"Catalina." Abel chased after me and hooked my arm, so I whirled around to face him. His expression was puzzled, his jaw was locked, and his eyes narrowed in on me.

"Ab—" He shot forward and kissed me. It happened so fast that it took me a moment to realize what he had done. I pushed his shoulders and stepped back. "Abel, I just don't feel that way any—" Again I was cut off with the sound of someone talking.

I pushed past him and came to a cold stop when I saw the scene in the library. My father was on his knees at the feet of his older brother Bash. A gun was stuck in his mouth, and my aunt was dead on the floor next to him.

"Huh." All the air was sucked out of my lungs.

"Ah, Catalina, what a gift. We have been patiently waiting." His thick accent barked through my fear. His haunting gaze swooped over my shoulder. "Good boy."

What? An acid wash flooded my veins, and I stayed stuck in a parallel that told me to run but also to stay still. Slowly, I looked over my shoulder, my heart crumbling from the bottom like sand through an hourglass to find Abel with a gun dangling by his side. He glanced at me, and I saw his face conflicted with emotion.

"Time for some truths." Bash pulled my attention back to him and grabbed my father by the hair, roughly pulling him back to look at me.

"Catalina! Save me!" my father pleaded desperately.

"Catalina, darling," Bash pulled my attention back to

him, "did you know your father was sleeping with my wife for the past nine years?"

I shook my head, unable to tell the truth.

"Lies!" my father hissed like the filthy coward he was.

"Did you know he killed his own son because he tried to make peace with the family?"

My emotional gaze fell on my pathetic excuse for a father, and all my hate came at me in one swift motion. With all my might, I swung my bag into my father's face. I heard the crack of the glass from the picture frame that protruded as it smoked his cheek. He fell backward, only to be hauled back up by Bash. Blood oozed from the gash, and I wondered if he had done the same to my brother.

Shattered glass could be replaced, but a shattered heart could not.

"Catalina," my father coughed, "you think I pulled the trigger to kill my son?"

I felt him behind me, and I whirled to find Abel about to grab me.

"Oh, my sweet, useless daughter, I don't do the dirty work in the family. My hands stay clean."

No.

Abel's face hardened, and I knew the truth. I felt my heart break all over again, as it had at seventeen. He didn't come for me then because he was weak, and he wouldn't help me now.

"I have to do as I'm told." He leaned against the doorframe like he didn't care.

Something clicked in my head. "What did you mean,

you were patiently waiting?" I looked at Bash, and he smiled.

"My dear brother sent for you, of course. What other card did he have to play? He offered you, my dear Catalina, his own daughter, to save his worthless life."

I turned to look at Abel once again. My mind flashed to the hallway when he kissed me, and fingers went to my lips to rub the memory away.

I almost felt my uncle make the connection to what just happened, and the shockwave from the bullet nearly blew me backward. Abel jolted with wide eyes before he slumped to the floor.

Holy shit.

"Why?" I tried to keep my mind moving. I felt like I was covered in mud again at the swimming hole, unable to move. "Why would you trade his life for mine? What value am I to you, Uncle?" I tried to understand.

"You have no value to me at all, Catalina, except to see how deep your dear father, my brother, would go to save his own worthless hide. It will fascinate me to watch him as I take his daughter's life before his own. I will wipe out all that was his."

"What's rich, here, Uncle Sebastian," I drew out his name and made my tone sickly sweet, "is that at the end of it all, I will be the only one still standing with the Esteban name."

"Women don't have any place in the cartel world," my father hissed like a snake.

"Who said anything about the cartel world?"

I shot him a devilish smile as it all clicked around him while Bash seemed still confused.

"Yes, father, I'm an American now."

My mother's sweet face appeared in front of me. She seemed to shout something, but I couldn't understand until I felt it.

It took me a moment to process what just happened. The walls in the library shook, the chandelier swung, and plaster from the roof rained down around us. My hearing went in and out as a loud boom hit my ears. The silence was now replaced with a loud hum. I struggled to stand, but vertigo attacked my balance as I reached for something to hold.

A gunshot rang out, and as I fought to stop the spins, I saw my father fall to the floor, his head and the floor red with blood. My uncle now pointed his gun at me.

"What did you do?" Bash screamed through the white powder that filled the air.

Shit, the cocaine stash has been blown up.

Quickly, I ripped my shirt and tried to use it as a filter. The last thing I needed was to breathe it in.

"It's nothing personal, Catalina." Bash fired his gun, but he missed.

Boom! Another hit to the house shook the foundation.

I threw myself toward the door as Bash flew backward and hit the bookcase. So much chaos filled the room that all rational thinking was blocked from my head. I scrambled to find my footing and stumbled toward the gun that was next to my father.

Boom!

I fell sideways and hit my ribs hard. "Ahhhh!" I cried, but I could tell they were only bruised, not broken. Again, I forced my disoriented body to stand, only to feel a hand wrap around my throat and something hard touch my face.

Cold, hard fear broke out across my body when I caught my uncle's evil face in the reflection of the cabinet glass.

My eyes looked to my angel on the library wall, and I called out to her. A surge of adrenaline flowed through me. For too long, I had taken the abuse my father had dished out to me, but now he lay in a puddle of his own blood next to his lover. Now I was in the hands of his brother, and I wasn't going to go down without a fight.

Boom!

We shot backward, and I cried out when I caught a glimpse of what was pushed against my neck.

No!

TWENTY-THREE

MIKE

"Raven One to Delta Six," Cole shouted at me through the radio, "what's your twenty?"

I pushed the two-hundred-grain roll up charge next to the door and raced out of the second room on the right with the scope to my eye ready to shoot.

"Thirty seconds to the next blast." I rushed to the next room with fear lodged in my throat. It too was empty.

Where was she?

So many scenarios raced through my head as I dropped to my knees and set another blast. I used my fingers as guides because the cocaine made the air murky.

As I let my fingers do the work, my head slipped backward.

"Irons!" Daniel called up at me from the ground. I was halfway up the mountain in the middle of a training exercise when he found me. I let go and rappelled down in a matter of minutes. Whatever it was, it must be important, because Daniel never interrupted a training day.

"Hey, what's up?" I rubbed my hands together to brush the dust off.

He placed two fingers in his mouth and whistled to gain Cole's attention.

"Yeah?" Cole threaded a line down to Mark.

"Irons and I need a moment, and then I'll need yours."

"Sure thing." Cole signaled to John to take over. He disappeared off the top of the mountain to hurry down the back side.

"I got a call from Catalina." Daniel held up his private cell phone. "I transferred her to Frank, so he knows, but we need to talk."

Oh, shit.

"Seems her father's got himself in a mess."

"How bad?"

"Well," he rolled his watch over, "she left twenty-two minutes ago, so we're pretty much at a ten, here."

"Wait," I placed a hand on his shoulder, "she left for Mexico?"

"Yeah," he nodded, and I felt the agreement we'd made poof into thin air, "but she did blow up Frank's

*phone pretty good before she left. She told me she
went to your father's because she couldn't get you,
then called my number trying to reach Frank. Frank
did get a moment to speak to her, though. She did
everything right, except listen to him about not
leaving."*

*"Maybe she didn't?" I wanted to call my father, but
when I turned my phone on, I saw I had endless
missed calls from Charlotte, my father, and Catalina.
We didn't have our phones on when we were
training.*

*"Her mother was murdered." Daniel broke through
to me. "Would you stay home?"*

The entire house shook again, and I knew it would only take three more blasts before the place went down.

"Beta Seven to Delta Six," Keith sounded off, "I have eyes on the sparrow. I repeat, I have eyes on the sparrow."

"Where?" I dropped all training.

"Library."

The six-second run down the hallway and into the library reminded me of when I was back in Iraq. I'd gotten separated from my troop, and I wasn't sure if they were dead or alive.

And just like then, I was brought to a dead stop when I saw her terrified face and a hand grenade held to her throat.

"Stop!" A guy I recognized from photos as Catalina's

Uncle Sebastian, or Bash, clearly unnerved with our presence, screamed, "One more step and we all go!"

Catalina's eyes were wide and kept sweeping the room as if desperately seeking a way out. That was when I took in that her father and a woman lay executed on the floor. Her friend Abel also had a huge hole in his chest.

What the hell happened here?

I slowly held up my hand and pointed to my neck to show him my intention. "If I don't radio to stop them, they will shoot."

He nodded for me to go ahead and stop the team.

"Delta Six to Raven One, do you copy?"

"Right behind you, brother. Exits are secure, and we have eyes on the mark."

"Stand down. Subject has a hand grenade."

"Copy that, Delta Six. We will wait for your signal. Pin in or out?" I didn't need to check a second time; I'd noticed right away.

"Out, copy that." Again, I lowered my hand slowly and moved my eyes to Catalina, who seemed to be in total shock.

"Why are you here?" Sebastian yelled at me as another one of my blasts went off. He rocked backward and almost pulled Catalina right off her feet. She struggled to breathe around his flexed arm. I went to make a move, but he found his footing and removed one of his three fingers from the spoon trigger.

Keith came into view behind, but I shook my head. I

was calm, and my head was clear. It had to be if we were going to get through this.

"Denton Barlow sent me." I lied, of course.

"The American?" He sounded confused, and what shocked me was that he used his nickname. "I find that hard to believe. He's in prison."

"Has that ever stopped anyone before?"

He shifted Catalina to cover more of his body. I wondered if he could feel my men moving in for the kill.

"Denton and I have been in communication, and he never once mentioned a US team coming here."

That so?

"It was a deal made with your brother. Why don't we ask him?" I dropped my gaze to Salvador's lifeless body. "Oh, wait, we can't." I was deadpan.

"Not possible." He spat on the floor, and I saw his pupils were dilated. He'd obviously had a good deal of cocaine even before the blast. "We had a deal. I take out my family, and in return, he'd ship me pretty USA girls. He's already got a container full. I just need to show him some proof."

Human trafficking was the lowest of lows.

"I want in. Where are the girls?"

"Mike," Cole warned, but we both knew if we had an opportunity to get some information before we blew his head off, we should.

"Why does he want your brother dead?"

He glared at me, and his mindless chatter came to a

halt. He whipped around, and he spotted Keith with a rifle pointed at his head.

"No!" He squeezed his eyes shut. "If I die, he'll know something has happened."

"That's fine." I shrugged and glanced at Catalina. "Are you okay?"

She didn't register me. I couldn't tell if she was high or in shock or both.

"Catalina?" I spoke louder, and her eyes snapped to life and tears broke through at what was happening.

"Mike?" she cried and tried to fight Sebastian's hold. A finger slipped, and I held up my hand.

"Stop!"

She froze.

Sebastian looked at me, then her, then me again.

"You want to know what connection my father made?" Suddenly, Catalina's fight was back, only I wasn't sure she knew what she was doing.

"Ten seconds to the next blast, boys. We need to move," Mark whispered, and both Keith and Cole shifted their weapons.

It was time.

"The only daughter of the Esteban family flipped," she hissed in delight as her words hit him hard. I saw the moment he realized who we were, and I saw his last finger make the move to release the grenade.

I leaped forward and dove at Catalina just as the blast from the other room went off, I tucked her under my body as we hit the floor.

The boom shot books in different directions, little sheets of paper fluttered around us like snow, and I waited, but the second, harder blow never came. Keith seemed just as confused as I was. I stood and saw it. The hand grenade was now in a tight grip in Catalina's hand.

"Shit." I knelt and pried it carefully from her locked fingers. "Give it to me, babe. I got it."

As soon as her hands were free, they went to cover her face, and a sad cry ripped from her chest as the last thirty minutes hit her.

"We need to move!" Keith yelled, and I scooped Catalina up and carried her out of the house, down the stairs, and into the waiting SUV that John had just arrived in.

"Take her!" I yelled and headed back inside to finish my job as he peeled out of the driveway.

Mark met me in the entryway and helped me peel back the floorboards. I dumped everything I had on me and lit a fuse.

"Did you get it?" I yelled over my shoulder as we raced back down the stairs.

"Yes!"

"Good." We jumped into the other SUV, and Cole sped away after John. Just as we hit the main road, we could feel the shock waves that flattened the Esteban house. Thanks to Catalina's call to Daniel, we were able to clear the house of all staff and baggers. No casualties except the ones we meant to take down. It wasn't the smoothest of operations, but it was successful and would never have worked if we hadn't had Catalina.

"John?" I clicked my radio.

"She's okay. Keith is with her."

I sank back in my seat and removed my helmet, thankful she hadn't been hurt and we hadn't lost any of our guys.

"Nice work, Mike." Cole kept his eyes on the road. We weren't out of the woods yet. "I called Denton's info in."

"Good." We could never be too careful with what we learned. We always called it in the moment we could in case anything happened to us on the way home.

Cole turned up the music, and *Same Blood* by Aloe Blacc pumped through the speakers, and I sank into the seat while a sense of relief crept over me.

The wind whipped Catalina's hair around as we escorted her from the truck to the helicopter. I stood next to her and lifted her by the waist to help her inside. She awkwardly shimmied to a seat Keith pointed to. She looked at the five-point harness with confusion.

"Here." I helped her get settled, and as I finished, she placed her hands over mine.

"I'm sorry," she whispered, and my heart ached for her. She had no idea what we were able to accomplish, thanks to her. I would make sure she knew the full extent of it when we were alone, but this wasn't the time or place.

"Get me out of here." Mark laughed as he took a seat next to her and smiled widely. "It's never a dull day on the Blackstone team!"

She returned the smile, and I could tell she was still worried about what kind of trouble she'd be in when we got home. I knew she must be devastated over the death of her mother and all that had happened these past days.

I moved to the other side of her and strapped myself in, then I placed my hand on her leg for reassurance as the helicopter took off. Reaching above her, I drew the earphones over her head and showed her how to put them on so she could hear us.

Although seconds later, I regretted it.

"I'm starving." Mark patted down his pockets. "Where the hell is my…"

"Oh, shit, this is good." John bit into one of Mark's beloved power bars.

"Son of a ripe shit, when the hell did you take that?"

"When the second blast knocked you down." John took a bigger bite.

"Wait," Mark tried to undo his harness, "I was down, and you robbed me? I feel so… used."

"You were fine."

"My pants were undone too, John." He snickered. "What else did you do while I was unconscious?"

Catalina covered her mouth as she laughed. Yeah, the guys were something else when we were in the chopper. However, lately, my head always went to…I leaned over and switched her channel to a private one. I unbuckled, despite Cole's confused look, and moved to kneel in front of her.

"Since we met, every time I flew, I thought of you." My voice cracked over the radio. "It was usually during the time I should have been mentally preparing for our next mission, but I couldn't. We may come from different worlds, Catalina, but that doesn't matter because we are both in this one together."

A single tear slipped down her cheek, leaving a small trail in the dust on her skin.

"My life isn't easy, I know that, but you make it so much better just by being in it. I don't want to go on another mission without knowing you'll be mine. I need to know you will be there when I come home." I looked around the cabin and spotted a loose piece of parachute cord. I used my knife to cut a small piece off and held it up in lieu of the ring. "Catalina Mendez, will you please marry me?"

She nodded, her eyes glistening with tears, then she seemed to realize she didn't answer me verbally. "Yes! Yes, of course I will!"

I slid the makeshift ring over her finger and reached to hold her face and kissed her hard.

"I'm so glad she said yes," Mark chirped over our private line. "That man scares me when he's pissed."

I removed one hand from Catalina's face and granted him the finger, which sent the rest of the crew into a fit of laughter.

"I love you." She kissed me again. "Thank you for saving me from my past, from myself, from everything."

"I will always save you." My heart nearly burst apart with joy.

TWENTY-FOUR

CATALINA

"Wait, am I dreaming?" Rail smirked as he pushed off his bike and met me at the door of the restaurant. He waved me ahead to go inside.

"Nice to see you again too." I spotted Tess at the bar and wove my way through the sea of people. I noticed John let me have some space, and I was thankful for that. It was strange having someone follow you around wherever you went, but I understood it was just for a little while. At least that's what they told me.

"Hey, girl!" Tess wrapped me in a big hug and glanced at my handsome escort. "Welcome to your new life."

"It's not so bad." I shrugged, and then she spotted my ring, and I held up my hand for her to see.

"Shit, girl, that's beautiful."

It really was, and I couldn't help constantly looking at it. It meant so much to me to see it there.

"Thanks." I glanced around and wondered how many bikers were in the bar at that moment. To say I was nervous about a gunfight was an understatement. Frank had insisted I visit the house psychologist before the wedding, and I would, just not until after this visit.

"Okay, are you ready?"

"Lead the way."

I followed her outside then across the street to a garage that looked like a 1950s barber shop complete with pinups, booze, and a strong odor of pot.

"Hey, Mud, this is Catalina. She's hitching up with Mike in a few weeks."

He moved the fat joint to the corner of his mouth and shook my hand while the other held a needle.

"She needs a little help fixing something."

"Yeah?" He squinted at me while I turned around, and my backless shirt gave him a clear view of my angel. "Damn, that's some tattoo."

"Do you know it?" I faced him and brushed my hair out of my face.

"The fallen angel," he stated before he stood and opened a beer and handed it to me. "I've seen a few, but never like yours. What do you want me to do to it? I kind of hate to mess with something that beautiful."

I looked over at John. He was on the phone, but he must have felt my gaze because he turned to look at me.

"She's not a prisoner anymore." I faced him. "I want her to be free."

His weathered cheeks crinkled when he smiled. "I think I could do that."

Tess didn't leave my side for three hours. We chatted a lot, and even Trigger came in to take a look. I was sure Mike had asked him to check in, but nonetheless, I was pleased.

"Mud, she doesn't pay," Trigger grunted when he was about to leave.

"That's very kind, Trigger, but I can't allow that."

He moved his intense green eyes in my direction, and I swallowed hard.

Why is he so scary?

"My oldest friend finally found someone he loves enough to marry, so you're family now."

"But…"

"Consider it a wedding present."

"Don't argue, Angel," Mud advised. "You won't win."

I shifted to get the uncomfortable feeling to leave, but I couldn't, so instead, I thanked him, and he kissed Tess and left.

Tess smiled at me when she caught me staring at the two of them.

"How is someone that intense?"

"Meh," Tess laughed, "you get used to it. Plus, it's a huge perk in bed."

I bet.

"So, when do you arrive in Asheville?"

Her face fell into a sad smile. "Thank you for the invite, but we can't come. You know, right? Just like how Mike couldn't come to ours."

"What? Why?"

She held her hand up. "There's the Army's line with tolerance," she drew a line in the air, "and there's Devil's Reach way over here."

"The Army has a right to say who we're friends with?"

She shrugged. "I don't take it personally. We get to see Mike and the guys a lot, just not at functions that might bring in the bigwigs."

That was crap, but I wasn't going to make a big deal about it. Rules were rules, and I understood that.

"Then we'll have to have a party to celebrate later."

"I think that can be arranged." She handed me an envelope. "Could you give this to Mike at the wedding?"

"Of course."

Another thirty went by, and I blocked out the pain. Well, to a dull roar, anyway.

The flight back home was less than comfortable. Poor John tried to help, but he was very careful about how often he touched me. I felt bad but just sucked up the pain and hunkered down the rest of the flight.

"Will Mike be there when I get home?"

"Should be." John checked his phone on the plane's Wi-Fi. "He had a lot to do in Washington, but I know he was trying to, so…"

"That's nice." I loved that he was willing to move mountains to allow us to be together. I just wished I could do more. The plane was quiet and dark, other than John's computer, and he tapped away as he answered a pile of emails.

I grew sleepy and pulled out my phone and tapped the audio icon. John plucked it from my hand with a laugh. "Let me guess, it was Tess who recommended this?"

"Yeah, why?"

"Did she tell you about it?"

"No, she just said it was really good and that I might learn a little bit more about the Army from it."

John gave a big booming laugh, which made a few people jump. Not caring, he handed it back to me. "I should be taping this."

I fumbled to turn on my Beats headphones. "What am I missing?"

He shook his head. "Just listen to it."

Chapter two had me shooting John a puzzled look, and the corners of his mouth lifted, but he didn't look over. However, in chapter five, I made John jump when my hand clamped down on his arm.

"What?" I nearly shouted. "But how?"

"The author made a compelling argument on why she thought she should write their story."

"But how?"

"Cole can't say no to Savannah," he simply explained. "She loved the idea of their story being in print."

"That's crazy!" I beamed at how romantic it was. "Okay, bye!" I tossed the headphones back on so I could block out the world and caught John smirking at his screen.

It was Charlotte who met us at the airport, not Mike. As disappointed as I was, I understood that Mike needed to jump through hoops in order for our marriage to happen.

"I have to meet Mark. Are you good?"

"I am. Thanks, John, truly. That was fun."

"I'm glad. I'll see you both soon."

Charlotte took me back to her parents' place where Mike and I had been staying since they moved me out of my basement apartment last week. The best moment for me was when Jeff saw the U-Haul then Mike and Keith. He backed down very quickly, and I even got my security deposit back.

After a quick dinner, I trudged my way to the bed, stripped down to nothing, and crawled into Mike's scent. I had never traveled so much in one year, and my body wasn't used to it.

Cold fingertips drew me from my sleep in the dead of night. I grinned into my pillow as they moved to the bandages.

"Can I see?" he whispered, and I nodded. Light filled the room as he gently peeled back the tape and gauze to see the changes.

"Wow," his warm breath sent a shiver across my skin, "she's so vibrant, so beautiful."

It was true. Mud had used a shimmer of thin white strokes which really helped to pop her wings and face.

He'd added tips to her feathers, so they weren't clipped anymore, and all along one of her wings were tiny letters which formed the words, *freedom comes in many forms; love was mine.*

I knew the moment he caught their meaning, because his fingertips stilled, and he cleared his throat. "He did a wonderful job," I whispered and waited for him to speak.

"He did," I could barely hear him, "and I'm honored that *you* did this." His fingers skimmed lightly below the words.

"It's the truth." I tried to fight the sleep that wanted to pull me under. "Will you come to bed?"

I felt the mattress dip, and he carefully covered my back with the cool sheet so I wouldn't get cold.

"I missed you." He kissed my cheek. "Did you have a good trip?"

I nodded.

"Good."

A stretch of silence told me I could give myself back to sleep, so I did.

———

The next three weeks were a whirlwind. Besides my work and my social life, our wedding was really coming together. Mike had to travel a few times, but I was all right with that. I barely knew if I was coming or going.

"Okay." Charlotte handed her mother a glass of champagne. "Okay, we're ready, let's see the dress."

With a glance in the mirror, I smoothed my hands down the non-traditional wedding dress, very pleased with my choice.

"What do you think?" I whispered to my mother who, I knew, was there.

The girl had called it an A-line or princess V-neck, sweep-brush train, sleeveless, lace chiffon wedding dress. I had to laugh at that. In reality, it was a lace V-neck with a short dress under and a long skirt over top. The long skirt had two slits up the sides all the way to my hips so that when you walked you could see the lace dress underneath. It was incredibly pretty and sexy all rolled into one. Soft pink heels peeked out, and I knew I wanted to wear my hair down and in curls.

I opened the door and stepped out to the two women who both sat speechless. Mrs. Irons—sorry, *Jackie*—started to cry.

"You look like an angel." She sniffed, and Charlotte nodded in agreement.

"I think I might need a necklace." I turned to the mirror to see.

"I know Mike has something in mind, dear."

I found her in the mirror. "Really?"

"Yes, so I wouldn't worry about it."

Okay, wow. I couldn't help but beam at the thought.

After the dress was handed over to Keith, who promised not to wrinkle it and insisted on being our driver for the day, we enjoyed a nice lunch, and, as much as I wanted to drag my feet, I knew it was time to go.

I had my head glued to my phone, reassuring Linda that I would definitely have the ad ready in time for our next big client when I got a strange vibe. Where were we?

"Wait," I turned around in my seat then back to Keith, "this isn't the way to the house."

"I know."

"Do I not have to go?" I grinned at him, but he just shook his head. "Come on, Keith, you know I know people. I can make you rich beyond your wildest dreams."

"That's messed up." He tried not to laugh.

"Meh, if you can't be dark with the bad stuff, when can you be?"

He laughed again as he tapped his earpiece. "Hey, man, we're five minutes away." He paused. "Well, she did try to bribe me not to take her." He eyed me playfully. "She's got a great dark side. I see the draw." He winked at me in the mirror. "Yeah, okay. Bye."

"Mike?"

"Daniel."

"Seriously, Keith, that's not funny! I still don't think he was pleased I called him."

"Oh, trust me, he was, and yes, it was Mike."

"Gawd," I hit his arm, "you're so mean."

He laughed harder then suddenly took a turn onto a dirt road.

"Where are w…" I trailed off when we came to a checkpoint, and he was waved through.

"It's a little cliché, isn't it?"

"What?" He seemed amused by me.

"Taking a cartel daughter deep into the woods," I joked darkly. "You're either going to whack me or torture me for info."

"Wow," he hit the wheel and laughed, "you spend entirely too much time with Charlotte."

"I really do," I muttered with a sigh.

"And whack?" He found me in the mirror. "Who'd say that? We don't whack."

"That's what the mob calls it."

"Last I checked, Cat, we were not the mob."

"That's what they all say, until one day they bring the girl to the woods," I did air quotes, "*just to chat*, and then whack! She's being buried in a barrel, in some remote area, and the only witness is a crow."

"Remind me to make notes on this session." He belly laughed.

Another twenty minutes, and we came to a clearing, and my jaw almost dropped on the ground.

"Welcome to Dusk, Catalina." Keith put the truck in park. "This is our second safe house."

"Holy shit." I stepped out.

The place was huge—no, gigantic—but before I got a chance to take it all in, an older-looking man in a tailored suit and a rather skinny tie approached me and offered a hand.

"Hello, Catalina. I'm Dr. Roberts. Welcome to Dusk. I'm sure you have many questions, but let's start with getting you inside."

Keith gave me a nod to tell me it was all right.

"This is the living room." The doc pointed to the massive, rustic-modern room. The giant windows looked over a lake. I also could see a pool and an outdoor gym. *Wow*.

"Somes?" a voice squeaked from behind me, and the cutest little boy smiled up at me and held out a cookie. "You somes?"

I bent down on my knees to get eye level with him and took a piece of the chocolate chip cookie and held it up.

"Is this for me?" He nodded. "Well, that's very kind of you." I popped it in my mouth and made a yummy noise. "Did you make it?"

"Savs." He muttered something I couldn't understand.

"I see. What's your name, cutie?"

"Gandon." He spat cookie out as he said it.

"Brandon, your name is B-B-Brandon," a pretty girl said behind him. "Hi. I'm Lexie," she offered a hand, "and this is Brandon. Keith's son."

"Oh!" I had a lot to learn. "Nice to meet you both."

"You too." She looked at the doctor. "Sorry. I hope he didn't interrupt."

"Not in the least," Dr. Roberts said softly. He held himself with such poise. His smile was warm and immediately put you at ease. He seemed to be a truly nice person.

"Say goodbye, B." She bent down and scooped up the little guy, making an airplane noise as she did, and he laughed. As she left the room with him, she muttered something about him needing a bath.

"You're good with kids," Doc Roberts said. "Did you grow up with a lot of little ones?"

I felt my back stiffen a little. *Here we go.*

"Dr. Roberts, if you want to get inside my head, you can. I have nothing to hide. You don't need to ask probing questions. Just come out with them."

He nodded politely and offered for me to follow him outside onto the patio. We took two seats that looked over the lake.

"I appreciate you offering to be so open during this session. It will make things a lot easier on my end."

"Okay." I shifted uneasily and wondered if I was ever going to get past being questioned about my background.

"Why don't we start from the beginning? Share your childhood with me."

I took a deep breath and let it go for Mike. I shared my most personal moments with a stranger because that was what *I* needed to do to make sure Mike and I could marry.

TWENTY-FIVE

MIKE

The aftermath of what happened with the Esteban family and their house was slowly starting to trickle in. Our North Rock team informed us the damage had really shaken up the drug side of the cartel world. Word spread that Denton Barlow was behind it all, so now we waited to see if he actually took the fall or not. Daniel's idea to plant a body that resembled Catalina worked perfectly. I didn't even want to know where he found an available corpse, but Daniel was resourceful that way. The town already had a memorial for her, and as strange and upsetting as it might sound, it was the right call to ensure her freedom. Of course, we hadn't shared all the details with her. She had enough to deal with. Just like we had with Savannah, we'd trickle the truth out as time healed her wounds.

The loud sound of ice in the blender pulled me back from my thoughts.

"What are you doing?" I rubbed my neck. Man, I was tired.

"This is Catalina's first session with Doc Roberts." Lexi poured more than half a quart of tequila over the crushed ice in the blender. "She's going to need this."

"True," I laughed, then yelped, "Son of a bishhhh." as I turned around and found that horrible Furby in my face.

"Sgot you!" Brandon giggled, "Ukle Johns give cookie." He tried to tell me the story.

"Lies!" John laughed from the other room.

I snatched the Furby and pointed at his mother. "Your son is a cookie junkie, you know that, right, Lex?"

"Like father, like son." She poured the margarita into four glasses. "I blame Savannah."

"Me too." I snickered and glared down at the addict. "You're a pawn in this sick game, little man. You know that?"

"Scookie?" His small hand came out and waited for his payment.

I scooped him up and brushed his hair away from his face. "I just so happen to know where your father hides the good ones." I made my way over to the pantry. "He thinks he's so sly, hiding them in the pasta box, but little does he know we all sneak them when he's in his office."

That gave me an idea. I grabbed the Furby and held it up to his son's mouth.

"B, say 'my cookies!'"

His little eyes lit up; he loved this game. "My scook-ies!" I laughed at his little monster voice.

"Up top." I got him to high-five me. "Now we wait to hear your daddy shriek like a little girl."

Lexie cleared her throat in a warning Keith was coming.

"Our secret, right, B?"

"Screcret!" He giggled and ran off with two cookies in his grubby hands.

"Hey, babe." Lexi bought me a moment to slip out of the pantry, and I nonchalantly grabbed a water from the fridge.

"Hey." He wrapped his arms around his wife and kissed her neck. "Mike, Doc is finished."

"Oh?" I peeked out to the living room where she and Doc where chatting.

"FYI, man, I want the CliffsNotes of that meeting." Keith laughed as he unfolded from his wife. "She had me cracking up in the car on the way here. All about how she thought I was taking her to the woods to be murdered. Well, actually, I believe the operative word was *whacked*."

"Sounds like she and my sister need to spend some time apart." My sister had a flare for the dramatic.

"That's what I said."

"Mr. Irons?" Elena appeared in the doorway in an oversized hoodie and yoga pants. "I just wanted to thank you again for helping my family escape. We should be able to leave soon. This is a really beautiful place," she spread her arms to encompass the property, "but we need to go."

"Please, Elena, call me Mike, and you're very welcome. You and your mother are welcome to stay as long as you need to, but I totally understand." We'd had this same conversation three times now, but I understood her need to get it out of her system before she could move on. "How's your mother?"

She shrugged. "She's okay. Luna's death has taken its toll on her, and on me too, but we've been working with the doc and Frank. We will, of course, keep our end of the deal."

"I don't doubt it. Are you hungry?"

"No," she shook her head, "Lexi helped me get something earlier."

Lexi shot her a smile, and I was happy to see it. Once again, her walls had come down. Lexi was the most complex of the three wives. She had spent years hating life and hunting her parents' killer. She had even joined a gang and dated the ringleader to find out the answers she believed were true. I was pretty impressed by her.

Doc Roberts had an incredible effect on those we brought to him for help. We were extremely lucky to have him on staff. He traveled, whenever he was needed, between our two safe houses, Dusk and Shadows. The incredible work he did with our rescued kidnap victims was the secret to them being rehabilitated enough to live a normal life again, especially after such extreme fear and violence destroyed who they were.

"Elena," Catalina called through the room, "is that really you?"

Elena broke down in tears and nearly jumped in Catalina's arms. "I never thought I would see you again!"

"Did they hurt you? Are you okay?"

"I'm okay." Elena pulled back and moved her shiny eyes to me. "She's the reason I survived that hellhole. She's a legend."

"Oh, yeah?" I was interested. Catalina certainly wasn't like any other woman. I took pleasure in the thought that I would have a lifetime to hear her story, and that made me a happy man.

"Yes. When I arrived at the house, I heard the stories about the dark angel." She reached out for Catalina's hand. "The dark angel had the blood of a monster but the heart of a saint. It was said she tended to their bruises, fed them when they were starved, and held them when they cried. Sometimes she even helped girls escape. I thought it was just a story of hope, until one day I saw her, in the study with her mother, and I saw the wings on her back. I knew she was the one, and the legend was true. She had returned, and now look," she started to cry again, "we are free."

"Yes, we are." Catalina hugged her again, and I had to cough as I felt my own emotions bubble to the surface. My girl continued to amaze me.

"I should check on Mama and let her know you are here."

"Okay." Catalina let her go and dried her cheeks. "I needed that."

"Here." Lexi handed her a large margarita, which instantly changed the mood. "The first session is always the hardest."

"First?" Catalina looked at me for help.

I shrugged. "We all have to see the doctor a few times a year, and since you are a part of this world, that means you too."

"Super." She sipped the drink and squinted at how strong it was.

"Wait for the second sip. It goes down like butter," Lexi said, laughing.

"Mr. Irons, may I see you a moment?" Doc called me over, and as I walked by Catalina, I gave her a quick kiss on the cheek.

"I'll be back."

I followed him, and Keith joined us as we went down the hallway and into my office. Cole was patched through on speaker phone, since he was traveling this way but didn't want to miss the outcome of the session.

"Should I be worried, Doc? My wedding is in a few weeks." I pointed politely to a seat, as the doctor never liked to be anything but formal.

"It was quite interesting. I found more similar traits between Catalina and Lexi," he adjusted his glasses as he pulled out his iPad to retrieve his notes, "as they both were around a lot of violence. Catalina, therefore, handles her PTSD differently than, for example, Savannah would.

Savannah shut down, lost trust, stopped eating, and lost the ability to function with people, whereas Catalina could roll with it, if you will, since violence was a normal thing to see."

"Is that a good thing?" I tried to follow.

"Yes and no." He glanced up at me. "You just need to watch her and report to me if you see any changes. She hasn't dealt with her mother's death but seems to have accepted her brother's. Their deaths were completely different. The brother knowingly walked into danger, while her mother was an innocent used as a shield by her own father to protect himself. That is a lot for one head to absorb. Not to even mention the violent death of her father and uncle and the end of their entire family. I still need to work on that with her."

"Okay."

"Now, her overall personality is quite entertaining." Doc laughed unexpectedly. "And I know the importance of this. She is still more than willing to hand over her family's information to you." He turned toward the phone where Cole was on FaceTime. "You might be interested to know she grew up with Denton's family."

"What?" Cole moved closer to the screen. "We have never found any information on his family."

"I won't hand over secondary information, but I do believe it would be important to speak with her on that."

"Will do, thanks." Cole started to type an email as Doc looked back at me.

"Honestly, Mike," he removed his glasses and turned off his iPad, "if I may speak candidly."

He waited for me to agree. "Please do."

"Catalina is a wonderful woman who has been through a lot. She fought like hell to do what she felt was right. Personally, I feel she is a blessing in disguise, not only for you but for the Army."

"So, you trust her?" I knew how important that was for both of us, that they trust her like I did.

"I do, without hesitation."

"Agreed." Daniel popped on the screen next to Cole. "When she called me, she was trying to do the right thing. I could hear her nerves, but she fought through them and gave us every last shred of information she could before we hung up. I think Catalina might be what we've been waiting for. Between her, Elena, and Martina, we just might be able to take down a major part of the cartel."

"So, you're saying…?" I needed to hear him say the words.

"I'm saying you found a gem in the unlikeliest place."

"Mike," Cole took over the camera, "I would like her to live at Dusk, and she should be supervised on her outings for precautionary reasons. Just because we removed her immediate family doesn't mean there isn't more out there, and it doesn't mean she didn't gain any enemies after all this."

"We need a club." Savi snickered from behind them, and we all broke out in laughter.

"Great." I felt the world lift from my shoulders, and the release was an incredible rush. "Now what?"

"Now," Doc continued, "you go marry the woman you love."

Later that night, the Logans arrived, along with Mark and Mia, and John and his twin sister. Abigail and June would arrive tomorrow morning, and I couldn't help but notice Doc Roberts looking a little more put together than normal. Of course, Mark noticed and needed to make it a thing, but Mia quickly put a stop to that.

Catalina continued to be in awe of everyone but fell into step with the other girls very quickly. I did notice a few times she'd excuse herself and wander down the hall, but I thought she just needed a moment. We could be a lot, and Catalina hadn't been around a big family in years. Our family wasn't even big, it was huge, and no doubt very overpowering.

I, on the other hand, relished it. I missed my little Livi and found myself on the floor roughhousing more than talking with the adults.

"Hop on." I was on all fours and waited for Mark's twins to climb on for a ride. Of course, Brandon was right there wanting his share of my attention. I really did spoil that little dude.

"Sseat." Before I knew what he was doing, he jammed a peanut butter finger in my mouth. "Syummy, Kuncle Ike."

My stomach rolled, and I tried not to think about how his hand was fuzzy from God knew what.

"Thanks, B, I wasn't hungry, and I don't think I will be now for a few days."

"Ride, pony, ride!" one of Mark's twins shouted as they both yanked at my hair. I bucked and wiggled beneath them and basked in their giggles of delight. I spotted Catalina across the room, watching me with a smile. Something about her look told me she was honestly happy to be here. Never did I think I would find love…or find a love that could work in my life.

"Ahhh!" Keith shouted from the kitchen. "Mark, I swear to God!"

I tossed the twins off my back, grabbed Brandon, and ran over to Catalina.

"What?" She grinned and tickled B's tummy.

"What did I do?" Mark shouted over everyone in the room.

"This!" Keith held up the toy and the half-eaten pasta container.

"I had no part in that, man," Mark moved closer, "but I would like a cookie."

"No!" He snapped the lid closed.

"Remember our secret," I warned B, who with his tiny mentality was putting the situation together.

"Daddy!" Brandon suddenly shouted. "Me scookie?"

"He's had, like, twelve today," Lexi piped in.

"You can have a cookie if you tell me who made you do this," his father countered.

Brandon looked back at me and wiggled to get down.

He clumsily walked across the room and raised his arms for his dad to pick him up.

"Scookie, me," he said again, and I saw Keith crumble.

"Who made you do this?"

"Kuncle John."

I let the biggest laugh go, outing myself to everyone, but I didn't care. That little boy was on my side.

"It's on, Irons." Keith handed his son a cookie.

I noticed Catalina had slipped out after John and I started our normal banter. I found her on the deck looking over the lake.

"Hey," I came up beside her, "everything okay?"

"More than." She looked down. "I never imagined a family could be like this. I'm just trying to let it sink in, that's all."

"I understand." I drew her to me and hugged her tightly.

———

Our wedding day came all too fast, yet not fast enough. I wasn't nervous; I was just ready. I'd waited my entire life to find the one, and now that I'd found her, I couldn't wait to make her officially mine.

With the wooden box in hand, I knocked lightly on the door, and my sister answered with disapproval in her eyes.

"Yes?"

"I need to see Catalina."

"No."

"Is she dressed yet?"

"No. But, Mike, there are rules."

"I respect that, but let me in. I have something for her."

"Hang on." She slammed the door in my face, and I cursed at her manners. "Okay, the coast is clear."

I found Catalina in front of a vanity, make-up and hair finished. I itched to touch her silky white robe. I swore my heart skipped a beat.

"Hi." Her face glowed. "What are you doing here?"

"I have something for you." I held out the box to her as her eyes brimmed with tears.

"How? How did you get that?"

"I had a little help. Before the last bomb went off, that is." I opened her mother's jewelry box and pulled out a pink pearl necklace, the same one her mother wore when Catalina was born. "Something borrowed." I hung it around her neck and awkwardly fastened the tiny clasp.

Tears slipped down her cheeks as her delicate fingers clasped the pearls.

"I can't believe you did this, Mike," she whispered. "Thank you so much."

"You gave up a lot and still will by marrying me, Catalina, and you have no idea what that means to me."

I wanted to kiss her, but I could wait. I wanted to do this right for us. We both deserved it.

"See you up there." I kissed the top of her head, and

despite my sister's fake anger about their schedule, she did give me a hug as I was about to leave.

"You've set the bar high for any man I might find, big brother. Thank you for that."

I full-on lost my voice as her words hit me in the center of my stomach.

"You will stay single forever." I kissed her cheek and looked back at my soon-to-be wife.

Just as I closed the door, my mother stood in front of me with a shoebox sized present of her own in her hand.

"Sweet Jesus, Mom," my heart jumped in my throat, "never sneak up like that."

"Don't curse, Banner." She pushed the box in my hands. "I have something for you."

"Oh, yeah?" I grinned like a child because my Mom always gave great gifts. I lifted the top, and my stomach twisted, and tears came to my own eyes.

Dammit, I was doing so good today too.

A bride and groom troll set lay nestled in black tissue paper.

"I know you don't need them anymore, as you have wonderful friends and now a wife, but it makes me happy to give them to you. It somehow completes their happiness too." She pointed at the little dolls.

I couldn't speak. Shit, I could barely think. My mother always knew just how to squeeze my heart and make me feel so incredibly loved all at once.

"I…" I cleared my throat. "This means…" Where the hell was my voice? "Thank you, Mom, they are perfect."

She grinned through a tear-soaked face. "I'm so proud of you, son, and you chose a wonderful woman to share your life with."

"I did, didn't I?" She went to take the box back.

"I can put them away for you."

I pulled it out of her reach. "You think you get to be the one to introduce the happy couple to the rest of the gang? Sorry, Mom, but that's a negative on that one."

She laughed lightly. "Okay, fine. I'll leave you to it."

I kissed her cheek and left to put my new additions in a safe spot.

TWENTY-SIX

CATALINA

Charlotte handed me my bouquet of dark red roses as she studied my face. "I've always wanted a sister. Who knew it would turn out to be my best friend?"

I hugged her with my free arm. "And who knew I would lose a sibling and gain another?"

"I'm sorry I never got to meet Javier, and if he was anything like you, I'd love him too."

"You two would have been trouble."

"Great, now I'm really bummed." She laughed, but I could tell she was worried about me.

"Charlotte, I know there are a lot of holes in my life that I haven't shared, but, if it counts, having you and Kyle as my best friends helped me get through some of the hardest times in my life. I've lost a lot, but I've gained a lot too."

"I'll take that." She nodded and dramatically fanned her eyes. "Have you seen Savannah's dress?"

"No." I leaned around her and spotted a beautiful woman next to Cole in a very chic blue dress. "Stunning."

"Okay," she turned to me when the music started, "ready?"

I pulled back the white curtain of the canopy and glanced at the guests who lined the walkway to the gazebo. Snow capped the mountains, reminding me that it was still January, despite the warm weather we had been granted lately. Mike's father, Ray, offered to host the wedding at the place where Mike and I fell in love. I wanted to cry for the fourteenth time that week. We happily accepted his offer.

"Ms. Mendez?" Ray offered me an arm, and we stepped out into the warm afternoon light where a hundred different pairs of eyes stared at me. I didn't care about any of them; I cared only about one particular set. I nearly tripped over my heels when I caught sight of Mike in his uniform. His eyes were shaded from the rim of the hat, but by the way his mouth curved into that smile I loved, I knew he felt the same way I did.

A violin and a cello set the pace as we slowly walked past a blur of happy faces. Jackie Irons snapped a hundred photos until Charlotte told her to sit and let the photographer do his job.

Just as I reached Mike, Ray turned to me and held both of my hands. "You came into this group as a friend, but you will remain in it as family. I knew one day my son would find someone special. Someone who would help wash away the stress of his job and love him unconditionally. Thank you for being that person, Catalina. Welcome to our family."

"Thank you, Ray." I leaned in and kissed his cheek.

"How can I top that, Dad?" Mike chuckled when he took over holding my hands. "Hey, you."

"Hey," I sighed.

They said your wedding passed in a blur, time sped up, and before you knew it, you were off on your honeymoon. Though most of that seemed true, there was one part that did stand out to me.

"Mike, are you ready?" Father Arthur asked.

"Love came easy to us." He cleared his throat. "I considered us lucky for that. On the other hand, we kept secrets from one another because we didn't want to take a chance of something spoiling it. When the truth came out, it hurt, and most would have run, but we didn't. We fought to the end. One bombshell after the other." He winked at his inside joke. "I'm proud of us, Catalina, because it shows me that our love knows no boundaries. That our love will last a lifetime."

And I'm a mess.

Drying a few more tears, I took a deep, shaky breath and tried to recall my vows.

"I thought I had things all worked out. New life, new job, new start. Until one day this handsome man at a bar was in my special spot chatting away to his mother." The first three rows made up of Blackstone and staff laughed loudly. "As much as I may tease, it showed me a lot about you. Mike, you are caring, sweet, loving, and a wonderful friend. You make me laugh and hold me when I'm scared. You gave me a family and a sister I never thought I'd have, new friends, and shockingly, a new side job." I chuckled and glanced at Frank, who returned the smile. "You saved me when my world crumbled beneath my feet, and I don't know what I would have done if you weren't there." I wiped a tear away. "Not all heroes wear capes, Mike. They come in many forms, and I'm so lucky to have landed myself my own true hero."

We didn't wait for the minister to say the rest. Mike dove in and kissed me with so much passion, I blushed down to my toes, but I never pulled away. I would never.

The afterparty was unbelievably fun. So many people shared stories about Mike and what he'd done for them… or to them. With every story, I found myself needing to be next to him, to remind myself he was mine.

"Shake it, baby!" Keith's Nan was once again in the middle of the dancefloor surrounded by men, young and old, while she shook her ass. Who knew she could move like that at her age? Seriously, that was a life goal, right there. Keith, on the other hand, still had her in the doghouse for something she did a while ago. I didn't even want to know.

I spotted Lizzy a few times. Charlotte had asked if she could come, and I was fine with it. Lizzy and Mike had a past, but that was all it was—a past. She had her shot and blew it. I did notice Ray lean in to speak to her when she tried to approach Mike at one point, and her face twisted with discomfort. I appreciated that. He wanted to make sure we had the perfect day.

Mike handed me a glass of wine, and I hesitated but took it, warming the red liquid between my hands. "You all right?"

"Mhm," I muttered, a thousand miles away.

"What's up, Catalina?" He removed the glass and leaned forward to grab my attention. "Out with it."

"Tess wanted me to give you this." I slid over the letter I promised I would give him.

"Huh." He tore the envelope open and scanned the words, and at one part, his eyes closed, and he paused, and I felt something special must have been written.

"Everything okay?"

"Yeah." He smiled and folded the letter back up. "You should read it later. It was really nice."

I settled into the silence, unsure how to proceed.

"You gave me a present." I touched my necklace. "I guess brides and grooms do that, huh?"

"I don't know. Do they?" He shrugged like he never thought about it before. "I don't need anything from you, darling. Is that what's bothering you?"

I strummed my fingers on the table and opened my purse with my other hand.

I think I might pass out.

"Um, let's call it a co-gift." I handed him a photo.

"Holy shit." His entire body went rigid, and I wondered if he was mad.

"I know it wasn't planned, but apparently you have strong swimmers."

"How far along?

"Three months."

"Whooo!" He suddenly jumped to his feet, then onto the chair, which thankfully didn't break, while he cheered again, and everyone stopped to stare.

"Three months, baby!" He turned the little photo around to share it with the entire wedding. "My baby is three months!"

Jackie and Ray both started to cry, and Charlotte and Kyle started making baby shower plans.

Yikes, this is all a little overwhelming. One celebration at a time, please!

While all the buzz happened, and I got re-hugged for the billionth time, and was told congratulations more times than I could imagine. Faces blurred together, and voices became a loud hum. I began to get overwhelmed again, so I slipped away and changed into a more comfortable dress then grabbed the letter from Tess and headed down to the dock, needing a moment to myself.

With my legs over the edge and the glass lake beneath me, I scanned the letter. I knew Mike wouldn't mind. I wanted to see how what kind of friendship they had.

Mike,

You were a friend when I didn't have one, and you were a friend to Trigger when he needed one. It took me a while to see how you two could be so close, but I see it now. You've spent the last two decades understanding the lines of black and white and created a gray area where you both could coexist. Though you might not know this, you were the one who taught Trigger how to be compassionate. You have a way of getting through to him like no one else, and for that, I thank you.

Do you remember our conversation about the trilogy? And how I asked why you weren't in it yet? Your words were, "Because my story hasn't been written yet." Well, guess what, Mike. You finally got yours, and what a story it is! She's wonderful.

We may not be physically there to celebrate, but you can bet your ass we are celebrating at the club in your honor. Cheers!

Much love from the DR,

Tess

Mike moved to sit next to me. He had changed into shorts and a polo.

"They're really good people." He took the letter from me and stared at it. "Different from us, but that's what makes them special."

"I agree."

"Tired?" He glanced at me, concerned.

"Actually…" I stood, and he followed. I set the letter under my glass, careful that it wouldn't blow away. "I need to talk to you."

"Okay." Concern deepened the lines around his eyes.

"I was, ah, talking to Mark about something I heard a long time ago, and he explained what it meant. Now," I brushed my hair out of my face from a small breeze, "it won't work that well because you're bigger, but I'm willing to give it a try."

"Give what a try?"

I stepped back a few paces and raced toward him before he had a moment to think, and I pushed us both into the water. When I came up, he had a look of pure shock on his face.

"What the hell?" He laughed in disbelief.

"I can't Code Forty-Five a man twice my size, but I apparently can push you into the water."

"Friggin Mark!" He went to grab me, but I dipped under the water and swam to my favorite place at the Irons house, under the dock.

He followed me, and when he came up, he wrapped his arms around my waist and pushed me up against the wall.

"Your dress will get ruined."

"It's okay. It will dry."

"Great answer." He dove in and kissed me hard.

TWENTY-SEVEN

Six months later

MIKE

"Congratulations on your little girl." John clinked his beer to mine. "I couldn't be happier for you, brother."

"Thanks." I grinned over at Catalina, who had Gabriella in her arms, rocking her to sleep. "Me too."

"Yes, thanks for giving Olivia someone she can team up with." Cole smiled as he raised his glass.

"Yeah, Liam and Ethan could use a little charm in their lives." John laughed at Mark's kids, who were wrestling on the grass below us. Poor Mia was about to deliver any day and needed to be on bed rest.

"Hey, my boys have swagger." Mark defended his little rascals. We all gave him the raised eyebrow.

"I know you've missed our Livy since you left Shadows, Mike," Savannah patted my shoulder then perched on the armrest of Cole's chair, "but now you have your own little girl to tease the heck out of you."

"That's for sure. I hope she is near as sweet at Livy."

"How's Elena doing?" Cole changed the subject.

"Much better. We held a wake for Luna, hoped to give them some closure there. All in all, they have each other, and with the help of the good doc, they are making it work." I couldn't keep my eyes off my little family. As soon as Catalina felt my gaze, she smiled and carefully shifted a little. I knew she was still sore. Our little Gabby was only three days old, but her Mama had made a quick recovery and was more than happy to be home.

Home. Who would have thought in only one year I would find the perfect woman and have an equally perfect daughter of my own?

"You want to go to Daddy?"

"Yes, pass her over. She needs to come to Daddy." I gently took the swaddled little bundle in my arms and kissed her tiny forehead. "Daddy will protect his girls until the end of time."

"Hey, John," Mark beamed, "I guess you're next!"

"Not sure it's in the stars for me, boys." John finished his beer.

"Yeah, it is." Catalina held up her phone. "Your story just hasn't been written yet."

I grinned at my wife, happy she just threw out a quote from one of my good friends. "She's right, John." I pushed my finger into my daughter's hand, and I felt myself falling head over heels for the little seven-point-something-pounder all over again. "You're next."

"If I can have what you all have, I'd be willing to give it a try."

Catalina draped her arm around my shoulder and rubbed our daughter's tummy. "If we made it work, anyone can make it work."

"Cheers to that!" Cole held his drink high, and we all toasted to happiness.

To say life was great was an understatement. It was perfect.

The End

ACKNOWLEDGMENTS

Jill and Steve Chamness—for all your help, reenactments, and laughter along the way! Jill, you're such a sweet, kind human being I just love to be around.

Steve, I'm still convinced we were siblings at some point. I like how we both view life and the darkness that surrounds it.

It's special when you can find someone as wonderful and warm as you two.

When we're together, I feel like I'm home.

Ceej—this was the first book I have written since you left for the stars. I have to say I struggled with the thought you didn't get to beta Mike's story, the one you have been waiting for. I hope wherever you are, you have a book in your hand and a huge Ceej smile.

Until we meet again, much love from below.

First and second round betas—for being my eyes when I couldn't use mine anymore. Your notes, opinions, and overall feedback were invaluable.

Blackstone Reader Group—for the support and love you show me every day.

My team—Ketura, Vanessa, and Kim for rocking another year and another release!

My friend Shannan—for your help on my "shelved projects" and giving me the boost to release them.

My mother—for sitting out on the balcony in Maui in the dark before anyone was awake, before the birds stirred, and listening to my endless storylines for this book. I will forever cherish that time with you.

My step-father—for listening, reading, and your constant honesty from a male's perspective.

My sister Erin—for helping me "dig out of my hole" when I just couldn't find my way out.

My sister Gillian—for your endless support in whatever I choose to write.

Readers—once again, for being so patient while I create another story.

I thank you!

J.L. Drake, born and raised in Nova Scotia, Canada, later moving to Southern California. Though she loves the weather in Cali, she would sell her left kidney for a good rainstorm. Jodi's love of the seasons back home in Canada definitely appear in her books.

When she's not writing, you can often find her sitting somewhere along the coast of Huntington Beach, reading, or at home curled up on a couch with her two children and husband, binge watching a good movie.

AUTHORJLDRAKE.COM

FOLLOW ME ON SOCIAL MEDIA

facebook.com/JLDrakeauthor

x.com/jodildrake_j

instagram.com/j.l.drake

tiktok.com/@authorjldrake

bookbub.com/profile/j-l-drake

BROKEN TRILOGY

Broken

Shattered

Mended

BLACKSTONE SERIES

Honor

Escape

Freedom

Courage

DEVIL'S REACH TRILOGY

Trigger

Demons

Unleashed

QUIET MAFIA SERIES

Quiet Wealth

Quiet Secrets

Quiet Power

Quiet Empire

DARK WATER SERIES

Shadows

Whiskey

Alpha

Tango

<u>HAVOC OF SINS</u>

Grim

Havoc

Sins

<u>DARKNESS SERIES</u>

Darkness Lurks

Darkness Follows

Darkness Falls

<u>STANDALONE BOOKS</u>

Behind My Words

Christmas At The Cabin

Omerta

For the suggested reading order, please scan the QR code: